RETROGRESS

THOMAS CONNER

websites
www.sc-fi-retrogress.com
www.thomasconnerbooks.com
www.friesenpress.com

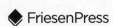

FriesenPress

Suite 300 - 990 Fort St
Victoria, BC, V8V 3K2
Canada

www.friesenpress.com

Moon icon by Saxon Evers from the Noun Project

ISBN
978-1-5255-0149-4 (Hardcover)
978-1-5255-0150-0 (Paperback)
978-1-5255-0151-7 (eBook)

1. FICTION, SCIENCE FICTION, TIME TRAVEL

Distributed to the trade by The Ingram Book Company

RETROGRESS

To Svea

Best Wishes

Thomas Conner

December 2017

For

STEPHANIE

Always

CHAPTER ONE

Silence, total silence enveloped the pod compartment, like snowfall on a windless night blanketing the ground turning the air into a soundproof zone. Deathly quietness prevailed until a single click signaled a prearranged sequence that brought the craft to life. Lights came on, sensors hummed and gauges started recordings.

A loud click from outside indicated the outer door being opened followed by the inner compartment door to the pod sliding open. The figure of a man peered in before sliding the door fully open, dark eyes scanned the interior before stepping inside

"Are you receiving this?" he said quietly.

"*Yes,*" replied another.

"The pilot appears lifeless, no movement, just a flashing light in the helmet. Name on the badge says Dr. S. Cooke."

"*Take a look.*"

He stepped up to the recumbent figure of the pilot and placed a gentle hand on the shoulder.

"There is no heartbeat, just as I detected from the outside. I will remove the helmet and check for signs of life."

Moving his hands around the base of the helmet, there was a click as he released the clips and eased the helmet off.

"It's a woman," he said.

"*I can see that,*" the voice replied. "*Now check her over.*"

The man leaned in and very gingerly eased down her eyelids and examined her for any vital signs.

"Have you ever seen such beautiful eyes? Vivid green with flecks of gold, one pupil darker than the other."

"Get on with it, Cal."

"Sorry. Looks like she did not survive the journey. Feels like her bones are broken."

"Get a BRB on her and get her back here quickly," the voice ordered.

Another man entered the cabin, dressed like the first in a gray-green suit with a name badge on the left breast. The first read Cal 244, the second Dal 160. In the cramped conditions of the compartment, they eased around each other without touching the pilot.

Dal carried a white pack and they carefully moved the pilot up and placed a collar around her neck with tubes attached. There was a hissing noise as they pressed a button on the pack. Cautiously, they unbuckled her from the seat and lifted her outside, trying to keep the body in a level position. Weighing just 140 pounds, she was no encumbrance to them.

After a few minutes, Cal resumed a careful study of the interior of the pod.

"I am placing the pilot's helmet in a position to record everything, if that is what it's doing, and I will talk through and explain everything," Cal stated.

The voice, coming from a speaker in his suit, spoke again.

"Her death has radically changed our plans. I will consult with the council and get back to you. Continue to scan the vehicle and send back the data."

"Principal Talan, there is a clock here counting down. We have forty-one minutes left. I presume that means the craft leaves then."

"Carry on. Explain our circumstances and I will return quickly." The voice clicked off.

Cal looked to the helmet and began.

"If this is being recorded, let me explain."

His head moved around and his eyes changed colour as he examined the instruments, gauges, and controls.

"We were expecting you after the first craft landed but we were not quick enough to reach it before it disappeared. We then set up a base close by and waited for your return. Our data stated you would come from the twenty-first century but records have been corrupted. We are in trouble and need your help. Planet earth is dying and we need solutions. Even our most advanced artificial intelligence systems have not found a way to save us."

Cal moved around the pod slowly, looking at the internal components."

"The Earth's magnetic core has almost depleted, which has affected the climate. The troposphere and stratosphere started to lower and all water began absorbing into the ground or evaporating away. It has become so bad that humanity has moved underground. As the air became unbreathable, huge oxygen plants were built to sustain life. The only people who can walk on the surface are humanoids like myself, of which there are two kinds. The first are straight humanoid with A.I. and are pure robotic, used primarily for keeping humans alive. The second, like myself, are hybrid-humanoids, called hubrids, which have a combination of artificial intelligence linked to a normal brain from people who lived a normal life. I do not have the time to expand further as the clock is ticking down."

He looked toward the clock then returned his gaze to the helmet.

"The finest human thinking took place between the industrial revolution and the twenty-second century. After that A.I. was used so much that we became lazy and left them to solve our problems." He placed his hand on some instruments and seemed to hesitate before continuing.

"That was until the climate has forced us to pay attention. Even with our combined intellect, we have only been able to come up with one solution to the crisis, and that is too catastrophic for us to consider. That is why we have been waiting for you. We need your innovative thinkers to look for solutions."

He hesitated for a moment then, putting his other hand into a compartment, pulled out a revolver.

"What is this? You sent your pilot with a weapon! We banned these a long time ago. Did you think we would be such a danger?" His face darkened in a grimace.

"I do not have enough time to discuss this."

Returning the gun, Cal continued to examine the craft. He stepped out into the outside compartments and drive components. Minutes passed by before he returned to face the helmet again.

"Your gyroscope is not functioning. Looks like it seized. That probably caused your pilot a lot of stress, maybe even killed her."

He glanced at the clock.

"Principal Talan," he said into his comm. "Time is getting close. Do you have any instructions?"

There was a delay before a voice cut in.

"*Not Yet.*"

"Then I think I should return with the craft, as I have all the data needed to explain our dilemma and ask for their assistance," Cal said.

"*We cannot ask you to do that. You may not survive. There is no data to suggest your body will make the return journey safely.*"

"I don't think we have a choice, do you?"

"*The council suggests we wait until they send another craft.*"

Cal walked out of the pod compartment and closed the outside door. Returning he then slid the inner door closing it as well.

"They may never send another. We have no records of that happening. I will take the chance," he replied. "I will shrink down, lock myself into the pilot's seat, and go into standby mode."

He waited through a long pause. "*The council wishes you good luck and a hope for a good ending.*"

"Thank you. I appreciate the approbation from all," Cal answered.

He looked to the helmet and sent a message before getting into the seat and strapping in. His body contracted, making him smaller. He lowered his head onto his chest and lay still.

CHAPTER TWO

PRESENT DAY

Anxious faces watched computer screens around the room, nervously anticipating the return of the craft. Empty paper coffee cups on each desk indicated the pressure to stay awake and alert.

"Everybody ready? Time is getting close," said Matt.

They all nodded, taking their eyes off their tasks for a moment. The nervousness in the room reflected how new all of this technology was. Although NASA had started the program in Florida, T.T. Labs provided the key studies into the viability of time travel. Their theory was that time only travelled forward, starting from the big bang and moving outwards in waves of time and gravity. Those waves could possibly be bent and stretched but the laws of physics demanded they must always return to their original form. That opened the possibility of time travel, but only into the future—never the past.

"Hope it all works," Sierra muttered, flashing her dark brown eyes at the team leader. Mathew Petronas looked back, nodding silently at his administrator.

"We all do," Carla said.

They were gathered in the control room of a powerful particle accelerator, designed to propel a craft into the future. But just as a wave hits the beach or an arrow attached to an elastic band, it would be dragged back after reaching its maximum trajectory. Their calculations suggested they would have a short time at the peak of travel, possibly an hour, to study and gain data, and maybe make contact with locals before being yanked back. At the beginning, numerous failures followed until a combination of a particle accelerator, the enlargement of quantum foam and the Einstein-Rosen Bridge could overcome the effects of the gravitational time dilation.

A Titanium-Lead shield was built to surround the craft and contain the gravitational field built up before the launch to propel it into the future.

"It worked for the probe so I'm sure it will be alright for the *Intrepid*. No reason for it not to," Matt said. "Just stay calm and concentrate."

Everyone went quiet again. Only the low hum of the computers filled the room and time seemed endless as seconds and minutes ticked by.

"It's late," Daniel grunted.

"Not yet,"' Billy replied. "Give it another few minutes."

Air in the middle of the room shimmered and a vibration shook the floor, all their hearts seemed to jump in unison.

"Prepare for arrival!" Matt announced.

The six teammates buzzed anxiously, waiting for the return of their seventh member. Stella had been chosen for the first manned mission because she was the only one without commitments to a spouse or partner— and for all the hours she had put into the project. She had joined the team early on in the research and theory before switching to the engineering and build stages.

Each of them had a task to concentrate on when the craft returned. Daniel Owens, already a NASA veteran at thirty-two, stood ready to test the craft for radioactive, bacterial, or other contaminates. His buzzed haircut and erect stature made him look like a marine ready for combat.

Billy's blue eyes were glued to the computer screen, ready to make contact with the pod as soon as it arrived. Carla and Katie had side-by-side desks, both tasked with downloading data from all the sensors onboard.

Desks were arranged in a crescent-moon to one side of a central space in the middle of the hanger where the craft had once stood. On the other side of the gray steel built aircraft hangar, set up against the wall, was all the equipment and spare parts used for the assembly.

Matt paced up and down behind the desks, coffee in hand, his hooded eyes and sagging face showing his agitation.

They looked at the camera screens trained inside the shield. Slowly, a form took shape and an outline of the craft became clearer. The air shimmered and the outline vibrated for longer than expected before settling down.

"Yes!" someone shouted. They cheered as they hugged and congratulated each other, getting up from their chairs and congregating around Matt.

"Great job everybody, but let's get back to work. We have so much to do before we can really celebrate. The priority is to get Stella out of there."

Dan grabbed his gear, pulled on a clear shield face mask and rubber gloves, and approached the craft to take readings. The others sat back down at their desks to concentrate on the screens and await Stella.

Matt flitted from desk to desk, glancing at the screens, burning full of energy as success boosted his adrenaline.

"Wait!" shouted Billy. "There's a message from inside."

He rushed over and so did all the others.

'Review the video recording before entering.'

The screen was highlighted in bright red letters.

"What does it mean?" asked Katie, looking over shoulders from behind.

"Don't know," Matt replied. "Billy, transfer it onto the big screen."

A large screen TV was set to the side and all eyes turned to it.

The screen was black for a few moments before lights came on, illuminating the interior of the pod. It was quiet except for the sound of instruments humming in the background.

"That's the outer door," Dan said. They had all heard the sound many times before.

Eyes stayed glued to the screen.

The sound of a sliding door broke the silence. Then a man's face came into view, with dark eyes peering into the camera.

There was an audible gasp.

"Are you receiving this?" his deep voice said quietly.

"Yes," said another voice, off screen.

"The pilot appears lifeless, no movement, just a flashing light on the helmet."

"There is no heartbeat..."

"No!" Billy cried.

The camera angle shifted and turned so most of the cabin was in view. Stella lay motionless in the pilot's seat.

"*It's a woman,*" the man in the video said.

The team could see him more clearly now, wearing an all-in-one suit, dark in colour. He had light brown short hair and a square angular face.

"*I can see that,*" the voice replied. "*Now check her over.*"

The group watched as the man lowered her eyelids and examined her. They felt powerless, deep in despair. Some looked away while others held hands. Some broke into tears when they saw Stella lifted gently out of the seat. The two men eased the body out the door, the second man carrying a pack with tubes and wires connected to Stella's neck.

They all stared quietly when the first man returned, moved the helmet recorder, and proceeded to stare at all the instruments. He continued talking to the camera, explaining what was happening. The team looked to one another in astonishment as Cal lowered himself into the pilot's seat and seemed to go to sleep with his head dropped onto his chest.

He placed his hand on the nearby helmet and said, "All you have to do is speak the name 'Cal' to bring me out of standby mode. I do not have any weapons, except for the one you left, and I wish you no harm. There is a desperate need to explain our circumstances, the planet's total life support systems are shutting down. We need your help!"

CHAPTER THREE

Matt paced back and forth behind them as they sat at their desks. Once or twice he started to say something, but shook his head and returned to his thoughts.

Finally, he spoke. "We have to follow protocol. Unauthorised entry to this facility requires us to call security. In this case, it has to be homeland security, the director of the local section."

No one objected as he made the call. After talking and gesturing with his hands, he put the phone back in his pocket and turned to face the team.

"They are on their way."

"Good!" a voice boomed behind them.

They spun around and Matt looked up to see the man's figure standing in the doorway to the craft.

"Please stay calm." The man said in a quiet, reassuring voice. "I mean no harm and would like a chance to explain."

"Armed security is on the way," Matt said.

"I know. I can hear them coming."

"I hear nothing," Billy said.

"Oh, but they are," the man replied. "My hearing is better than yours."

He stepped down from the craft and approached them, his face turning and scanning the building and its contents. It seemed to become taller as he got closer. The gun from the spacecraft came out in his hand. Everyone froze.

"Do not worry," he said. He turned the revolver around and offered it to Matt. "I have no use for things used to destroy."

A smile creased his face as Matt took the gun and the tension in the room dropped.

They heard sirens approaching. The man retreated a few steps and held up his hands in surrender.

"My name is Cal."

"What do you want?" Dan asked. "And what happened to Stella?"

"First, I want a chance to explain why I, and the planet, needs your help." Cal looked at them each individually. "Unfortunately, your pilot did not survive the journey to my time. When I examined her, she had many broken bones, including the rib cage, and that stopped her heart. I am sure it was because of the forces exerted due to the failure of the ship's gyroscope."

He looked at Billy. "You will find some solutions to this problem as well as some modifications to your craft already downloaded on your computer."

Billy looked confused as he stared at the computer. "How?" he asked.

"The same way I know there is a text message on Matt's phone from his daughter." He smiled and then looked serious. Pointing to his head, he said, "What is in here is all yours, the rest is freely available. I want you to know that I'm here to help."

"What about Stella?" Carla asked. "What was that thing you put on her neck?"

"A brain recovery backpack. It's used in emergencies to preserve brain function until we get a patient to a medical centre. Our technical knowledge is far greater than yours, but I cannot say what her prognosis is. I can only tell you she will get priority treatment, as we would provide to any of our ancestors."

He looked toward the door. "Your guards are here, Matt. Please ask them to stay calm until Homeland Security arrives. We do not want bullets flying around here, do we?"

The side door opened and two guards entered, guns drawn and pointed at Cal.

"It's okay," Matt said. "We have everything under control."

"What's the situation?" one of the guards asked.

"We have an unauthorised person in the facility." Matt pointed at Cal. "Homeland security is on the way, so let's just wait for them to get here."

"May I suggest that you open one of those hanger doors so they can drive in?" Cal nodded towards the end of the hanger.

"Who is in charge here?" the other guard asked.

"I am," Matt said. "Just do it."

The guard nearest the door pressed a control and the door started to slide open.

"Can I step outside for a moment?" Cal asked.

"Why?" Matt asked.

"Because it's raining," he replied. "Just for a moment. You have all the guns. Please."

Matt waved the gun towards the door. "Don't try anything."

As a whole, the group walked slowly to the door and Cal stepped outside with three guns pointed at him.

Raindrops hit Cal and turned to a myriad of lights. As they bounced off, the lights faded to droplets again before hitting the ground. He held his arms outstretched and the light show continued, then changed colour, his face smiling like a child meeting Santa Claus. He spun around and the lights twirled in a spiral. He started to laugh.

"What the heck is going on?" one of the guards asked.

No one answered. They stood mesmerised by the show in front of them.

Cal moved towards a grassy bank with a tree close to the hanger and laid down. The rain bounced all over his body, changing colours through the rainbow. Then he started to disappear, his legs at first, then hips and lower torso.

"What is happening?" Matt stepped out into the rain towards him, gun pointed.

Cal stood up and moved towards him, colour returning to his lower body as they walked back inside. "I'm sorry," he said. "I can make my suit change colour and blend into the background. I did not mean to scare you, but I have never seen real rain before."

The group stared in stunned silence and walked back inside.

"The others are here now," Cal said. "I can hear them at the gate."

They stood in silence for a minute until a group of large black vehicles wound around the roads and pulled into the hanger.

Swat team members in full riot gear jumped out and surrounded the group with machine guns trained on everyone. A well-dressed man got out of the lead vehicle and approached.

"Which one of you is Matt Petronas?" he asked.

"I am." Matt raised his hand but was careful to keep the gun pointed at the ground.

"I'm Jack Branigan, Director of Homeland Security. What's going on here?"

"Sir, this is an experimental facility engaged in the possibility of time travel, and this man," Matt pointed at Cal, "is from the future!"

CHAPTER FOUR

Jack Branigan stood five foot five, a hundred and eighty-five pounds, and rotund in stature. He had a round face, a ruddy complexion, and round horned-rimmed glasses, through which he stared at Matt.

"You're joking, right?"

"He is not," Cal said from behind.

Branigan swiveled around to look into the man's dark eyes.

"I was not talking to you, sir," he said. The homeland security chief looked him up and down, drawn to the name badge, which was level with his eyes. He examined it closely.

"Fancy suit you have on. What does the badge mean?"

"That's my name," Cal replied.

"And the number, 244?"

"That changes every year," Cal responded. "Next year I will be 245."

Branigan's face turned red. "Any more wisecracks, mister, and you are going straight to jail. In fact, you are going there anyway, but you're not making things better for yourself."

"Jack." Cal turned serious. "I am here on a mission to save the planet. I need to speak to this group of scientists."

The security chief looked at him briefly, then burst into a fit of laughter, doubling over and holding his belly. The security detail seemed to find it funny as well.

"Cuff him, boys," he said.

"Wait a moment," Cal said.

"No moments, son," the chief replied. "You are under arrest for trespassing in a restricted facility."

Two large soldiers came from behind and grabbed Cal's arms, but instead of restraining him, they were lifted off their feet and held in the air. Cal grew in height until he towered above everyone. As the group shrank back in fear, he swung the two guards around and placed them down.

"I wish no harm to anyone. Just give me a chance to explain."

As the guards retreated, the giant frame contracted and walked back a few steps.

"Before you start shooting at me, know that my suit is bulletproof." He pointed to a guard. "You, take a single shot at me on the side so it ricochets away from everybody."

The guard looked at his superior, who nodded. The gunshot echoed around the hanger, followed by a ping against the far wall as the bullet struck.

"Right!" Cal said. "Now let's all settle down and have a chat. Jack, I will go anywhere with you, jail if you like, but let me talk to the group first."

The chief nodded.

When they sat down and seemed to relax, he smiled and began.

"I am a hubrid. Not a robot, but a humanoid hybrid. That is, I have a humanoid body but retain my human brain, in the usual place." He pointed to his head. "I have a worker class body that allows me to complete tasks in high or low places, hence my ability to get smaller or larger.

"I also have an artificial intelligence unit that is housed in my body just below the neck and is coupled to the brain. They are both fed by a recirculating fluid that conducts electrical pulses between them. This gives me access to all of humanity's digitized data going back through history."

Some smiled, while others looked at him with incredulity.

"Coupled with sensors that improve hearing, sight, smell, and touch, I am able to do things beyond biological humans, but there are a few drawbacks."

"Like what?" Dan asked.

"I have no genitalia, for a start. We cannot breed. This type of body is made to suit the person who wants to carry on at the end of their normal life. Although my body is new, I retain the same appearance as I did when I was a normal human."

"Then you lived as a man before you were changed to a robot?" Matt asked.

"I am not a robot, Matt. I am a hubrid, and there is a big difference. But yes, I lived a full life and was married to a beautiful woman, but never had children. She died when I was one hundred twenty-eight, and I then decided to become a hubrid."

"That's ridiculous," Jack said. "That would make you over three hundred years old!"

"Three nighty-two, actually. Jack, I did not make the change until I was one hundred forty-eight. I could not decide until then. You see, hubrids, human-oids, and robots are tasked with protecting the humans."

Cal gave them a moment, then he continued.

"After about the twenty-second century, A.I. was doing all the work and decision making, so humanity became lazy in their thinking. They concentrated more on improving themselves through art, sport, music, religion, and entertainment. We focused on those pursuits instead of science. That is, until the planet started to die."

"That's enough," said Jack. "This is utter nonsense. Pure dribble. I'm putting a stop to this right now. Surrender or I will have all the guards shoot you until you drop."

"Alright, chief. Let me just say one more thing, then I will go wherever you want." Cal turned to the group. "I do not know if Stella can be helped, but if my people can, they will. I want you to repair the craft before I return. Also, I need to speak with as many scientists as possible so I can explain the situation to them. We need to find a solution and are unable to do it by ourselves. Can you help me with that?"

Matt hesitated for a moment, then nodded.

"Thank you. Alright then, Director Branigan. Do your worst."

The chief point towards a black SUV. With the guards surrounding him, Cal walked towards it and got in the back. Another guard pointed a rifle at him, then got inside beside him. The chief got in the front. As the convoy pulled away, the door locks in the SUV dropped down, then popped back up again.

"Not necessary," Cal said. The doors locked again, then immediately popped back up.

"Are we going to play this game all the way there?" He smiled, but Jack didn't find it funny.

CHAPTER FIVE

"Doctor Cooke, can you hear me?"

The voice gave her the impression it was far away but she was sure it was quite close. Confusion filled her mind and she hesitated.

"There is electroencephal activity. She can hear you," another said.

"Can you tell us your name?"

"Name? Stella Cooke," she replied.

"Stella, my name is Doctor Jevoah Amrid. I need you to relax and listen carefully to me. Can you do that for me?"

"Where am I? What is happening?"

It felt like she was in a deep dark hole and someone was talking down to her.

"You had an accident and now we are helping you recover. Things will feel strange and that is normal. Please stay calm as we talk you through this."

Jevoah's voice was soothing, as if this was a normal everyday occurrence.

"Did I die?" Stella felt panic rising within her.

"What are you last memories?" he asked.

Stella had many strange thoughts running around in her mind.

"I don't remember."

"Okay. Try to open your eyes slowly, and do not be afraid. You are restrained in a bed but that is only a precaution."

Her eyelids gradually opened. Two figures stood over her, one male, one female, almost in silhouette. She looked around. There were bars across her and a glass cover on top.

"What is happening to me?"

"You were in a craft. Do you remember that?"

Pain, she recalled. *Unbearable pain and noise.* Then memories came flooding in.

"Yes. What happened?"

"Stella, look up. I am going to show you a hologram of your body."

A translucent image of herself floated above her. Small but intricate internal parts shone through.

"Your body went through tremendous force, crushing your bones, collapsing the rib cage, and piercing your heart."

"I died? Is this heaven?" She felt a scream growing within her.

After a few moments of silence, the doctor spoke softly. "There is no easy way to tell you this, so listen and try to stay calm. Because of your helmet, we were able to save your brain. You have undergone a procedure to make you a hubrid humanoid."

Stella's arms came up banging against the bars, her legs flailed around and her body squirmed to break free. Panic imposed itself in every movement and now she did scream, intensely and shrilly venting all her emotions at once.

Her caregivers waited patiently while the restraint bed strained against the forces within. The metal on the sides of the bed bent outwards and the bars buckled as she pulled.

"She is going to break out!" the lab assistant said with concern.

"Wait, it will subside," he replied.

Slowly, her rage decreased. Her face was distorted in a grimace that displayed her frustration.

"Why did you do this to me?" she yelled.

"It was our only option, Stella. We need your help. The planet needs your help," said Jevoah.

"What do you mean, the planet needs my help?"

"You jumped into a future on the brink of a disaster. Earth is dying and we need a solution. Our scientific knowledge has been unable to find an answer."

The doctor implored her with his eyes, and she paused, trying to understand.

The lights and display screens of the operating theatre buzzed. "I need more information," she said finally.

"Of course, you do," the doctor replied. "When you are feeling stronger, you will work with a woman who has been through the same procedure. Nyla knows a lot about our culture and technology, and will mentor you as you learn about our world."

He waved a hand, gesturing someone to come forward. A woman's face appeared. Bright white teeth smiled and sparkling deep brown eyes set in a dark oval face looked down at Stella.

"Hello, Stella. My name is Nyla and like you, I am a hubrid humanoid."

Doctor Amrid cut in. "We will leave to you two to get accustomed and caught up on your unique circumstances. We will be back later to help you get up."

As they left, Nyla came more into view and spoke soothingly. "I know you have a million questions, but let me try to help. Is that okay?"

Stella nodded in agreement.

"We have had humanoids for hundreds of years. They have an artificial intelligence system and work well doing all the tasks humans did not want or were unable to do. They don't require rest or pay and have been effective in keeping the world peaceful. Humans were able to devote themselves to what was thought more meaningful pursuits like sports, art, religion, entertainment, and the progress of human evolution. However, when the planet started to lose its atmosphere and deteriorate, humans realized there was a problem A.I. could not fix.

"It was thought a combination of artificial intelligence and human brains could solve the problem. Scholars with years of experience were the first to undergo the procedure. Then others who saw the benefits of living on past their normal life span decided to become robotic."

"What are the benefits?" Stella asked.

"For one thing, the humanoid body is powered by a fusion-energy induction system that is viable for a thousand years."

"What? A thousand years?" Stella exclaimed.

"Yes," Nyla said. "There are two chambers of compounds that when fused together in small increments produce all the power required. These chambers are situated within your chest cavities and make breathing oxygen unnecessary. This mean you have the ability to go anywhere."

"In space, you mean?" Stella asked.

"Yes, even there. But there's more. Your brain is in the normal place but is linked to an A.I. unit situated below the neck and at the top of the chest cavity. This gives you unparalleled access to knowledge and data. You are more intelligent than any computer from your era and you only have to think the question to access it. The A.I. unit and your brain are kept alive by a fluid able to oxygenate the brain and transmit electroencephal communication between them."

"Is that why I feel so confused?"

"Yes," Nyla answered. "There is a lot more to get used to and I am here to help you with that. You are also stronger than any normal person and have enhancements like improved vision, better hearing, touch sensors that can transmit signals and diagnosis ailments, and more. You will learn how to control them all in time."

Stella looked confused and lost.

"Are you ready to begin?"

Stella acquiesced.

CHAPTER SIX

Cal did not take any notice of where they were going as they left the hanger; he was fascinated by the buildings. It appeared that they were in a business park with cars parked outside steel gray units and tall hangars on each side of the road. They travelled past three smaller office blocks and approached the exit gate. It rolled apart and allowed them access to a main road. That's when he really got excited. There were shops and lights and groups of people walking out in the open. His eyes followed each of them. It was unbelievable—people out in the open!

They drove for fifteen minutes and Cal was awestruck. He had seen this type of thing on old film but to witness it first-hand, that was a thrill he never thought he would ever witness.

No one spoke but they tensed up as they came to a tall fence with barbed wire running along the top. The vehicle slowed and turned into a tall gate that opened to let them through. They pulled up outside a large door situated on the side of a tall, plain structure. The sign outside said 'Blackwater River Correctional Facility'.

Branigan got out and opened the door for Cal, who was then surrounded by security as they walked inside.

They breezed by an entrance desk with a brush of the hand from the security chief and strode down hallways with high glossy walls. At the end, a steel gate was unlocked by a large man in uniform. Above the steel bars a sign read 'Solitary Confinement Unit'.

"The first one on the right is open, sir." The guard motioned to an open cell.

"Thanks, Sargent."

Squeezing around him, Cal was ushered into the cell. The guards exited and left the homeland security chief alone with him.

"Anything you want to say?" Jack asked.

Looking around the bare ten by eight room, Cal turned to face him.

"I could ask for a lawyer but he would not believe me either. Would he?"

Branigan scowled. "You would not get one anyway. Not until I get the truth from you. Want to confess?"

"I spoke the truth, but you cannot bring yourself to believe it. I need you to confer with your superiors and get me back to the facility. You can ask me any questions you like and I'll answer truthfully."

"No, I think we'll let you stew awhile." The chief smiled and stepped backwards out the cell. "Close her up, Sargent."

A steeled bar door started closing from the side, sidling along until it reached the end. With a clunk, it latched closed. There was another clunk as it opened and started back.

"Sargent, close it," Jack shouted.

The door switched direction, closed, then latched before it unlatched again and began sliding open.

"You're wasting your time, Jack. You can't hold me. It would be better to put me under house arrest until we reach an understanding, I'll be more cooperative, especially if you let me go back to the facility" Cal said.

With an angry look, the chief turned toward prison guard.

"Do you have a mechanical lock cell?"

"Yes sir, bottom one on the left. I'll bring the key."

The chief nodded in the direction of the cell and Cal followed him. Once he was inside, the door swung closed and the key turned, locking him in. A metal window in the door slid open and an irate face stared in.

"We will see how you feel in a few hours." The window slid shut and the chief strode away.

A few minutes later, the Sargent was entering the new prisoner's information into his log. He looked up from the computer screen after he heard a click and was shocked to see Cal standing in front of him.

"What the fuck?"

Cal stretched over the desk and placed his hand on the big man's shoulder, keeping him down in the chair despite all his efforts to get up.

"You look tired. You need a nice restful sleep. When you awaken, you will feel restored and relaxed."

He placed a finger onto his skin and the guard slumped down in the chair.

CHAPTER SEVEN

The architecture, shops, and restaurants, all grabbed Cal's attention as he wandered the streets. He tried to take it all in, absorb the ambiance, and file it away to be scrutinised at a later date. He came upon a café with tables outside.

"Fancy dress ball last night or going to a comic-con convention?" a patron yelled.

"Neither. This is the latest fashion; comes in any colour," he replied with a smile.

Everyone returned to drinking their lattes and eating their buttery scones.

Entering an older district, he noted the taller buildings had year markings across the top—1886 or 1890. This shocked him and he analysed them intently. Walking slowly, he came across a bank that looked like a roman structure with huge round columns stretching up to a pyramid portico. Fascinated, he walked in and was greeted by a security officer.

'Can I help you, sir?" he asked.

"No," Cal replied. "I am just curious about the architecture." He looked up at a dome ceiling.

"Yes, grand, isn't it? They say Italian craftsmen were brought in to sculpt the interior in 1891."

"Amazing." Cal wandered into the middle, under the centre of the dome. Frescos were painted around the lower base depicting scenes from sailing ships, ancient landscapes, and people dressed from an older era.

Suddenly, there was a commotion near the entrance and voices started shouting.

"Down on the ground, everybody. Now! This is a robbery! Everyone down on the ground!"

Cal looked away from the dome and watched. The guard by the entrance was already splayed on the floor with a gun at his head and two others were waving assault rifles around. All three had ski masks over their heads and were advancing on customers, who all dropped to the floor. Cal thought it prudent to do the same. Too many innocent people, not enough time.

The leader, who had done all the shouting, strode purposely towards a desk with an elderly man on one side and a young woman on the other. He grabbed the woman by the arm and motioned with the gun for the man to get up.

"You're the manager?" he asked.

"Yes," stammered the man, trembling.

"You're going to open the vault or the girl's life is on you!" He lifted a revolver to the woman's head.

"I can't, it's on a time lock." The manager was shaking, eyes wide and staring at the robber.

"You're the manager, which means you know the override. Open it now." The robber was getting angry.

Visibly unsteady on his feet, the manager looked as if he would faint. "I can't."

"Do it or she gets it," the man shouted.

"I can open it," Cal called.

All eyes swivelled towards him. The leader swung the girl around so he could see him.

"I am familiar with these systems and can open it no trouble."

The leader waved Cal over and, rising slowly, he moved towards the group.

"How do you know?" the robber asked.

"I used to work on them. I can open it, really I can."

"Let's go." The thief looked at his companions. "Watch the others and don't let them make a move."

Marble steps led down to the vault. The manager led the way, followed by Cal, then the girl with a gun still held to her head. The stairs took a turn to the left and then a steel barred gate blocked the entrance to the vault. Pulling keys from his pocket, the bank supervisor unlocked the gate and pushed it open. He went through first, followed by Cal.

As the thief and the girl entered, there was a sudden movement. The girl turned and found the robber slumped over the arm of the strange man.

"Take his guns," Cal said, motioning to the girl. "I do not like touching them."

"What?" the manager said loudly.

"Shush, quiet down," Cal said. "What are your names?"

"Harold," the man said.

"Irene." The girl was still agitated but getting it under control.

Unhooking a bag from the robber's shoulder, Cal offered it to the girl.

"Put all his guns in the bag, quietly, while I move him further in." Taking the ski mask off the man, Cal slid him effortlessly along the ground.

The girl and the manager stood in amazement as Cal's clothes changed colour to the same as the robber and he slipped the ski mask over his head.

"Wait here and do not make sound." Cal lifted the bag and went upstairs.

Eyes shifted towards him as he reached the top step. Pretending the bag was heavy, he laid it down and motioned to the middle robber to follow him. Trying his best to remember the lead robbers' voice, he said, "Bring your bag. I need help."

Turning back downstairs, the other robber followed obediently and scrambled quickly after his boss. As he turned the corner, a hand grabbed him and he lost consciousness.

Dragging the two robbers together, he frisked them. He removed their weapons and put them in the second bag.

"Wait here," he told Irene and Harold.

Striding across the foyer towards the thief at the entrance, he offered him the bag. Instinctively holding out his hand to take it, he was grabbed and slung over Cal's shoulder.

With a quizzical frown, the security guard got up as Cal pulled off the ski mask.

"Wait here, I won't be long." Cal went back down the stairs.

"What's going on?" Irene asked as the third robber was dumped.

"It's over," Cal said. "Give me a hand to make sure they are all unarmed, then lock them in here, Harry.'

"What did you do to them?' Irene asked.

He turned to look at her in detail for the first time. She was slim, blonde, with azure blue eyes, and very pretty with an oval face and pale pink lips. She made him hesitate for a moment.

"I used a laser on them. Eh, no that's not the right word. I used a Taser on them." He felt flustered.

The other two looked at him with hesitant frowns.

"I have to go," he blurted out. "Harry, calm your customers down before the police get here. I have to go; I'm not supposed to be here. Irene, take care."

Upstairs, he went to the security guard.

"Tell everyone it's over. Calm them down and wait for the police to come. Tell them the getaway driver will be the one outside asleep at the wheel."

Without waiting for an answer, he strode out the door as the sound of sirens started to fill the air.

CHAPTER EIGHT

Sensors in his nose and mouth told him he was close. He could smell the sea breeze and taste the salt in the air. If only he could see it once in his lifetime and feel the waves lapping at his feet. It would be such a thrill.

All the films he had seen, the artificial underground lakes, and the data he could access could not replace the real thing. He was already overwhelmed with sights, sounds, and smells, and had an intense desire to witness a real ocean.

"Cal, Cal!" A voice broke his thoughts. He looked in its direction to see Irene sitting in a car.

She called again and waved him over. "Get in. The police are looking for you and you stand out like a clown at a wedding."

"How did you find me?" he asked, getting in.

"I was lucky. Dressed in that outfit, it won't take long for the police to find you." She looked around nervously.

"What happened?" he asked after they had made eye contact. "Back there."

"The police arrived and took away the bad guys, got statements from us all, then examined the video footage from the bank's security cameras. And now they are looking for you! You should not have left. Who are you and what are you running from?"

"I'm not running, I just don't need the hassle right now. I have things to do and I will be in trouble for walking away."

They sat in silence for a few moments, contemplating the situation.

"You need to get out of those clothes. You are too conspicuous." Irene nodded out the window. "There's a menswear shop over there."

"I can't, I don't have any credits."

"Money, you mean?"

"Yes," he replied.

She smiled. "I guess the least I can do is buy you a new outfit, after you saved my life."

"Your life was never in danger," Cal said.

"With a gun at my head I would have to disagree. C'mon, let's go." She opened her car door and got out, Cal followed her.

Inside the shop, he chose a long-sleeved shirt in a plain blue colour and darker blue pants to match. In the changing rooms, he put them on overtop of his suit. When he emerged, she looked him over.

"That's better. You don't stand out now, but you could have taken the suit off underneath."

"Can't," he answered, not offering an excuse.

After paying, they got back in the car.

"Thank you. I have never had a woman buy me clothes before." He was amused at the thought.

"You're welcome," she replied.

Looking intently though the windshield, he asked, "Is the ocean close?"

"Not far, why?"

"I really want to see it, but should get back." He thought for a moment. "They are probably already looking for me, so another hour won't make a difference."

"I know someone at the marina," Irene said. "If you want I can take you there."

"Would you?"

In less than ten minutes, they entered a car park alongside boat docks with yachts and various watercraft moored up. Mesmerised, he sat unable to move, captivated by the sights and sounds of ocean activity. He saw the beach and people were in the water, swimming, playing with balls, and resting under umbrellas. People were actually in the water!"

"Are you coming?" Irene was already out of the car and waiting for him.

"Sorry, it's just overwhelming."

"I know someone with a boat. Let's go see if he's aboard."

Like a small child following his mother, he dragged his heels, wanting to stop at every new encounter with things he had never seen before.

"You coming?" she asked, turning around to find him lagging way behind.

He caught her just as she drew level with a bright white yacht named "Seahorse."

"Craig? Are you here?" she called.

Within a few seconds, a head popped up from an open galley slide.

"Irene, is that you?" A blonde haired young man, his face tanned, emerged from the steps. "What are you doing here? It's not the weekend."

"Just popped by on the off chance you were here. This is Cal and he is fascinated by all things nautical."

The two men shook hands. "Are you feeling better?"

"Pardon? How'd you know I was sick?" Craig asked.

Cal felt a little flustered, realizing his error. "You look a bit green around the gills."

Craig eyed him suspiciously. "I was sick earlier, but I didn't know it showed. I'm better now, thanks." Turning back to Irene, he grinned, his bright white smile flashing.

"You're in luck. I just did some repairs to the engine and was going to take her out for a half-hour if you want to come."

Curiosity got to Cal and he tried to avoid hampering the sailor as they got underway, but Craig had to go around him a number of times. Cal apologised but he could see it was annoying the other man. Finally, he sat beside Irene and observed.

She scrutinised him, still unable to understand what he was all about.

"What you looking at?" she asked.

"That young girl on the pier in the pink swimsuit. Is she skipping? Is that a skipping rope?"

Irene stared in the direction he was looking.

"Where?"

"Over there on the pier."

"Craig, do you have any binoculars?"

"Of course," He handed them to her.

She focused on the pier for a while, moving side to side, then stopped, adjusted the glasses, and dropped them before turning to Cal.

"You can see that? That little girl skipping?"

He nodded.

"Craig, can you see a girl skipping on the pier over there?"

Craig looked over and squinted. "No, of course not. That's a mile or more away."

Irene stared blankly at Cal. Embarrassed, he tried to change the subject.

"Is it okay if I swim in the ocean?"

"Go ahead," Craig said, cutting the power. "I want to check on the engine anyway."

Cal stood and stripped off his shirt and pants then walked towards the edge.

"Aren't you going to take off your suit?" Irene asked.

"No, it's waterproof," he replied.

"Oh, I just wanted to see you skinny dipping."

He smiled, shaking his head before jumping over the side.

Instantly, he knew he had made a mistake. He sank like an anchor, straight to the bottom. It had been hundreds of years since he last swam as a human and he had forgot he had no air to keep him afloat. He thought that by kicking or pulling with his arms, he could swim upwards but found he was unable to.

Facing upward, he saw the bottom of the boat outlined against the surface of the water. He jumped as hard as he could, but could not reach the vessel and fell back to the sea floor.

Looking around, he knew he had to walk back to the shore. At least he could observe the marine environment for longer than he had anticipated.

CHAPTER NINE

"Craig! Craig!" Irene shouted down to the engine room.

" What is it?"

"It's Cal. He hasn't surfaced after jumping in. I walked around the boat and can't see any sign of him."

Blonde hair came up the steps followed by the usual bright smile. He studied her and looked around before reaching the deck.

"Are you sure?"

"Yes! It's been nearly ten minutes since he went over."

They went around the boat's edge, searching for any sign of movement.

"I'll jump in and have a look around," Craig said.

He took off his shorts and had a swimsuit underneath. Grabbing a face mask, he slipped it on and jumped in. Irene leaned over the ship's side to watch him dive down and back a number of times before finally climbing back onboard.

"No sign of anyone," he said, breathless. "Who the hell is he, Irene? He seems very weird!"

"I don't really know. I only met him today."

She told him the whole story about the bank robbery and everything that had happened after.

"He saved my life, stopped a robbery, and disabled three men with guns. I can't explain it, but I trust him."

They sat wondering what to do next when they heard a whistling noise. They looked toward the shore to see Cal waving his arms.

"How in the heck did he get there?" Craig said, incredulous.

Astounded, Irene tried to calculate the distance to the shore and how long it would take to swim there. It did not seem possible for anyone but a world class swimmer.

"We best get back," Craig said.

It took twenty minutes to reach the dock where Cal was waiting. He jumped back onboard to retrieve his shirt and pants.

"Sorry about that. I got disorientated and found I was closer to the shore than the boat, so I came here."

"What were you thinking," Irene said, irritated. "We were worried about you. I thought you had drowned."

Sheepishly, he tried to make excuses. The other two listened as he put on his clothes, then he tried to give them a reassuring smile.

"I have to get back, so I want to thank you both for everything. I'm already in trouble. Everyone will be searching for me."

"I'll take you," Irene said.

"No, I can make my way back," Cal said.

"Don't argue," Irene said. "Let's go."

They drove back the way they had come, passed the bank and some policemen, but weren't stopped. They didn't speak except for directions given by Cal as he retraced his steps. As they got closer to his destination, he felt obligated to say something.

"I didn't mean for all of this to happen. I want to thank you for being accepting of the situation. Perhaps you will understand later."

She was still confused and his comments did not bring any more clarity.

"What situation?" she asked.

"Just pull over here," Cal said.

Irene looked around and saw the high fences and lookout towers.

"But this is a prison. My father sometimes comes here for his work."

"Yes. I'm something of a house guest."

"That explains some of it, like why the police are looking for you. What have you done?" Irene asked.

"Nothing, really. It's all a confused mess that will get straightened out soon."

As they got closer to the main entrance, she pulled over to let him out. With his hand on the door handle, he turned to her.

"I am grateful for your understanding. Thank you again and please thank Craig next time you see him." The car door open and he went to step out.

"Wait," she said. "Where did you get that suit? I want one like that, one that changes colour."

"You can't," he replied.

"Why not?"

He looked her straight in the eye. "You have to be dead!"

***

The Sargent looked up from his desk as he heard footsteps approaching.

"Ah, you're back then. Had a nice little jaunt, did you?"

"Yes, Sir. How are you feeling now?" Cal replied.

"Better than you will feel when they get through with you. You are all over the news and the chief is having a fit. I've never seen him so agitated."

"Better let him know I'm back then. I will wait in the cell until he gets here."

He settled down to wait in the cell with the door open. He had done things that day he never thought could happen to him and if he had done wrong, it was worth it. He probed the recordings in his mind, examining every moment.

Soon there were footsteps as a SWAT team entered, guns pointed at him, eyes glued for any movement. He lay motionless on the bed. Jack Branigan was right behind and strode up to Cal, his face showing no emotion.

"You are all over the news," he said.

"I know. I did not mean for any of this to happen. I was just taking a look around; you know, a recce.'

"A recce! A little recce! The whole world wants to know who you are and you went for a little recce!"

"Sorry," Cal said. 'You said you were going to leave me for a few hours. I could not let the time go to waste."

"Well, you got some attention. The Homeland Security Committee wants to interview you tomorrow morning. In the mean time, you are to be put under house arrest with me. That means at my house, under my supervision."

Cal smiled. "You should have done that in the first place. I asked you to. I knew we were to be best friends."

CHAPTER TEN

Legacy Woods was a residential neighbourhood of estate homes on the northwest outer limits of town. Jack Branigan had worked his way up to settling his family around a private school, golf course, and all amenities needed for a cozy life.

As the black SUV pulled up to his drive, there was a police cruiser parked on the road outside. Getting out of the front, the chief indicated for Cal to follow and they both walked to the cruiser. The driver's window slid down.

"Officer..." Jack looked at his badge. "Officer Jarvis, are you assigned to patrol this area tonight?"

"Yes sir. Another car will relieve me later."

The chief pointed at Cal.

"If you see this man leave the house, call it in. There is a SWAT team nearby. Do not approach him. He is dangerous."

"No, I'm not," Cal said.

Jack ignored him. "My driver is leaving, so you are on your own outside the house. Understood?"

"Yes sir."

The house's front door was a double steel entry, reinforced and surrounded by cameras. He showed his face to one before inserting a key and opening the front door.

"Hi, I'm home."

Cal heard a couple of people approaching. A woman appeared, blonde and slim, with an oval face.

"This is my wife Laura. And this is Cal, not sure what he is."

They shook hands and Cal held on for longer than normal.

"And this my daughter..."

"Irene!" Cal called, looking past Laura. "Long time no see."

"Yes, well, I know you have already met. Now you see why I agreed to look after you. I would have been pretty mad if it had been anyone else you rescued."

"No, you wouldn't," Laura interrupted. "You're happy when any civilian gets rescued."

Cal let go Laura's hand and reached out to Irene.

"How are you feeling now?"

"Still confused," she said. "Maybe we will get some answers."

"Maybe." Cal replied. He turned to face her mother. "I can see where she gets her good looks from."

"Flattery does not work on me, but keep trying," Laura said. "Suppers ready so please come through."

They crossed the foyer and entered a room with a set dining table, plates and dishes all laid out and tureens of food set it the middle. Irene indicated for Cal to sit next to her.

"Help yourself," Laura said to Cal.

"Mrs. Branigan, I have to tell you something."

"What, you don't like duck?"

Cal looked embarrassed. "I do not eat."

Everyone froze, staring at him.

"Let me explain, but please do not spoil your dinner. Don't let it go cold."

Cal indicated for them to resume their meal and slowly the others filled their plates and settled down.

"I am not human," Cal said. They all stopped again and stared at him.

"I knew it!" Irene said. "I knew all along there was something strange about you."

"I am a humanoid hubrid and as such I am powered by non-metabolic systems. I have sensors in my mouth for taste and in my nostrils for smell but no digestive system. I can put the food in my mouth and taste it, but would have to spit it out."

They stared at him as if he had two heads.

"Please carry on. I feel awkward not letting you eat your meal."

The family reluctantly carried on picking at their plates, slowly chewing but not taking their eyes of him.

"Also, I do not breathe oxygen. It is not required when I have a separate power source, but that can have drawbacks—as I found out today."

Cal hesitated and Irene burst out laughing, lifting her serviette to her mouth.

"That explains a lot."

The parents looked at the other two with confused looks and Cal went on to explain.

"When I was human before converted, I used to love to swim in a pool, but never in the sea. Today on a boat with Irene and her friend Craig, I just wanted to swim in the ocean. When I jumped in, it had been so long I had forgot I would sink to the bottom."

"Craig and I searched all around," said Irene. "There was no sign of him and Craig even dove down looking for him."

"It was very embarrassing," Cal said. "I had to walk back to the shore along the seabed."

They all had a polite laugh and Jack turned to him.

"Explain what you did to those criminals and my officers."

All eyes were once again on him.

"It's called tonic immobility," Cal said. "The most common knowledge of it refers to sharks that when flipped upside down become immobile, if left they will die. Even whales and orcas know of it, and after flipping them over, they wait for them to die before eating them. There are many other instances of this phenomenon in other animals. Lobsters, for instance, turned on their heads also go into a state of catalepsy. As with animals, it can also be induced in humans. Hypnotists can induce it on people already in a trance. I can induce it by sending a neurologic signal to the brain and, depending on the strength of the signal, can set the time for the person to be in a cataleptic state. I have to be able to touch the skin to transmit and have to be careful not give too strong a jolt to cause memory loss. If you Taser someone, you shock their whole body; I merely induce a light trauma to their consciousness."

They all reflected on this while finishing their meal.

"Can you teach me to do it?" Irene asked.

"No," Cal replied. "You have to have receptors and transmitting sensors in your fingertips. When you convert to a hubrid, your body is all wires, mechanical systems, and power convertors. They are all packed into this suit, which I cannot take off."

"Tell me," Laura asked, "what was your name before being converted, and why was it done?"

"My name was Callum Moorcroft; I think it referred back to my ancient Celtic roots. But we have our name shortened to a designation so that humans can recognise us for what we are."

Jack opened his mouth to speak but Cal stopped him.

"Save it for tomorrow's meeting. There is one other thing. I do not sleep, it's not necessary. Laura, if there is any housework or jobs you need doing, I can easily help."

"No, there is nothing," said Jack, intervening.

"All right. Well, I promise not to leave the house while you sleep, but I have one request."

"What?"

"Can you turn on your internet? I want to do some research on scientists that can help."

"I can turn it on but you cannot use any computers, they are confidential."

"I do not need a computer; I have my own."

***

Later that night, Cal wandered the house. He had heard Jack and Laura go to bed in separate rooms, and crept upstairs. Listening, he knew she was awake, and he quietly opened the door.

"Laura." he whispered.

"Don't come any farther. I have an alarm button in my hand."

"I only want to talk. You have nothing to fear from me."

"What do you want?" she asked.

"I know about the tumour." He waited.

"How?"

"When we shook hands, I scanned you. I do it automatically. Sorry."

He heard a quiet sobbing.

He slowly approached her bed but held back before invading her space.

"Who knows?" he asked.

"Only Jack, not Irene." She paused. "And it's inoperable."

"Maybe at this time, but will be cured one day," Cal said. "But I can help."

"What, how?" Laura stared at his face in the dim light.

"I can stimulate your immune system to fight the tumor and kill it off. There is only one problem."

"What's that?" she asked.

"It will make you very sick. You will feel bad for about a week before starting to feel anything like normal again."

"You can do that?"

"Yes, but I need a promise that no one will ever know. I don't need the hassle of people coming after me for cures."

She paused for a moment.

"Alright, do it." There was determination in her voice.

"I have to put both my hands on your skin. You will feel a tingling sensation in your chest where the tumor is attached to your liver, but it will only be a minute. Then I will put you to sleep but you will wake up with headaches, nausea, and sickness. I'm sorry."

Cal placed his hands on her bare arms and sent the signals. She tensed slightly before settling and going to sleep.

CHAPTER ELEVEN

Nyla had been talking for over an hour. Stella listened carefully while taking note of her surroundings. They were in a hospital but like nothing she had ever seen. It had glass walls and doors outlined in a blue light. Instruments and tables, desks, and equipment were all luminous and yet user friendly and inviting to touch.

"Are you ready to get up?" Nyla asked.

"I think so," Stella said.

Her mentor pressed a button and the transparent screen slid back, then the steel braces across her body retracted to each side.

"Easy does it," Nyla said.

Slowly the bed tilted, bringing her up to a standing position. With hands holding the sides, she took a step.

Instead of walking forward, she flew outward as if she was shot from a cannon and hurtled across the floor on her stomach. Sliding frantically towards a double door, which sprung open at the last second, she carried on straight through. Hands outstretched, she stopped about twenty-five feet from where she started. Nyla came running.

"You're okay, you just don't know your own strength yet. Baby steps. Move slowly and easily."

She felt like an idiot and apologised, gradually getting to her feet.

"I don't know what I'm doing," Stella said. "It's so strange."

"That's why I'm here." Nyla comforted her. "It will take time. You have to think about the physical act of walking first. After a while your A.I. unit will get used to interpreting your thoughts and turning them into actions. Soon all of it will become natural and you will not only do every action normally, but without thinking."

"I hope you're right because it feels completely unnatural to me," Stella said.

"Let's take a slow walk to the rehabilitation gym and work on getting you acclimated to the new you and you can return here anytime." Nyla took her arm and they walked steadily down the corridor.

Entering a large open room, Stella noted what looked like exercise equipment. Some of it was being used by two women and three men. The workout apparatus was bent and old and did not look as if it were useable.

"What's with the equipment?" she asked.

"They recently had the same procedure and don't know their own strength either."

They had all stopped and were looking at Stella curiously.

"We hope you can help us," one called.

"I do too," Stella replied.

"They all know who you are." Nyla told her. You are the biggest story in the world."

"I am?"

"You are! Just say to yourself 'news network' and you will see."

Stella looked at Nyla, mystified, and then silently mouthed the words. A hologram jumped out in front of her. Stunned, she watched a video of her being lifted out of her craft and loaded onto a stretcher vehicle, accompanied by commentary.

'Doctor Cooke, we believe her name is Stella, arrived from the past. The journey is so perilous and she is suffering from grave injuries, but is being treated as a great ancestor in the reclamation clinic. With recovery, it is hoped she can shed light on and aid our scientists in earth's revival.'

"No pressure then," Stella said ruefully.

Semi-transparent blue walls went on endlessly. Doors were spaced evenly along the corridors and by each one there was a small round light. They looked like doorbells, but each had a red diagonal line through it, like a no entry road sign.

"What are these doorbells?" she asked, turning to Nyla.

"They are not doorbells, but indicate whether or not the apartment is occupied. No red stripe means you can use it. You know all this. Everything you need to know is already in your A.I. databanks. Like I told you before, you just have to ask yourself the question and it will spring into your mind."

"I keep forgetting," she said. "How much further is it?"

Her final meeting before finishing the guidance and re-introduction program was to meet with the Elders Committee. She was apprehensive and wary. What did they expect from her? Could she ever go back to her own era? Her mind was filled with endless questions, none of which could be answered by her A.I.

"Not much further. You have to meet with a prominent elder first," Nyla said.

They turned a corner and at the end of the hallway were a large pair of entrance doors marked 'Congress Halls'. Nyla ushered her into a different, smaller room on the right.

They were met by a tall man wearing a suit like their own, but he seemed to glow in a silvery light. The man had white hair, a square jaw, and deep dark eyes that seemed to penetrate into her soul.

"Good morning, Stella." He gave her a radiant smile. "My name is Talan. I will guide you through the meeting today."

They shook hands and he guided them to a desk with a scroll rolled up in the middle and a small pot beside it. They sat down with Stella facing the other two.

"First, let me say I was in charge when you arrived and it was my decision to convert you. If you are angry or disapprove, you are free to vent at me."

Stella stared him in the eyes and gathered her thoughts.

"I was mad at first, thinking you had no right to make that decision, but I have tried to rationalize the situation and am curious to find out more."

Silence filled the room and a discordant ambiance seemed to bristle between them. Finally, Talan broke eye contact.

"Back in your era, according to historical data, your entertainment media had a fascination with superheroes and super powers. I have to tell you that you do not have super powers. You cannot fly or break down buildings or have x-ray vision. None of that is available to you. Do you understand?"

"That's disappointing," Stella said with a smirk. "But go on."

"However, you have great abilities denied to normal humans. We have progressed for a thousand years, and now you are at the pinnacle of that development. Stronger and faster than any human, your senses can outperform any one, even some animals. You are the top of the evolution chain. More than that, you have an intelligence capability that exceeds anything that we have produced before. Even we are not sure what is possible and what can be developed when you set your mind to it."

"I do not feel that," Stella said.

"It is early days," Talan said. "Clarity of thought will increase with use and your performance will be enhanced through challenge. We have great hopes for you."

They sat in silence for a minute or two. Stella tried to understand everything that had happened.

"Let us continue with the ceremonies, shall we?" He picked up the scroll. "This is usually explained to people before going through the conversion and they have to agree beforehand. You have to swear to a covenant, pronounce it to a council committee, and sign it. Basically, it states you will protect life and humanity above all else, even yourself, and devote all your efforts to restoring planet earth. Is that understood?"

Stella concurred.

"Do you agree?"

She wrestled with thoughts of commitments, to a new life and past loyalties, to making new friends and remembering old friendships, in the end there was no choice.

"Yes."

The elder smiled. "There is one last stipulation we go through with every conversion. We need to bring closure to your previous existence." He hesitated. "Next door is a line of drawers, one of which contains your old body."

Stella froze, her eyes widening at the thought of what she would have to face.

"We expect you to confront that body. By placing your hands on it, you may discover the cause of your death. You then decide how you wish your body to be interred, which allows you to begin a new existence. The pot you see here holds a sample of your blood, which you will use to sign the agreement on the scroll."

"This is rather macabre, isn't it?" Stella asked.

With a sombre expression, the elder continued. "This is a binding agreement between you and humanity. The DNA from your blood is a testament to your conviction and may be called upon if you are charged with any crime against humanity. Do you understand?"

"Yes."

"Do you agree?"

"I don't think I have any choice, but yes, I agree to all the stipulations."

Talan looked relieved and stood up, lifted the scroll, and walked to the next room. The two women followed. A drawer in the wall was partially open and the elder pulled it all the way out. Stella held back and watched in horror. A body bag enveloped the corpse and Talan motioned her over.

"The bag is cryogenic and will preserve the body until we can enact your wishes. Are you ready?"

Stella nodded and tensed up as he pulled down the zip in the middle.

Her face looked calm and at peace. Her skin was coloured as if alive and her hair pulled back as she normally kept it. She knew there was no brain inside the skull, and she wondered about her soul. Did she have her own soul with her? Was there even such a thing?

"What does the religious community think about this and a person's soul?" The question tumbled out of her mouth without thinking.

Stella stared first at the elder and then Nyla.

"Most religions have had to rethink their positions on the soul," Talan started. "The soul has never been proven to exist and there are many arguments by scholars and scientists. It is left to each person to believe or not, but even non-believers admit to the existence of a soul as a possibility. My view is that all religions believe that God is love and the soul was thought to reside in the heart. In our present state, our human minds still feel emotion, including love, we don't feel physical pain but every other feeling is still in our minds and memories.

Our thoughts and actions portray love to humanity and grace to God. Therefore, I believe our soul is within us at any stage of living and we grow exponentially with acts of love."

He pointed with his hands for her to touch the body.

Trembling hands reached out and touched the hands crossed in front of the body, sensors flooded her brains with data.

She saw confirmation of broken bones, torn ligaments, contusions, a non-beating heart, and pierced lungs. If she were able to cry, tears would have rolled down her cheeks. Her eyes turned upward and a silent prayer formed within her, bonding to the body beneath her hands.

"If possible I would like my body returned to my era for my family to have closure," Stella said.

"Of course, We will hold it here and carry out your wishes. If and when your ship returns." The elder closed the zipper and pushed the drawer into its slot.

Lifting the scroll and indicating for them to follow, he stepped out towards a door into the main chambers.

CHAPTER TWELVE

The black SUV approached a legislative building in the old part of town. Once a mayoral and town council department, it was now used primarily for civic functions. Police waved the vehicle through a large gate and around the back to a private entrance sometimes used to usher criminals to courts.

"You have gained this audience because of the notoriety from TV, so don't waste it," Jack said. "Some members of the committee have flown in specifically for this meeting. I managed to get nine and that is enough for a quorum to make it legal, but they will probably not commit to a binding agreement on your status. The best you can hope for is to be allowed to state your case to the scientific community."

Cal nodded and they exited the vehicle and entered the building. They were led to a large boardroom with a desk in the middle. Two chairs were behind it and a long bench was set up in front. Cal and Jack sat in the two chairs at the desk while the Homeland Security Committee took the seats behind the bench. Some had coffee and others had water in coloured containers. They settled down with a woman chairperson in the middle. Three men and a woman were on her right and two of each gender on her left.

"My name is Patricia Niven and I convene this meeting to order." She named the other members attending.

She had a stern countenance but a pleasant smile, short hair with grey streaks, and blue-grey eyes that focused on Cal.

"Please state your full name, origin, and date of birth."

"Cal 244 is my designation as a non-human. My previous name was Callum Moorcroft. Florida state. Fourteenth of November, thirty-six seventeen."

Mutterings spread around the room.

"How do you expect us to believe that?" Patricia asked.

"If I could explain recent developments, maybe we can get passed this."

"Alright Mr. Moorcroft, we're listening."

Starting from when the craft arrived on a desolate desert, Cal described everything that had happened. Behind the desk, some gasped, others listened intently, and some almost choked while trying to take a drink.

"You have seen video coverage of some of the events that has happened since my arrival and Director Branigan can vouch for my actions while in his custody," Cal said finishing his speech.

Patricia smiled at him. "Can you prove who you are? Do you have any proof of where and when you are from?"

"If I may approach, ma'am, I have some evidence that I wish to share with you and the scientific community."

They agreed and he approached the bench. Placing his right hand on the left side of his chest, Cal swiped his hand across, pulled out a palm-sized thin box, and laid it on the desk. It began to unfold until it was about a foot square, then lights came on at each corner. A hologram of earth appeared, hovering above the board and rotating slowly. Distinct lines appeared to cross the globe.

"This is what we call a holook, producing a hologram that shows the earth of the future—forty sixteen, to be exact," Cal began. "It is a desolate place, covered in deserts and only small pockets of water where the deepest parts of the oceans used to be. The atmosphere is unbreathable and humans have taken to living underground where air is decontaminated and recirculated. Water is purified and reused again and again. Cities have been built using materials reclaimed from above ground. The only beings able to go to the surface are humanoids or humanoid hybrids like myself. Droids and other robots are used to maintain human life until we can revive the planet."

"Around the year thirty-five hundred, the earth's magnetic field started depleting rapidly. It was a loss of seven billion kilowatt hours per month instead of per year. It was expected to last until thirty-nine ninety and possibly reverse polarity and strengthen."

"The last time that happened was around seven hundred thousand years ago, but instead of reversing, it degraded slowly until the climate changed to what you see now."

Using a laser pointer from his index finger, Cal pointed to lines on the world.

"These are underground monorail links to all underground cites, of which there are thirty-nine. Most major cities were re-located underground and retain their original name, like London, Beijing, New York, and so on. But the population has decreased dramatically. People did not procreate for many years as fears of the earth's demise continued."

"When we realised people were coming from this century, we waited and hoped that inventive thinkers could come up with a solution that our AI systems missed. We had found that artificial intelligence is incapable of imagination and abstract thought. Even our combined AI and human brains have not found solutions."

He switched the view to a landscape of starkness and desolation.

"Here is a normal landscape. Cities are no more and the ocean floor is exposed and littered with wrecks. Mountains are swept by solar winds, and the planet looks more like Mars does today."

The chairperson seemed to pull herself together. "Mr. Moorcroft, any magician can put on a show like this. I am sorry but we are not convinced that any of this is factual. Have you any other way to prove your story?" Others muttered in accord.

"I could do some party tricks if you like. For instance, I can tell eight of you have mobile devices on your person and three are turned on."

"I'm sorry, but you will have to do better than that," Patricia said.

Cal got up from his chair. Standing in front of the committee, he shrank down until only his head showed above the desk. Reversing the motion, he grew taller and taller. They shrank away as he towered above them.

Guards rushed to him with guns drawn, but Jack Branigan held up his arms to calm the uproar developing around him.

"I guess magicians can do this as well. You see, humanoids are made for different tasks and one of mine is to work underground or reach high areas," Cal said.

"Alright, you have made a point." Patricia motioned for him to return to normal.

Quickly, he diminished to his normal size. "I swore an oath to protect people, not hurt them. I need to speak with specific people and agencies to complete my mission."

"I understand your request. Please leave the room while we confer," said Chairperson Niven.

Jack and Cal exited, followed by guards holding their guns and glancing nervously at them.

They did not have to wait long before they were called back in and stood before the committee.

"We have considered your situation, Mr. Moorcroft," Patricia started. "And our ruling at this time is to leave you under the protection of Director Branigan. You will undergo scrutiny by military investigators and submit to a psychiatric evaluation."

Cal did not object but turned and left, returning out to the vehicle waiting outside and they drove away.

When they were back in the car, Cal turned to Jack, "You need to check on the guy on the far right, Mr. Allen Cox. He was recording the meeting secretly and I do not trust him."

Branigan ignored him, seemingly deep in thought.

CHAPTER THIRTEEN

Exiting the elders' chambers, Stella sounded a sigh of relief. Reading and swearing an oath to humanity—not to mention signing it in blood—seemed so unreal. Being introduced to the elders and having her designation imprinted on her suit left her in awe of the new world she had entered.

"That was so overwhelming and weird at the same time," she said to Nyla. "I feel like I became a citizen of a new country."

"Well, you did in a way. It was a huge deal for us as well."

"What do you mean?"

"Not everyone gets to become a hubrid. It is a huge honour," Nyla said. "They have to be able to contribute to society and be academic, to understand laws and governance. It's a first step to becoming an elder and part of the cost of the life extension you have been given."

Stella shook her head in disbelief.

Through another door, Stella was surprised to find herself in a parkade or garage of some sort. What looked like strange vehicles were stacked all around.

"I thought I might give you a tour of the city before we go above ground," Nyla said.

Stella examined the nearest vehicle and was perplexed. "They remind me of a vehicle back in my era but before my time. They were called bubble cars and had a front opening door and a steering wheel that folded out with it. Only these are all glass and have no wheels."

Nyla laughed. "Yes, I know what you mean, but these are powered by fusion and thrusters that lift and hover the vehicle. We call them flyhovs as they can fly and also hover, for short we call them hovs. Variable thrusters push them in any direction. They come in various configurations. We'll use a flyhov 2, which it the smallest two-seater."

She went to the nearest small vehicle and waved a hand in front of it. A click sounded and the front glass door slid upwards. Inside was a bench seat and they sat down as the door closed and latched.

"The joysticks on both sides control the vehicle and either can be used," Nyla said. "These are great fun above ground but inside are driven automatically to prevent accidents. I'll just take us out of the depot."

Pressing a button, the controls lit up and the vehicle silently raised off the ground. Holding the joystick forward, it gradually built speed.

They approached a double exit, one of which was marked *Surface* the other *Lower Levels*, and she took the lower. Driving towards a door, it opened automatically and light flooded in as it slid aside. A voice said, "State your destination."

"Downtown wildlife park," Nyla answered and let go the controls. A slight nudge indicated a change and the flyhov increased speed.

Stella tried to look everywhere at once, gawping from one side to the other and staring upwards.

"How come there is some much light?"

"You know it's all in there." She pointed to her head. "But let me explain a few things. It's easier. We are underground in a huge cavern excavated under a mountain. The rock was left to act as a brace and help support the roof. Where possible, glass apertures are inserted and lights are fitted at the correct locations and alignment of the stars. At sunset, the lights brighten to give the illusion of a night sky and illuminate the city. Solar power from panels outside store energy for use by the city and utilities."

Stella stared in wonderment at every new vista. Buildings rose up from every locale, from a few storeys to high rises, mostly fronted by glass or brightly covered mosaic tiles in unusual patterns. Fountains and trees lined avenues, and green spaces with walkways separated the buildings. They caught up with some traffic and the flyhov took up a fixed distance from the one in front, shortly after it took a turn to a winding road leading up to a green space.

"This is the closest parking spot to the park," the woman's voice said from a speaker behind them.

They sat for a while as Nyla explained. "We have tried to preserve as many species as we can from around the world. Some are in wildlife parks, such as these, some in aviaries or aquariums, but others we have had to store in containment, either as eggs or DNA for re-introduction or cloning. Unfortunately, the world was so diverse and we may be unable to save it all. The vast majority of genetic material is stored under a mountain up north where the temperature is steadily maintained below freezing without using any power. We hope to repopulate the planet at a later date."

Stella was musing on this when she spotted a man running towards them carrying a small boy bleeding from his leg. They got out to help.

"Let me use the flyhov, I have to get my boy examined. He fell in the playground."

Nyla stopped him. "Let us have a look."

The man stopped, realised they were hubrids and lay the boy on the ground.

"Stella, check him out while I get a first aid kit."

She stared at Nyla with a questioning quizzical look.

"Go on," her mentor urged.

Stella kneeled down and placed her hands on the boy's leg. Data flooded to her brain and within seconds, interpretations came to her via AI.

"No bones broken, just a nasty gash. I'll seal it after we clean and sterilize the wound." She did not know why she said that but Nyla came out of the flyhov with a kit.

After they cleaned the dirt, blood, and grime off, Stella placed a finger over the wound and sealed it up, though she did not know how. She then lifted the boy to his feet.

"There you go. What's your name?" she asked.

"Kevin," he replied. "Thank you..." He looked at her badge. "Stella."

"Hey, you are the woman from the past, aren't you?" asked the boy's father.

"Yes."

"I sure hope you can help us."

"Me too."

"Can I take your hov to get Kevin home? His mother will be worried."

"Of course," Nyla said. "We can call for another."

Standing back, they watched as the boy and his father got in and the flyhov backed out and drove off.

When they were out of sight, Nyla said, "It's getting towards sunset. Best we wait until tomorrow before going above ground. We can either walk around all night or find an open apartment and stay there."

"Let's do a bit of both," Stella replied.

CHAPTER FOURTEEN

"Are you listening? Jack? Jack!"

"Yes, give me a minute. I'm thinking. I'm worried."

"About what?"

The SUV exited the main gate and the chief turned to the driver. "Take us home." Then he turned to Cal. "I'm worried about a number of things. My wife was very sick this morning so I want to check on her. Second, if the military takes you away, there is nothing I can do to help you. You have earned my gratitude and respect for helping Irene, but once they have you, it's out of my control and anything can happen."

"Don't worry about it," Cal said. "Laura will be fine and they can psychoanalyze me all they want. But the military will not be getting their hands on me. Not going to happen. Just like you thought you could lock me up." He smiled.

"If they bring orders to me, I'm obliged to hand you over or I will lose my job," Jack said.

"All I really need is to state my case, submit my data to the scientists, and hope they can come up with ideas to resolve the crisis facing the planet. Then I can get back home. I need to visit the T.T. Lab as soon as possible."

They stared at each other for a while before Jack spoke again.

"Let me check on Laura first. As for Allen Cox from the panel, he is CEO of a large aircraft business and I'm sure he wants some intel. He has aroused my suspicions before. We'll keep an eye on him."

They rode the rest of the way in silence, Cal still trying to take in everything around him.

Arriving at the house, Irene was waiting at the front door with anxiety written all over her face.

"Mom's really sick and has been all morning. I think she needs to go to the hospital."

Cal said nothing as they went inside. Jack went straight upstairs to his wife and Irene followed Cal into the kitchen.

"She will be fine." Cal wanted to reassure her but it wasn't working.

Irene paced around as they waited for Jack to come down. Eventually he entered.

"She says she is okay and refuses to go to the hospital. Typical stubbornness of your mother," he said, looking at Irene. "I'm going to stay home in case she gets worse."

Cal looked at him with a knowing stare. "You know I need to get to the T.T. Lab. Can Irene take me? You know it's urgent."

The security chief thought about it for a while.

"I can't do it. I'm held responsible for you."

"Then I will go alone. You cannot stop me." Cal walked towards the door.

"Wait, wait, wait." Jack moved sideways to block his path. They scowled at each other.

"If you will promise to look after Irene and not to get involved in anything public or make a nuisance, then I'll allow it, but only if she is willing to take you there and bring you straight back."

Both looked toward Irene and she faced one then the other.

'Only if you keep me informed about mom. This is going to cost you, both of you.' She pointed out.

'What?' Both men replied.

"I don't know what yet, but I'll think of something." She grinned. "I'll just get my handbag."

Jack had phoned ahead and the security guard gave them a cursory glance before waving them through the gate. Driving around the grounds, they came to T.T. Labs and Matt was waiting outside for them.

Inside, Irene looked around but focused on the craft in the middle of the hanger. Shaped like a blimp, it was about thirty feet long. The front and back were the same smooth shape and it had a round snout with blunt tips. The word *Intrepid* was painted of the side of the grey body, intersected by a single door. It had what looked like scorch marks in a few places.

Matt made introductions all round. The staff were all interested in Irene.

"You guys are famous now," Billy said. "You're all over the TV and stuff. How does it feel?"

Irene blushed. "We're not famous, nobody's asking for autographs. It's embarrassing, that's all."

"Well you're still in the news. Everyone is wondering who you are."

"Billy," Cal said. "How are you doing with repairs?"

"Good. I had to send out blueprints to make a couple of the parts. I'm just waiting for them to come back, then I'll bolt them in and we should be all set."

"Matt, did you get that list of scientists I sent you? And did you contact them?" Cal asked.

"Yes, and Yes," Matt replied. "But they aren't all available at the same time, so I suggested we make a video and send it to each of them."

"I will have to send them data, including experiments we have done and the results. Can we do that?"

"Yes."

"When?"

"Now," Matt answered. "We just have to set it up."

"Good," Cal replied. "Let's get started." That started a flurry of activity.

While they were setting up a desk, camera, and computer recording equipment, Irene wandered around. Still drawn to the craft, she went all around it and was met on the other side by Sierra.

"I'm not technical so I'm getting out of the way, but I find all this stuff fascinating. Do you want to look inside?" she asked.

Irene nodded. "Is it true this machine went into the future?"

"Yes," Sierra said as she opened the door.

They both took a step inside.

"Don't touch anything!" Billy shouted across the room, making everyone turn to look at them.

The inside was packed with machinery. In the centre was a steel ball with a seat inside, around which various parts were strewn around.

"All this stuff," Sierra motioned to the parts, "are part of a gyro-thingy, whatever that is. It holds the crew-cab ball steady while everything else turns or twists or whatever it does. Apparently, it did not work and killed Stella, our pilot."

"No!" Irene exclaimed, holding her hand to her mouth. "What happened?"

"She's still in the future. Cal 244 came back in her place. We don't know what has become of her."

"That's terrible," said Irene, backing out of the craft.

They were ready to start so everyone except Cal went behind the desk and the camera. Daniel signaled for quiet and cued Cal to start.

Once again, he pulled out the hologram recorder and laid it on the desk. It unfolded itself and lit up, causing a few murmurs from the audience.

Irene was mesmerized by the globe and listened intently as Cal explained the plight of the planet. This time he went into more detail, explaining time-lines, atmosphere changes, ocean level drops, and the depletion of earth's magnetic field. He switched to scenes of desolate landscapes devoid of any vegetation, sea beds with wrecks strewn around, and bones of dead whales. He pointed out the underground rail links between cities and indicated spots around the globe where deep drilling had been used to set off multiple fusion-bomb explosions, none of which had changed the situation.

"Finally," he said, "I will send you the data that accompanied the experiments with the hope that you may offer us a solution or a new line of approach to revive the planet. We can only come up with one fix and that is too catastrophic for us to contemplate."

"And what is that?" Matt said from the background.

Cal looked up at the audience, then straight into the lens of the camera.

"I will put it like this: The last time it happened, it caused the demise of the dinosaurs!"

CHAPTER FIFTEEN

The apartment they occupied was sparse and minimal with just the bare essentials for an overnight stay, but this was normal according to Nyla. Most people lived a nomadic lifestyle, moving around to congregate around communities with similar likes and dislikes. If a person or family were interested in certain activities, they would move to be around similar groups and expand their knowledge and abilities. If people found an area or part of the city they liked, then improving the accommodation was encouraged. Otherwise, the apartments were kept clean and repaired by teams of androids.

After wandering the streets for most of the night, Stella knew why different districts attracted similar minded people. In some traditions, it was similar to how neighbourhoods became established in her own era.

"It's getting light out so I summoned a flyhov," Nyla said.

"Do we have to check out or anything?" Stella asked.

"No, we just have to make sure the vacant light is on when we leave."

"Don't you have to pay?"

"I told you, accommodation is free, as is food. We all get a certain number of credits each month and you can earn more by performing in sports or arts or making merchandise. All these add up. If you are, say, a top athlete and attract big crowds, you get more credits. You can use them to purchase furnishings or your own butler droid. Get the idea?"

"I'll get used to it I guess, but my AI is not giving me all the nuances, or maybe I'm not asking the right questions."

"That's what I'm here for. It takes a while to get to know a new culture. Shall we go?"

A flyhov 2 was waiting curbside as they exited the building.

"Above ground," Nyla said.

"You will need a pass to exit the city," the voice advised as the vehicle moved off.

Stella was again preoccupied with her surroundings and focused on the new sights and sounds. Nyla sat quietly, letting her soak it all in. Eventually they reached the exit gate and she held up her hand to a scanner. The gate opened, then closed behind them.

"This is an air-lock gate. We have to wait while air is pumped back into the city. Then we can exit." The outer door opened, flooding in sunlight, and Nyla nudged the vehicle on.

Stella was shocked at her surroundings. It was bare rock in every direction. No buildings, no vegetation, no trees, no birds, and not a cloud in the sky.

The sky was not blue, but brown and dirty. Dust funnels of various colours were blowing wherever she looked. There were no roads to follow, just wasteland and endless vistas of desert.

Scanning the horizon, she spotted some movement and focused on an industrial area in the distance.

"What is that over there?"

"I'll show you." Nyla pushed the joystick forward. They flew across the landscape at breakneck speed and covered the distance in no time. Pulling back on the stick, the vehicle slowed almost to a stop.

"This is what we do to salvage what is left up top." Droids and robots were moving around a skeleton of a building. Cranes were lifting metal girders and placing them on top a number of large flyhovs.

"Anything and everything of use is taken underground to be reused or recycled. It is our only resource above ground, the city was big and there is quite a good supply."

They moved on, through what was left of it as a city. Dust covered broken buildings with no glass in the windows and crumbling walls.

"Is anything habitable out here?" Stella asked.

"No, but we build temporary stations to house equipment and robots as shelter from gales and dust blizzards," Nyla answered. "We built a station close to where we expected you to arrive. Monitors noted a disturbance when your probe arrived but before we could get there, it disappeared, so we built a station and waited."

"Is it close by?"

"Yes, but I will take you there later." They sped on.

There was no speedometer but Stella guessed they were doing over three hundred kilometres per hour—at least, that's what her AI said.

"How fast does this thing go?" she asked.

"Way faster than this." Nyla grinned. "We can space travel in it. Wait until we get to the sea-beds. I'll let you drive."

Soon they came to what had once been a shoreline. As far as the eye could see was flat muddy land. Bare dry patches were visible but mostly the sea-scape was dark brown-black sludge with humps strewn around that were the remains of long forgotten wrecks.

"You take over and get used to driving the flyhov," her mentor suggested. "There are no walls for you to run into. Have fun!"

Stella pulled back slightly on the joystick and the vehicle slowed. Pushing all the way forward, they fell back in their seats as they shot forward. Easing back, they swung left then right in a violent motion as she moved the stick.

"Wow, this is faster and more maneuverable than any car I've driven," Stella said, excited.

"Wait until we get in flight. Then you really can see what the flyhov can do."

They zipped along faster and faster as she grew more comfortable with the controls. Sitting in silence, they travelled miles before Nyla spoke.

"I'm guiding you towards the last bit of ocean here, to what was the deepest trench. We also have the deepest monitor for underground magma data available for this part of the globe. Not far now."

"What is that over there?" Stella pointed to something sticking out of the mud.

Nyla focused in, then looked worried.

"Better take a look." Stella swung in the direction and slowed as they approached.

"Is that a human?" Stella asked.

As they got closer, they could make out the top half of a man with only his bare torso showing. His body was bloated and blotchy, the skin grey. The face was scrunched, mouth partly open, with dead, staring eyes.

"Call to Talan," Nyla said into her internal communications.

"Yes Nyla, what is it?"

She motioned for Stella to hover around the body.

"You better take a look at this. Switching to visuals."

Circling the body, Stella moved in and out to better display the bruising, cuts, and lash markings on the back.

"Is he dead?" Talan asked.

"Pretty sure, but hold on and I'll check."

She pressed a button and the glass door hinged upwards. She eased forward to sit on the floor with her legs dangling out. Indicating for Stella to close in, she stretched out to touch the body and signalled again to go around the back.

"Yes sir. Dead and for some time, and the chip has been removed from his spine."

"Then it is murder," Talan said angrily. "We have not had a murder for a hundred years."

"Looks like he was dropped here, possibly alive and left to sink. Whoever did it expected liquefaction to suck the body in and hide it forever."

"I will send an extraction crew over. We will get a DNA sample to match the missing chip and find out where it is now. There are no missing persons registered on the censuses. I want you to carry on to your destination."

"Yes sir," said Nyla. She turned back to Stella. "I'll take over. I know where we're going."

"I don't like leaving the body out there," Stella said.

"They will not be long getting here," her mentor said.

"What did you mean about his chip being removed?" Stella asked.

"At birth, a DNA sample is taken and a unique chip inserted into the spine just below the neck line where you cannot remove it yourself. Finger and foot prints are taken and the data is stored securely. That is why everyone is allowed to move freely around the globe without hindrance. If you get into an accident or get lost and family wonder where you are, then humanoid support groups are available."

A little later, they came across what looked like a large lake surrounded by mountains. The far side was barely visible.

"This is it, what is left of the ocean." Nyla pulled up outside a small building mounted on a rock.

"You're not joking, are you?" Stella stared around in disbelief. "Are there any fish?"

"Not many. Some bottom dwellers, I think."

There was a hiss as the glass door opened upwards and they got out. Stella stood for a while, taking in the surroundings before walking to the station.

Inside were pipes sunk into the ground with gauges, workstations, and computers.

"I could have accessed the data remotely but I wanted you to see for yourself," Nyla said.

"You have certainly made your point," Stella said. "Is the whole planet this desolate?"

"Yes. In fact, it is worse in many places."

"I cannot believe that the planet could degenerate this fast. There has to be more to it. I want to scrutinise the data, dissect and analyse all of it."

"There is more," Nyla said. "Apart from the environment there is more to see from space. Come to the door and I will show you."

Upon exiting the station, Nyla pointed skyward.

"See that blob in the sky? That's a starship, and we're going there next. It is equipped with a LISA—laser interferometer space antenna—to observe gravitational waves. There is a public interstellar ship above each city ready to evacuate the populace if we find a habitable planet.

We have been building them for years in preparation of an exit, and each one is named for the city below. That is *Orlando One*, and it is already partially occupied. But that's another story."

CHAPTER SIXTEEN

The flyhov shuttle eased through the spaceship's outer door into a wide hanger. They had taken a regularly scheduled transport rather than the smaller vehicle. Bus flyhovs were longer, held more passengers, and had side doors instead of a front opening. Stella got more information travelling this way.

Because there were no humans on board, they had entered an airless hanger and had to go through another air lock door to enter the ship's interior.

"I know you have access but I will fill you in on some of the nuances of the *Orlando*," Nyla said. "It is discus shaped for movement in any direction. It also rotates inside to give a gravitational pull, meaning we can walk around normally. Engineering and flight control is situated in the top and bottom domes where gravity is lower, and the ship can be controlled from either one. The crew is mostly humanoid and commanded by hubrids like ourselves.

"There are twenty-six levels of living accommodation, all alphabetically systematized with outer family suites with windows and inner single units. The centre hold blocks of elevators to the various levels and innermost from that are shops, parks, hospitals, and schools."

"I know all that," Stella said. "What don't I know?"

"You may have noticed there are a lot of people around. They can come and live here, usually for a short time to acclimate. But we think there is a revolt happening, as most of the city is already here. Didn't you notice how quiet it was back there?"

"How would I know?" Stella said.

"I suppose you're right. However, there is a nobility faction of certain people who believe they can trace back their lineage to royalty. They feel they deserve certain privileges. They demand better accommodation, robotic servants, and a more upscale lifestyle than everyone else."

"You have that here? I thought we were done with all that."

"No, and it may be even worse now. They have taken over the finest rooms, moved robots and humanoids in place to take care of their needs, and are trying to regulate the whole ship community. We think they are afraid of being left behind and are getting a jump on migration before it begins."

"I'm not really into politics, I just want to find solutions." Stella said.

Making their way towards the middle of the spaceship, she noted how huge it was.

"How many people can it hold?" she asked.

"The whole city, including robotic staff. That's more than a million, I think the exact number at the moment is ,1356,725 with more to follow.

"I suppose you would need that capacity, is it enough?"

"There are thirty-nine ships but if we did have to move everybody then it could be cramped."

Arriving at the elevators, they stepped into an open unit.

"Top or bottom?" Nyla asked.

"Either."

Her mentor hit a button and they began to ascend. It went all the way to the top before the door slid open. Engineering was signposted to the left so they entered and were faced with a wall of displays and staff seated at control desks.

Nyla and Stella introduced themselves to an approaching engineer. His name badge was marked Tula and he ranked among the senior controllers.

"I was expecting you. This way." He led them to a small cubicle office with another desk and a large monitor on the wall.

"This is the LISA room. We are triangulated to other ships around the globe and can swap displays from any three connected ships. The display shows the local gravitational waves, and by turning this dial," he pointed to a rotary switch, "you can observe any of the thirteen windows and see the whole globe. Can I leave you to it? I am needed elsewhere, your clearance is highest priority, so help yourself."

"Yes, thanks." Stella said, sitting at the desk. "I know I am only here on a tour but let's start diagnostics."

"It's up to you, might as well while we are here." Nyla replied.

After he left, she studied the monitors, checking each window in turn and asking her AI for information. Nyla found a chair and sat close by, observing the displays. It took over an hour before Stella began making progress.

"According to historic data," Stella said slowly, "the waves should be constant with very little variation but these are pulsing at regular intervals. I want to download and study previous data and work out what should be normal. If this is abnormal, then what is causing it?"

"Looks to me like a heartbeat," Nyla remarked.

"I agree, but it seems to be fading!"

As they were downloading the data, a voice spoke to them in internal communications.

"*Talan for Stella, Talan for Nyla.*"

They both replied together. "Here. Yes?"

"*Mute the outside speakers please.*" They complied.

"*Stella, two things. First, the Intrepid has arrived with a request for your return. I think it was a test run after repairs. What do you want me to do?*"

She did not reply straight away and sat still, considering a response and looking at the displays, then at Nyla.

"I cannot get back down in time." She hesitated. "Send my body back with a request it be forwarded to my family. Also, please ask the *Intrepid* to be sent back in one week's time from now and ask the hubrid you sent to stay there. I have the start of an idea and will explain later."

"*His name is Cal and yes, I can do all that. Wait a moment while I send the order. I want to speak to both of you.*" Talan cut off.

Stella was quiet, wondering if she had made the right decision.

"*Still there?*" Talan said.

"Yes," they both replied.

"*I got the results of the DNA of our victim and his name is Alfred Drake, a flight Officer on board the Orlando. His chip reading is still working and moving around his cabin. Can you check? It's FL 041 in the lower quarters. I do not want to alert ship security until we get more information.*"

They looked at one another.

"Of course," Nyla replied. "We will do that right now."

"Get back to me as soon as you can, please." Talan switched off.

Leaving the room, they were met by Tula.

"Finished? Anything I can help you with?"

"Yes," Stella started. "How long have you been working here with the LISA system?"

"I have been here twenty-five—no, twenty-six years."

"And have the gravitational waves fluctuated during that time?"

"No," he replied. "They were mostly steady when I first started, then began wavering about ten years-ago."

They thanked him for his help and turned back to the elevators. Finding one open, they got in and pressed the button for lower FL. Alone in the elevator, they began discussing the murder.

"What do you think?" Nyla asked. "We know Drake cannot be in his quarters."

"I don't think anything at the moment." Stella turned her eyes towards the cameras in the corners. The rest of the way down was spent in silence.

CHAPTER SEVENTEEN

"Can I drive?" Cal asked Irene after they pulled away from the security gate.

"Why?"

"I may want to make a quick getaway, you never know." He smiled. "And I fancy a drive in one of these antiques."

"Antique!" Irene sounded hurt. "This is almost new. Dad bought it for my birthday and passing exams."

"New for you, not me. Please let me try it."

Giving him an annoyed glance, she pulled over and they swapped seats.

"I've studied how you do it so I don't need a lesson. You just put it in gear, press this pedal to go, and the other to stop. That's it."

Moving the lever to drive, he stomped on the gas and the wheels lit up, smoke pouring off them. The vehicle shot forward as traction took hold.

"Whoa!" Irene shouted. "Hold up! Slow down! This is not a race car!"

He eased off the pedal and the car slowed, then held a steady pace.

"Sorry, I did not think it could do that."

It moved across lanes as he tried to control the steering with excessive counter-moves. He got used to the controls quickly and settled down to a steady pace. Irene gave him pointers about traffic.

After a quiet period of reflection, she asked, "Do you think the pilot of the *Intrepid* is dead?"

He glanced at her. "She was dead when I got to her."

"That's awful, don't you think?"

"Yes, but she may not be," he answered.

"What? Is she dead or not?"

"I said she was dead when I got to her, but that may not be the end." He slowed down and took a right turn into a wooded picnic area. "Let's take a walk. I saw this spot when we passed it before. I need to see the trees. They are alive! Isn't that wonderful?"

She hesitated, considered him before getting out. They started walking along a path toward the trees.

"There is a chance, and I mean only a chance, that the pilot was saved. It would mean she becomes a hubrid like me." His head was turning this way and that as he spoke. "First, she could be brain dead before they got her to surgery, but then..."

"What?" Irene asked as his voice trailed away.

"The rule is that you have to request the change first and pass all the requirements before the elders agree to it. However, the extreme circumstances could force an override. I don't know, but I hope that is what happened. Please do not say anything to her team. It's only conjecture and we should not raise false hope."

Irene nodded. As they reached the treeline, he took off like a kid in a playground. With one hand on a tree, he danced around it, then ran to another to do the same.

She smiled at him as if he were a child.

"Irene, these are alive! Living outside in all weather and breathing just as we—sorry—you do. Their branches reaching up to the sun, and their roots soak up nutrients from the earth. They're living a normal life cycle like everything else. It's so beautiful."

The pleasure in his mood lifted her with euphoria as well.

"Irene, Irene, come here." He stood with both hands on a large tree.

"Irene, I'm older than this tree. I scanned the rings and I am older than it is." It was almost as if he were laughing but didn't know how. "Can you believe it?"

She said nothing but carried on along the path, leaving him to his adventure. The sun was breaking through the trees, a dappling light enveloping her all over. Turning to check on him, her breath was taken away as he jumped up into the tree branches at least twice her own height and landed softly beside her.

"Look, is he not a handsome devil?" He held a squirrel in his palm that seemed strangely undisturbed.

"How'd you do that? Oh, never mind." She realized it was just one more thing she needed to accept.

They both stroked a finger over the animal's head, along its back, and around the curly tail. They were both smiling.

"He's so cute," she said gleefully. "But he's a wild animal. Now put him back."

He duly placed his hand on a tree and they watched as the animal scooted up the trunk in leaps and bounds.

Carrying on, they reached the end of the trail at a picnic bench overlooking the sea.

"If only," he said, gazing over the water. "If only."

"If only what?" Irene asked.

He sat on the bench and bowed his head. She sat beside him and placed an arm on his shoulder, sensing he needed comfort.

"If only people could see the future, as I have, they would realize they are living in paradise."

Facing each other, their eyes locked.

"I glimpsed it on your hologram," she whispered.

"Irene, you are living in heaven."

Nothing more was said for a long time until he broke the silence.

"Can I ask you a big favour?"

"What is it? No promises; you have already gone way beyond your quota." She smiled.

"I have not been with a pretty girl for over three hundred years and..."

"And what?"

"Would you kiss me? I cannot hurt you in any way, I'm incapable."

She looked at him incredulously.

"Why?"

"I want to complete this occasion with something special."

She leaned forward as if to kiss him.

"Hold on, can we stand? And first place your hands on my face because my body runs at ambient temperature and it might surprise you."

"What? I have to take your temperature before I kiss you?" She chuckled as she stood up.

Closing to each other's body, she held her hands up and cupped his face.

"You're hot, but not that hot," she said. He did not get the implication.

Irene leaned in and kissed his lips, holding it as he gently lifted his arms and pulled her in tighter but gently until she broke off.

Looking into his eyes, she asked, "Well?"

He hesitated. "You have a deficiency."

Her face changed from expectant to incredulous.

"What?!"

"You have a hormone imbalance, but it's not serious. Do you have times when you feel tired? I sensed it in the scan."

"I kissed you and you gave me a medical? Is that what you do with everyone?" Indignity spilled out with every word.

"Wait, wait. It is just a natural part of touching people. I cannot help it. Hold on... just sit down."

They sat opposite each other at the picnic table. He put his hand inside his shirt and pulled out the hologram book. Opening on its own, it came to life and they saw themselves standing together, her hands on his face, kissing.

She was incredulous. "How did you do that?"

"I made it from my memories. I shall never forget this day, nor you, and can always remember it clearly with this." He played it through again.

She grinned. "It's like an old fashioned silent movie. It's lovely."

"I can add sound but you don't want to hear us slurping, do you?"

"No," she replied with a smile.

"I have other memories but this will always be special to me."

"Can you show me? Do you have one of your wife? Sorry, I should not have asked you that."

He focused on the hologram and an image appeared of a woman with dark short hair, curly but soft. Her eyes were bright and sparkling with warmth as she looked at a statue of a harlequin she was holding.

"It is so nice." His wife looked up at him. "Can I have it for the home?"

Her eyes lit up again as he agreed.

"Thank you." She leaned forward to kiss him then it went off.

"I cannot watch it." Cal said with sadness in his voice.

"I am sorry," Irene said. "I should not have asked, but she was very beautiful."

"She was to me," he replied.

Shutting the hologram book, he slipped it away under his shirt and turned his face to her.

"We should be getting back."

They stood and started back up the trail. As they passed the tree with the squirrel, she slipped her hand into his.

"You know," he said, turning to her. "If you were to work out some, you could increase your lung capacity and..."

"Will you stop it?!"

"Sorry."

CHAPTER EIGHTEEN

Cal got in the driver's seat and fiddled with keys till it started then reversing out put the lever into drive. Just as he was about to drive off Irene's cellphone pinged, she retrieved it from her handbag and pressed then slid her fingers over the screen.

"Hold on a moment." She glared at the display.

"What is it?" he asked.

"Dad sent me a text message. He never texts me though. It says, 'Come home soon, your mother is feeling better.'"

Cal stopped the engine and thought for a moment.

"Your dad is sending me a message to stay away. Why would he do that? It would mean trouble for him."

Irene did not know what to think. "I don't know, it seems weird. Mom might have something to do with it, she always gives him guidance if he is not sure."

"I cannot go home with you. If the military is waiting, there will be trouble." Cal stated.

"I will have to hide until after you go home. You know that shopping centre close to T.T. Labs?"

"Yes."

"Will you buy me some more clothes?"

"Yea, but from the cheap store, I'm not getting you a new wardrobe." She smiled flippantly.

He restarted the engine and turned back onto the main road heading back towards the T.T. Labs complex.

"I'll get lost in the mall while you go home and check things over."

He stared over the steering wheel, searching the traffic for anything suspicious.

Suddenly there was a wailing behind them as a police cruiser turned on the lights and siren. Cal hesitated and, sensing his thoughts, Irene leaned over and touched his arm.

"Don't run, Cal. It will only make this worse. Never try to run from the police. My dad taught me that. It's a sign of guilt and will bring on more forces than you can cope with."

He nodded, slowed the car down, and pulled into a deserted gas station and drove behind it. The cruiser slid in behind and after a few moments, a constable opened his door and got out. A huge guy, six-six and two fifty pounds sidled towards them.

"I will handle this," Irene said. "Open the window."

The policeman bent down to look in. Irene leaned over from the passenger's seat with the paperwork in her hand.

"It is my vehicle, officer. Here is the registration and insurance."

Warily, the policeman studied them both, looking especially hard at Cal. Without speaking, he reached in for the paperwork. Cal grabbed his wrist and he went limp. He slumped to the ground in a heap, Cal still holding his arm.

"Did you have to do that?" Irene said furiously.

"He was tired. I could tell he needed a short nap."

She got out of the car and tried to cover the officer from prying eyes.

"Open the back door of the cruiser, please," he said.

"I hope you know what you're doing."

Cal got out of the car and lifted the police officer as if he were a baby. Irene held the back door of the cruiser open and he gently deposited him on the rear seat.

"He works long hours. The poor guy needs a rest."

She scowled at him but he looked away.

"I will follow you to the shopping centre. We can't leave the cruiser here." He passed her and got in the cruiser. After playing with the controls, the lights went off and everything was quiet.

Irene glared at him. Her expression spoke volumes as she walked back to her car and got in. They eased back into traffic and drove off.

It was mid-afternoon and the car park was not full. Cal found what looked like a designated parking spot for security and pulled in. Checking on his passenger, he closed all the doors and jumped in beside Irene.

"Drive around the other side."

She did as he requested and parked close to a big department store that took up one end of the shopping mall.

Entering, they were right by the men's section, but he guided them towards the children's area.

"But.'" She signalled back at the men's.

"I'm going small today," he said.

Browsing around he picked up long pants, backpack, sports team ball cap and hoodie, all to fit a ten to twelve-year-old. After paying for the items they entered into the mall and he looked around.

"Any idea where the washrooms are?" He asked.

"By the food court, follow me." She replied and strode off towards the middle of the mall.

He dived into a cubicle and stripped off his clothes and put them in the backpack before shrinking down and putting on the youth's clothes. The young boy exited the washroom, backpack on, ball cap on and he dumped the plastic bags in a trash can.

"Hello, Mummy," he joked, taking her hand.

Irene looked down at him, amused and confused. "I don't know how you do it."

"Deep breaths," he replied. "Your heart rate is elevated and you need to stay calm."

"Will you stop it? What do you expect? I hate this cloak and dagger stuff."

Walking hand in hand, they headed for another exit and back to her car, nobody paying any attention to a normal mother and child.

"What are you going to do?" Irene asked at the mall doors.

"Hide out in the mall. I noticed some powered wheel chairs for rent. Do you have any credits?"

"You mean money." She pulled out a wallet and handed over what she had.

"Thanks. You go home and make sure your family is all right. If the coast is clear, you know where to find me. Send your father, you have done too much for me already. I cannot put you in danger anymore."

She bent down and kissed his cheek, then walked to the car and drove off. He watched, waiting until she was out of sight. As she reached the road exit, a cruiser pulled in front, then another blocked the back. In horror, he saw her being pulled from the car, arms pressed behind her back, handcuffed, and put into the back of a cruiser.

He stood there pondering what to do. What had he done?

CHAPTER NINETEEN

Exiting the elevator, they went in a slow circular route until they found room FL041. The accommodation light had a red cross through it.

"What does that mean?" Stella asked.

"It's a do not disturb indication for if the tenants are sleeping or away," Nyla answered.

"Try the intercom."

Nyla pressed a button above the light. "Anybody home?"

There was no answer. Instinctively, Stella put her hand to the door light and mentally instructed the door to open.

They were confronted by a domestic android blocking the entrance.

"There is no one home. State your business or leave. The resident requests no visitors."

"Stand aside," Nyla commanded. "We are from the census office looking for Flight Officer Drake."

"He left instructions to deny entry until he returns."

Stella put her right hand on the android and turned it around."

"No need to go in," she said. "I think I have found what we're looking for."

With her free hand, she stretched up and pulled off the chip stuck on the android's back.

"Who put this on your back?" Stella asked the droid.

"I know nothing."

"Who visited last?"

"I know nothing."

"Who instructed you to know nothing?"

They received no answer, but heard footsteps approaching. They turned to face one man and three humanoids. The man seemed to be the leader, tall and distinguished with gray wavy hair, clean-shaven, and wearing a multi-coloured cloak.

"What's going on here? Who are you?" he asked.

The group walked into the room and looked around, trying to look concerned, then turned back to face the women.

"We are from census office looking for Flight Officer Drake. And you are?" asked Nyla, staring him down.

"Earl Laurence Cavendish of the Royal Commission."

"Who is head of security around here?" Nyla asked.

"I am. Now, what are you doing here?"

"Then I would like to talk to the ship's commander," Nyla said with authority.

They stood in silence, face to face, neither backing down. Finally, the earl stepped back.

"Follow me."

They went down to the flight deck as a group with the humanoids taking up the rear. The command centre for the ship was more like a business hub than a cockpit, with computer stations set all around a central core. There were people entering and leaving the central axis, each giving orders to assistants. The ship's commander stood out in a bright red suit with military ribbons and decorations. He was walking amongst the desks, checking screens. The group approached him.

"Commander Roach, we found these two trying to get into Flight Officer Drake's quarters."

Roach's upright stature was obviously meant to intimidate. He looked down at them and made a gruff noise before speaking.

"My office." He made a bee line towards an office close to the entrance. It was blacked out with dark glass but once inside the whole flight deck was visible. He sat behind a large desk with a computer keyboard. Touching the desk, it lit up. The earl followed them and stood casually to the side.

"Talan said to expect you but you could have done me the courtesy of seeking me out first. I could have enlightened you."

"Sorry." Nyla said. Stella said nothing.

"Flight Officer Drake is on suspension and is to report to training for an update on protocols. He was not following instructions from the royal guard and is probably on the planet."

"Is the royal guard in the personal directory as security?" Nyla asked. "I cannot seem to find them."

The flight commander's face reddened and his manner turned ugly. It was obvious he did not like to have his authority questioned.

"I deputized them myself to beef up security."

"Did Talan explain our presence?" Stella asked.

"He said you were here to study LISA, no more."

The commander studied them and checked their designation.

"You are the new arrival. Right?"

"Yes," she said.

"Good. We have been looking for you. Now you can give us the coordinates for the habitable planet." His eyes flashed with a gleam of satisfaction.

"I don't have any such coordinates."

"That's not what we have heard, is it Laurence?"

"That's right, sir," the earl replied.

"Well you are both wrong. I'm here to assist with the planet's revival."

"We only want to get a head start before the other ships leave," the commander said, trying to be pleasant but failing.

"Sorry, I cannot help you," Stella replied.

"Oh, I think you can," Laurence said. Roach nodded.

The earl put his hand behind his cloak and pulled out a handgun, then pointed it at Nyla's head.

"Where did you get that? I thought weapons were illegal," Stella said, horrified.

"Exceptions can be made. We only want information, then you can leave. If we get a head start and get there first, we can set up a civilisation how it should be, with the right leadership in place. You can join us if you like."

"No thanks," Stella said.

"Pity," Laurence said. "Now give us what we want and you can return to that pig sty of a planet—or I blow you friend's brains out."

Stella looked from one to another, trying to figure out the best course of action.

"All right, but promise we can return to earth."

Commander Roach smiled. "Certainly."

Stella held out, not wanting to make it seem so easy before giving a sigh of resignation.

"The planet which used to be Kepler 22b..."

"Nice try, Stella," the commander interrupted. "We know all about Kepler 22b. That is old news. It's the same size as earth but is on the outer edge of the habitable zone. It is too dark. No more ruses. Try again."

"I was going to say," Stella began again. "If you go past Kepler on the same trajectory, there are two super earth planets. One is Tau Cetin, located 11.9 light years away, so with your boosted speed of .75 lightyears, it is only about fifteen years away. That is the best bet. Next is Gliese 581-d, which is 20.2 light years away.

The first one is definitely in the habitable zone and that makes it the closest confirmed habitable exoplanet to earth. These are the old names, I do not know what they are called now"

The men looked at each other. The commander opened a drawer and pulled out an electronic pad.

"Write down the coordinates and we will check it out."

"What I told you is true," Stella said as she wrote.

"The computer says it's correct." The commander looked from the notes to the earl.

"We will leave now," Stella said. "Earth is our priority."

Roach smiled. "No, I think we could use your expertise on the journey. What do you think, Laurence?"

"Certainly," the earl replied with a wry smile.

Both men looked at the women. "You're coming with us!"

CHAPTER TWENTY

"I should have known better," Stella said with resignation, looking at Nyla for reassurance.

Her mentor nodded and lowered her shoulders in submission. The men smiled at each other and Laurence lowered the gun.

As soon as the revolver was below the level of Nyla's head, Stella pounced. In a blur of motion, she grabbed the earl's hand. He collapsed in a heap, poleaxed by a sudden jolt of neurologic signals to the brain. Pulling the gun from the floor, she pointed it at the commander, who had not moved an inch.

"You cannot do that," he stammered. "You are not allowed to hurt a human."

"I guess there are other exceptions to the rules, Commander," Stella said, exaggerating the term.

"Have you killed him?" He nodded towards the earl.

"Him? No, he is only sleeping. You know we are not allowed to kill humans," she replied. "But, there is a judgement to be made between the life of one human and the rest of humanity. You may have a disregard for human life but do not make me have to make a decision between your life and the human race. It could be bad for you."

Nyla seemed stunned and shook herself out of it before speaking.

"What are we going to do now?" she said, eyeing up the commander before turning to Stella.

"We are going back to earth and he is going to help us." She pointed the gun at him. "Get up, we are going for a walk."

As he stood, his hands secretly pressed a button on the side of his desk. Grouped together, they walked out of the flight deck and towards the elevators. The commander was in the middle with the gun pressed against his back, hidden from view.

"You will not get away with this." Roach said in the elevator.

"Neither will you," Stella replied. "Care to tell us who murdered Officer Drake?"

"What are you talking about? Drake is on the ground."

"His dead body is, but not his chip. I just detached it from his domestic droid."

"I know nothing about that."

"That's what the droid said. You can explain it to the elders," Stella said as the elevator slowed to a stop.

As the doors slid open, they were confronted by the three humanoids that had accompanied the earl. They were blocking their exit.

"Stand aside," Nyla ordered. "We are on elder business."

Not moving an inch, the commander just smirked.

"Hold him." Stella passed the gun to Nyla.

"I cannot shoot him," she replied.

"I said hold him, not shoot him. You're way stronger, so just hold him."

Nyla took the gun and grabbed the commander's arm.

Stella stepped onto the threshold of the elevator door and confronted the middle humanoid.

"Did you not hear? We are on elder business."

"We belong to the commander and take orders from him. Let him go." The voice was squeaky and high-pitched.

Grabbing the first humanoid by the arm, she swung around and tossed him into the back of the elevator. The other two ran at her, and she pushed them into the elevator, knocking down Nyla in the process. Roach tried to run off but Stella grabbed him. Nyla jumped up and took hold of the commander again. The humanoids stood up and attacked Stella. She picked up the first one like he was a rag doll and threw him at the other two, knocking them to the floor. Pressing all the buttons, she stood back as the doors closed and the elevator moved off. A dent appeared on the door as if punched from the inside.

"I've always wanted to do that," Stella declared.

"What, fight?" Nyla asked.

"No, press all the buttons on an elevator." She grinned. "Let's get out of here."

People gave them strange looks as they moved towards the outer flight locks.

As they approached, there were air locks marked human and non-human, so they went straight to a human door and pressed the enter button. A single controller stood to the side when he saw the red uniform in the middle.

"Earth. Flyhov for three," Nyla said. The attendant pressed a control panel and a door slid open.

"You can use any of them. They have all been checked over."

They entered the airlock and chose a flyhov 4 closest to the outer door. Nyla got in the front and Stella with the commander were in the back.

It rose quickly and edged towards the exit door, which started to open as they approached. It was not quite open enough to let them through when it started to close again.

Stella looked back to see the three humanoids, one holding a gun at the attendant, the other two smiling at them through the glass.

"Damn! I thought they were out of the way," Stella said angrily. Turning to the commander, she grabbed his hand and he slumped forward. Lifting him back up, she wrapped a seat belt around him and snapped the buckle.

"When the outer door is open, slip outside and wait for me," she said. "I'll sort this lot out!"

There was a gush of air as she was getting out the flyhov side door, she tried to walk to the air lock entrance but found she was weightless and floating. Holding the door again, she turned to Nyla.

"Take us up to the control door."

Turning sideways the flyhov moved close to the door and Stella hopped off closing the flyhov door to keep air inside. The entrance door to the control room was locked and the humanoids were grinning the other side of the glass. She gave them an angry stare while moving her hand towards the lock. There was a loud click and she pushed the door inwards, knocking two of the humanoids down. Jumping at the other one, she grabbed the gun from his hands and turned it on them.

"Nyla, is there a way to turn these buggers off?"

She held the one with the gun and was examining it, her mind searching for information on their construction.

"No, not without their permission for repair."

Faced with a dilemma, she tried to buy more time.

"You boys need to go away before I really get mad."

"Three of us can bring you down, no matter how strong or fast you are," one said.

Stella pointed the gun at the attendant. "Open the outer door."

He looked nervous but slowly pressed the controls to open the door.

"Sorry, boys I've got to go."

She lunged into them. One fell down and the other two grabbed her. She grabbed an arm and twisted until there was a crunching noise as it came away from the body. Throwing it aside, she seized the head of the last one in both hands and pulled upward. It came off and for a moment she glanced into its eyes before discarding it.

Shrugging off the rest of the restraining hands, she pulled open the door to the air lock. There was a whoosh of escaping air until she entered and the door slammed shut behind her. Then crouching down and placing her feet on the back wall, she pushed off like a swimmer making a tight turn, heading toward the open door.

The door seemed to be closing faster than she was moving towards it. With no means of propulsion, there was nothing to do but wait for a collision.

Stretching towards the gap, her fingers felt the edge and she pulled, even though the opening looked too small. She squeezed through just as the door slammed shut.

Momentum carried her past the waiting flyhov and into the void of space, the enormity of the universe fully evident in this moment.

She froze as the view of waterless earth confronted her. Continents stood out in vivid relief above blank ocean floors. No clouds swirled around the sphere of dark insipidness, no white tips of polar ice or eddying waters.

Nyla pulled the vehicle alongside her but Stella was lost in wonderment of being alone in the cosmos.

With a slight bump, she became aware of the flyhov and opened the side door to slip inside.

"That was interesting," she said, smiling at Nyla.

"Which part?"

"All of it," Stella remarked and opened her internal communication. "Better report this. Stella to Talan, Stella to Talan."

"*Yes, Stella,*" the elder replied.

"There is a revolt brewing on the *Orlando One*. Humanoids with guns are running around and we just managed to escape."

The elder paused. "*We will look into it. Get back here.*"

"We also have Commander Roach with us," she said.

"*Did he threaten you?*" Talan asked.

"Yes."

"*Then we have much to discuss. You better get back here quickly.*"

CHAPTER TWENTY-ONE

Troops clad in camouflage khaki uniforms wielding assault rifles and helmets with radio communications surrounded the balcony overlooking the food court. An officer with a squad of soldiers stood on a raised platform in the middle of the tables. Off to one side, a kid in a wheelchair was observing the group with interest. The lieutenant coughed into his mike and addressed the detachment.

"You all have an image of the man we are looking for." He held up the A4-sized portrait. "Search every shop, every backspace, every washroom. Leave no stone unturned. Let's find this guy and remember, we want him alive. Now go!"

The troops scattered in all directions and the lieutenant stepped down from the dais and towards the wheelchair.

"You seen this guy, kid?"

He looked at the picture. "No, but he looks like me, don't you think?"

The soldier looked between the boy and the photo.

"Yes, he does look a little like you, but he is a dangerous man. If you see him, let my guys know, okay?"

"Sure. What has he done, sir? Is he a terrorist?"

"Maybe. We only have orders to bring him in. You be careful now."

Cal smiled and pushed the joystick forward, guiding the chair towards the exit. Watching the troops and the consternation they caused amongst the staff and shoppers, he glided by and towards soldiers stationed at the entrance. They were checking people entering and leaving. He joined the tail of a group waiting to exit. When it came to his turn, they gave him a perfunctory glance before waving him through. He wheeled past them and parked by a disabled loading sign.

Irene's car was still there and he decided to wait and watch. They had to move it sometime. He waited for what seemed like a long time and one of the soldiers approached him.

"You alright, son?"

"Yeah, just waiting for my mom to pick me up."

"Good job it's not cold, eh?" the soldier said before turning away and walking back to the mall entrance.

Shortly after, a tow-truck drove past him and went to Irene's vehicle. Sneaking behind parked vehicles, he sidled up to Irene's car, opened the rear door, and quietly eased in, lying on the floor.

After a minute, he heard the whirring noise of a crane and felt the front of the car rising off the ground. There was a ping on the roof as the tow-truck driver fixed a set of lights. They drove off and Call eased off the floor and lay across the seat.

Trying to judge time, distance, and route, he had a good idea how far they had travelled when they pulled into a compound. He pressed between the front seats and removed the keys from the ignition as the car was lowered to the ground. After removing the lights from the roof, the tow-truck driver opened the driver's door and, not finding the keys, closed it again and drove off.

Cal waited until it went quiet and slipped out of the car. Checking around, he found it was a compound behind a police station and there was no one on the gate. He threw the backpack on and manoeuvered around until he found a door on the side of the building. Trying the door handle and finding it locked, he asked his AI to open it and a short click later, he was inside.

A corridor seemed to lead to the cells on one side and the front desk and offices on the other. Calmly, he turned towards the cells and cautiously walked down the corridor. He sniffed and noted Irene's scent, so he chanced a look around the corner into the first cell. Empty. Passing two more cells, he found her sitting dejectedly on a bunk. He unlocked the door and it started to slide open. She looked up.

"Hello, Mummy." He smiled as he walked in.

"What? How? Oh, never mind, what are you doing here? Dad's on his way in."

He sat down beside her. "I came to get you out. This is all my fault. I'm so sorry."

"You certainly are to blame, but it's not all your fault. I understand your predicament, and my dad will help."

He handed her the car keys. "It's in the lot behind the station and I could sneak you out, but I guess we owe it to your father to wait."

She took his hand. "Now you're getting it. It's no good fighting it; just go with the flow."

Looking into her eyes, he nodded. "Nice to see you have calmed down. It's much less strain on the heart."

Taking her hand out of his, she formed a fist. "Stop playing doctor before I give you a beating."

He held his hands up in defeat. "Sorry, ma'am. Won't let it happen again."

They both smiled, but it didn't last. They heard approaching footsteps.

A police officer and Jack Branigan appeared and they walked into the cell. Both looked concerned.

"I would offer you a seat gentleman, but there's hardly room for me and the boy." Irene smirked.

Both men were dumfounded and at a loss for words, so Cal jumped in.

"This is all my fault. I'm sorry, we lost track of the time."

The police chief who accompanied Jack was confused and had no idea who Cal was.

"I thought it was only your daughter here."

"I thought so too. I guess you never know with family; they get so attached and go everywhere together," Jack said.

"We will get you out of here and back home. I will inform the army you have picked up your family." The officer stated.

Walking out of the cellblock, they gathered at the front desk, where Irene retrieved her belongings. They left the building after thanking the police chief for his help.

"What the hell were you thinking?" Jack said angrily, but in a hushed voice.

Outside it was dusk. Long shadows etched their silhouettes along the ground as they stood by the black SUV.

"I cannot let myself be taken by the military. You know that. What could I do? I tried to protect Irene and disappear, but they caught up with us." He looked up at Jack. "If I can just get to the T.T. Labs, I can hide and work from there."

Jack looked thoughtful and apprehensive.

"I promise not to leave there, "Cal said. "The research needs to carry on and I can coordinate with the other scientists."

The chief turned to his daughter. "Irene, you best get home. Your mother is worried and needs you."

"How is Laura?" Cal asked.

"Better, but still sick."

"I'm glad she's feeling better. Irene, your car is just over there in that lot. You best go."

She bent down and kissed him on the cheek. "Good luck."

Jack and Cal got into his car and sat looking at each other.

"I cannot risk my family anymore. All right? I will drop you close to the business park, then you are on your own. Understand?"

"Understood, and thank you, Jack."

Waiting until Irene had driven off, they pulled away in the opposite direction. It was getting dark and headlights flashed in their eyes. As they approached a tall chain link fence surrounding the complex, Jack pulled over. Cal got out and the black SUV drove off without another word.

CHAPTER TWENTY-TWO

Waiting until the coast was clear, Cal jumped the fence and crept into a dark space between buildings. There he took off his small clothes and stowed them in the backpack. Dressing in adult clothes and resuming normal size, he made his way around the complex. He went to the side door of the T.T. Labs hanger, unlocked the door, and slipped in. He expected darkness, but instead found the lights on and voices speaking behind the *Intrepid*, so he went to see who was here. Finding the whole team, he searched for any strangers and found none.

"Good evening, everyone." Trying to sound normal, he revealed himself by stepping out. Everyone jumped in surprise. They all tried to talk at once, each with a different question, before Matt held up his hands to ask for quiet.

"Where have you been? Everyone is looking for you. The army has been here all day. They just left called away by Homeland security. What's going on?"

"I will tell you what I can," said Cal. "They took me to prison and I did not like it much, so I went for a walk. That's when I got into trouble with the law. I was only trying to help and now the whole of the country it seems are after me."

"We saw it on TV and it's all over social media," Billy said. "You're supposed to be an alien or something, and now there is a bounty to see who finds you first."

Cal looked anxious and turned to Matt. "I need to stay hidden and work on the project I came here for. This is the best place for me. I don't need food or water, only to hide. Can I stay?"

The team leader looked thoughtful and glanced at everyone for a reaction or approval. Each person nodded.

"If the military turns up, I cannot hide or cover for you. What does Homeland Security say?"

"I am on my own, same as you. I promised to stay out of trouble. I only need to work with the scientific community. I will cause you no hassle if you let me stay."

"Okay, but if you want you can go back," Matt said.

"What do you mean?" Cal looked confused.

"We did repairs to the gyro and we are doing a test run tonight. We have to do the launch at night because a ten second burst of energy is required and it blows the city's electricity grid. It puts the city in darkness until the circuits reset. We had to get special permission for this but they do not know what we are doing." Matt smiled wryly.

Cal was quiet and thoughtful as he weighed the options. "I cannot go back without answers, especially without getting feedback from other scientists."

"I understand," Matt replied. "We've put a journal in the craft explaining what has happened so far and asking to get our pilot back. There is only room for one in the ship so we hope Stella will be returned."

The rest of the team each wished Cal luck. Refilled their coffee cups, they sat back at their desks and resumed the procedure to launch the *Intrepid*.

Matt went around each station, checking progress. Sierra, who had no duties during the launch, stood by Cal.

"Do you think Stella is alright?" she asked.

"I do not think so, but there is a possibility. What time will they launch?"

"Not until at least 2:00am, when city power use is at its lowest," Sierra replied.

The team worked quietly until just before the launch, and then it kicked into high gear, each one calling out the status of their areas. Monitoring power settings, start up readiness, and gauge recordings, all systems prepared for launch. Finally, after a last check, Matt started the send-off sequence. A machine buzz started low and built up to high-pitched whine. A ten-second electrical hum broke off when circuit breakers tripped. Then the air around the ship shimmered.

Cal watched in fascination as the ship's outline faded in the flickering light until it disappeared completely.

"No one is to enter the ship zone until after it reappears and has been checked for hazards," Matt ordered as the team relaxed in their chairs. "Now we wait."

The hour passed slowly, as if each second was a minute. Everyone stared at the ship zone as if it would appear right that second. Then at last the air began to glisten and vibrate, short bursts of sound were followed by the gradual reappearance of the *Intrepid*.

As soon as everything settled, Daniel donned a hazard suit and tested the perimeter of the ship. Finding no concerns, he signalled the team leader he was entering the ship. Opening the door, he stepped inside and disappeared. Everybody waited with baited breath for his reappearance and shortly after, he stepped out and walked straight to Matt.

"There is a body bag inside."

The team turned to each other in dismay.

"I will bring it out because it is in a tight space and I can manage the weight on my own," Cal said. "Can you clear a table please?" He looked at Matt, who nodded.

He stepped inside and noted the body was on the floor, too stiff to place in the seat. He also found a message book. Gently and respectfully, he lifted the body and carried it out of the ship. Tears and sobs met him as he placed the body bag on the table.

"There is a message that came with the body. Shall we play it before doing anything else?" Cal asked.

Matt nodded before anyone else spoke. Cal laid the hologram book on another table close by and the team gathered round.

The hologram unfolded and lit up at each corner. A figure appeared, a stately silver-haired man dressed in a silver suit similar to Cal's.

"Greetings. My name is Talan. I am one of the leaders in the elder council governing the state that used to be Orlando. Let me first offer my condolences for your colleague. In a way, I feel responsible for her, even knowing it was not my fault. This is a tragedy of scientific progress. She stands as testament to our desire to move forward and push the borders of human understanding.

"Dr. Cooke is a true heroine. She put herself at risk knowing full well the possible consequences. She will be honored by us, as I am sure you will too. Her story has already been told around the world and tributes have been written. We hope this news will be passed to her family." He paused.

"Our wish is that you may help humankind by assisting Cal 244 in his quest for knowledge and a remedy for the terrible situation facing the planet. We request that you send your ship in one week's time and that you keep Cal there until it arrives back. Finally, I have a message for Cal, if he is present."

The sound then broke into a noise that sounded like a fax machine buzzing through a message. Cal listened intently. Thinking for a moment, he turned to the others.

"I have more news. Talan asked that I should pass it on in person rather than in a recording. Stella has become a Hubrid." He waited until it sank in. "This is a great honour in my era. Let me explain."

He carefully explained how Stella was transformed and the responsibilities of her new position. He answered questions about her and tried to console the team.

"Trouble is Stella never agreed to or requested the change, she was dead when I lifted her from the ship after I had put a brain survival kit on her. Talan admitted it was an executive decision made by himself and some other Elders, they thought the extreme circumstances warranted it."

After a pause to let the implications assimilate in he continued.

"There is also a message from Stella. She requests that her body is returned to her family. She also wishes everyone to know she is fine and coping with the changes to her life. At first, she was angry but has now accepted the challenges that face her and the planet. She also hopes to one day be reunited with you all."

Cal then walked back to the body bag and unzipped the top half to expose her face. He placed a hand on Stella's body and sensed all the damage and changes, including the missing brain.

"You should all come and make peace with Stella's body and find closure within yourself and with whatever religious beliefs you have."

CHAPTER TWENTY-THREE

It was late and the team had spent all day winding down from the *Intrepid*'s voyage. The recordings were downloaded to be analyzed later and mechanical checks were completed, searching for any failures. The team had gone home exhausted and for a well-earned rest before returning. Matt had started the process to send Stella's body home and vexed over how to tell her family the news.

Cal had spent the day trying to contact scientists who had been sent the data but without much success. Not many had made progress or had had time to study it yet. Cal tried to convince them of the urgency. He was working through the night to contact others in different time zones.

After another fruitless call, he decided to step outside for a break. He hoped he might feel the rain on his face. Opening the side door, he stood still out in the open. Immediately, he knew it was a mistake. Eyes were on him.

Using his senses, he searched for the cause of his concern, not sure how many or what malevolence was directed towards him. Thinking it better to find out than be caught inside, he strode out away from the building and towards the complex entrance. Once out in the open, he ducked down between buildings and waited, not sure if the eyes were in a vehicle or on foot. He heard a car door open and footsteps coming in his direction. He knew it was only one person, so that made it easier. Blending into his surroundings, he waited until they were close before speaking.

"Mr. Cox, do you really like that cologne you're wearing? It smells like an animal to me."

Allen Cox nearly jumped out of his skin but controlled himself and spun around to face Cal.

"The women seem to like it."

He did not seem to be armed so Cal emerged from the shadows.

"I can't say I like it. What do you want? And how did you get in here?"

"I have security clearance through being on the committee of homeland security." Cox slowly walked up to him. "I want to help you."

"Help yourself, you mean. I know you recorded our last meeting. Are you after some intel on future products to develop?" Cal asked.

"I will not lie, Cal, of course I want to be at the forefront of technology and get a jump on the competition. But I am also a humanitarian and I have viewed that hologram of yours many times. If you are to believed, the planet is in trouble."

"Of course, it's true. Do you really think we would put ourselves at risk to come back here and seek help? Now, what do you want?"

Allen Cox hesitated, as if considering his reply. "I have resources. I been following everything you've done from the moment you arrived. The military could not find you, but I could. If I wanted the military to get you, it would have been easy. Believe me, that's the last thing I want. I have research facilities that may be of help. In fact, I have someone that may have answers for you. We looked at the hologram together and she thinks she knows what's happening. I'm asking you to come with me and see for yourself. I promise to return you before dawn."

Cal thought it through. "Alright. I have nothing to lose and any help can only be good. What do you want me to do?"

"I will drive you to my facility and bring you back. Follow me."

"No," Cal replied. "I don't want to be seen leaving here. I will meet you on the other side of the fence."

Allen Cox got back in his car, drove out the security gates, and back up the road to find Cal waiting for him.

After driving for thirty-five minutes, they pulled up to the gates of an airport business center with signs for Cox Aero Industries. They were ushered straight through, even in the middle of the night, and drove around to a low brick office building with just a few lights on.

Allen card swiped a lock to gain access and they walked through the main reception, which was unmanned, and past some outer offices. They came to a large glass room with his name on the front door. The lights were on and a woman was waiting for them. She was five four, one hundred ten pounds, with long dark hair tied back in a pony tail, her face was oval with dark hazel brown eyes. Cox did the introductions.

"Cal, meet Lara Holden. She is a prominent geologist. Lara, meet Cal244, the man from the future."

"Nice to meet you at last. I've heard and read so much about your escapades on the news and TV." She smiled and held out her hand. They shook but Cal held on.

"You have a lung infection. Have you been in a hot country?"

"What do you mean?" she asked "Yes, I just got back from a work project, but I feel fine."

"I am sorry but when I touch people I automatically scan them and you have an infection in the lung, maybe a virus. It may be MERS, and you need to be checked before it gets worse. Do you have a cough or shortness of breath?"

"A slight cough but nothing much."

"If it gets worse, go to a doctor straight away," Cal said.

She eyed him warily, withdrew her hand, and looked at Cox for help.

"If you have finished your diagnosis, Cal, we can begin. Lara has examined your hologram and made some deductions."

They sat and Cal fixed his gaze on the woman. She now seemed uncomfortable under his scrutiny but coughed lightly and began.

"I have studied rocks and magnetic field reversals for many years, and that includes earth's magnetic depletion. There are, as you probably know, three fields around earth—magnetic, electric, and gravitational. They are all measurable to a certain degree. The electric current and associated magnetic field have been decaying since earth was formed. The current rate of energy loss is seven billion kilowatt hours per year. We believe, at that rate, the magnetic field would be gone in the year 3991AD. What year are you from?"

"4016," he replied.

"There is a theory that as the magnetic field diminishes, it induces a voltage that opposes the decay, extending its lifetime by about 1400 years.

I have studied magnetic reversal in rocks, which is difficult because not all rocks are the same and can be undependable. The last known magnetic reversal was 700,000 years-ago. It's possible there will be another reversal before it gets depleted.

She hesitated. "From what I have seen, that has not happened. In your time, the magnetic field, by all predictions, should be low if not completely depleted."

"You're saying all of this was predictable?"

"Yes, but the consequences do not match your predicament. I do not think this is your cause or even its effect. There is more going on here than just magnetic depletion. Much more."

"Like what?" Cox asked.

"I can only theorise at this time without data to back it up." She turned to Cal. "There has to be something having a dramatic effect on the planet's gravitational field. The loss of atmosphere, lower stratosphere, and troposphere all point to lower gravitational waves. This is the real cause, but what is the source?"

They sat in silence, letting it all sink in and contemplated the next step.

"Any idea what is having the effect?" Cal asked eventually.

Lara frowned. "I can only guess, which may be completely wrong and throw us in the wrong direction. What it is, cannot be seen or measured." She leaned back and hesitated before carrying on. "That leaves a couple of possibilities: Dark matter or dark energy. Dark matter makes up the biggest percentage of the universe and is not considered malevolent, however, virtually nothing is known about dark energy."

CHAPTER TWENTY-FOUR

An auditorium was set aside for the inquiry into the flight officer's death. A semi-circle of forty seats surrounded a central raised platform. Elders from each city had travelled to be there and were all seated, with Talan in the middle. Stella was on the platform to answer questions from all of the elders and she related the events as they happened.

"Did Commander Roach ever threaten you or Nyla during the interview with him?" Talan asked.

"He nodded to Earl Laurence Cavendish, who then pulled out a gun and threatened us," Stella answered.

"Was the earl in control or taking orders?"

"I thought they were in it together. The humanoids who attacked us were under the commander's control. But they were also taking orders from the Earl."

"We will ask the commander to take the stand, but first, the elders would like an update on the crisis. Have you made any progress?"

Stella looked at the elders. Each seemed eager for information and gazed back at her expectantly.

"I need to make a full examination of the data, and then calculations have to be done to confirm my theory before finding a solution. I set a deadline of a week to complete the theory but need help with the calculations. It is only a theory at this stage and I do not wish conjecture to give you false hope."

Murmurings spread along the line and Talan held up his hand to speak. "The full use of the qubit central computer system will be available to you and we hope you can give us good news then. In the meantime, Commander George Roach, please take the stand."

They swapped places. The commander glowered at her as they passed. He was sworn in and faced the elders.

"Can you explain to us, Commander, why a civilian, a so-called earl, should be in a supervisory position and able to order crew and humanoids around?" Talan asked.

Commander George Roach stood erect and in his bright red uniform. He made an imposing figure as he stared at the council.

"The *Orlando* is almost at capacity with occupants who do not want to leave. I needed a liaison to control or coordinate between the crew and the public. The earl had an authority I thought would fulfill that role. He asked for some humanoids to help him so they were authorised but under my command."

"What can you tell me about Officer Drake?"

"The earl brought to my attention that he would not follow instructions and said that he would not obey the so-called nobles, only flight control. The earl said he had sent him to the planet to re-train in leadership command. That was all I knew until the ancestor and her mentor appeared, brought in by the earl."

"Then what happened?" Talan asked.

"I knew of her task to monitor the LISA modules but nothing else. She questioned me about the flight officer and I told her what I knew. There was a rumour that the ancestor had the coordinates of a habitable planet and I challenged her on that, and she eventually agreed to give it to us. My only ambition was to make a head start on the migration and become the lead starship for humanity."

"And did you agree to let her return to earth?"

"I thought her more useful to the *Orlando*."

"But you had agreed to let her return to earth."

The commander remained silent and looked at the Elders until a specialist entered the room and went straight to Talan. He listened for a moment, stiffened, and gave some orders to the technician, who left promptly. Talan then faced the commander.

"If you want to remain in command of your ship, you had better get after it. It has left orbit and is moving outwards!"

"What?!" The commander stood and seemed lost for words.

"It seems your faith in the earl was misplaced."

The commander stormed out and the meeting ended.

Stella and Nyla were led away by Talan to the main city computer control section.

The hub of the qubit central computer system was a lot smaller than Stella had imagined. Thirty-nine large screens surrounded the walls with a small circular desk arrangement in the middle. Seating in the desk area was for six at the most and Talan, Nyla, Stella, and two humanoids stood together. Talan addressed them.

"Each city has a super-computer system and all are linked to this central hub. You can use individual systems or link them together to increase computing power. If needed, you can link yourself via hand control unit to your own AI."

He looked at Stella. "This may be useful for downloading the data stored within you and you can order computing instructions through mind control. What is your strategy?"

"First, I want to download all the data we have accumulated, including past monitor records, all up to date sessions that were already inserted, and all the new recordings we have.

Once that is done, we will apply theorems to be calculated and provable to a set of axioms until we can prove our assumptions are correct. We will keep doing that until the math is irrefutable. Then we will know what we are up against."

"After that, we will work on a strategy to rectify the situation and revive the planet. It sounds easy but the task is monumental, if I cannot come up with some answers in a week, we need to reconvene and form a new approach." Stella was apprehensive.

"At least you have some ideas, which is more than we had before," Talan said.

"Einstein once said that imagination is more important than knowledge I have the imagination; let's hope we can come up with the knowledge."

"I have given you a couple of humanoids to help with download inputs so I'll leave you to it. Good luck."

"At least we don't need to stop for sleep," she said to the rest of the team. "Let's get started."

After figuring out the interface, Stella dove into the mind connection, finding herself like Alice in Wonderland, lost in an infinite universe of quantum properties of angular momentum. Not knowing which way to go, she started throwing theories out there, starting with a known gravitational equation which came back with the correct answer. That gave her confidence to try other approaches.

CHAPTER TWENTY-FIVE

True to his word, Allen Cox delivered Cal outside the fence to the complex before sunrise. Light beams were beginning to pierce the dark blue morning sky.

"I expect tonight has given you food for thought, has it not?" Allen asked as he pulled up and parked the car.

"More than I had before," Cal replied.

"Lara and I will research this some more, or at least Lara will. I have to go to a Homeland Security meeting in Washington and I'm taking Jack Branigan with me. We are flying up in my jet and returning late. Can we meet here at midnight?"

Cal nodded.

"I will try to get a personal meeting with the president," Allen said. "I'll take Jack with me if he is on board, and see if I can get the military off your back."

"It would be great to be left hassle free to pursue my mission," Cal replied.

"If I can get a chance to show him the recording of the hologram, perhaps he might be amenable. I will explain that it would be of no use to us if you just went back, and it's better we assist you rather than fight with you."

"I could not agree more." Cal opened the car door and got out. "See you tonight."

Once Cox had driven off, he surveyed the surroundings before hopping over the fence as if it were an everyday occurrence. Then he carefully went back to the lab and slipped in through the side door.

He thought over the night's events and previous days. Could he trust either Cox or Branigan? Did he have any other choices? As an entrepreneur, Cox was ambitious, but seemed to have a softer side. His relationship to Lara appeared to be deeper than work. She had no background in aeronautics, and what interest did he have in rocks?

Branigan was at first aggressive and only relaxed after Irene was involved. He was definitely a family man. Yet his position as head of Homeland Security for the area drew a conflict of interest that suggested he may turn against him in a critical situation. Cal knew he had to be wary of all situations and people involved.

Seven o'clock saw the first of the lab staff appear. Sierra came up to him carrying a white lab coat, the same as she was wearing.

"Here, put this on. You will blend in with the rest of us if anyone comes by."

"Thanks." Cal slipped it on and inspected himself.

"You look normal now," she assured him. "But what about the other clothes you have on? Don't you need a change?"

"Well yes, but I have only a little money that Irene lent to me."

"That's okay. Tell me what you want and I'll put it into our lab expenses."

Cal thought it over. "All the guys seem to wear those Jeanie things and sports tops."

"You mean jeans and team shirts?" Sierra laughed.

"Yes."

"What sport do you like, baseball, football, hockey or what."

"What is hockey?" Cal asked.

"I don't know much about it." The woman said. "It's a game played on ice with sticks and a piece of rubber instead of a ball." Her face was scrunched up.

"Oh, sounds intriguing, I think I did see a game on ancient history, anything will do as long as its not conspicuous."

She assured him she would find him something suitable and went to work things out.

Noticing Matt at his desk, Cal went over.

"You are part of the team now, I see. That's good. Did you have a good night?"

"I did, thanks. Matt, what do you know about dark matter or dark energy?"

"You could look it up and probably find out as much as I know about it. Dark matter is what most of the universe consists of and is just a cold void of nothing or partial debris. On dark energy, on the other hand, almost nothing is known. What I have read on the subject is that it could be energy floating around the universe, possibly in the form of clouds or similar. If enough of it accumulates, it can morph into or become part of a black hole, but all of that is speculative. I have arranged a desk for you over there. Why don't you look it up for yourself?"

To onlookers it appeared Cal was doing nothing, just sitting at his desk studying a computer screen, but going behind him, one could see that the computer screen was flashing page to page in furious action.

Why had this not been investigated before? There was no plausible explanation except that not being quantifiable, the artificial intelligence systems had ignored it. They had become too reliant on AI, but why had humans or hubrids not questioned the possibility? Dark energy was a possible threat and needed more investigation, but how? In this era, they were not so technically advanced and he searched his own AI for methods of research.

Close to the end of the day Sierra turned up at his desk carrying a couple of clothing bags which she dropped in front of him.

"Here you go try these on." She offered.

Opening up the bags he found a pair of faded blue jeans and a long-sleeved sports polo shirt, going around the desk he took off the lab coat then started taking off his shirt and pants.

"Don't you want to go to the locker room to change?" Sierra asked.

"Why?"

"You know, are you not embarrassed to get changed in front of everyone?"

"Why, I have nothing to hide, my suit is part of me like your skin and embarrassment is only your concern not mine." Cal stated.

He pulled on the jeans and shirt, adjusted his body to fit then paraded in front of the desks.

"You look like a real twentieth century dude now." Billy claimed.

"Thank you so much, everyone." Cal said happily then went over and gave Sierra a hug.

"Your very fit." He said to her.

"What does that mean?" She asked. "Is that a compliment or a hook-up line?"

"What's a hook-up line?" He asked.

They all laughed, bonded by the fact they all knew what it meant.

"A hook-up line means, are you trying to pick her up, you know get a date with her," Daniel said.

"Oh, if I were a human it certainly would be a pick-up line." He joked.

"Now that's a compliment, Sierra." Matt piped up.

They all laughed this time.

"And will you take it back after?" Cal asked her.

"What do you mean?"

"Well, the shirt, it says "property of the Florida Panthers" don't they want it back or did you steal it."

CHAPTER TWENTY-SIX

All the staff had gone home. Cal was all alone, still working at his assigned desk, and all was quiet. It was just getting dark and he had no more leads to pursue. Perhaps tomorrow he would get in contact with the scientists to whom he had sent data.

A noise attracted his attention from the main gate. He could tell heavy vehicles were entering the complex.

Leaving by the side door, he waited until they were in sight. His worst fears were confirmed: Military vehicles.

Backing up towards the rear of the building, he searched for a place to hide and thought about the roof. There were no ladders to get up so it could be a good observation platform. Jumping up, he found it at the limit of his ability. Gathering all his reserve, he pushed off again and this time barely made it. There was a walkway along the edge so he moved toward the front. Crouching, he watched and listened.

The lead vehicle stopped in front of the lab. A group got out of the rear and a couple got out the front. He could see Matt Petronas amongst them and a supervisor leading him up to the side door.

"Open the door," he ordered.

"There is nothing here. You have already been through here once," Matt protested.

"We are going over the ground again until we find him, so open the door."

"This is a top-secret establishment and you need clearance to enter. You only have permission for random checks."

"Stop screwing me around or I will take the keys off you myself. I have orders from higher up, so open the door."

Reluctantly, Matt complied.

"Sergeant, search the whole complex. You two, with me," he said, pointing to the troops.

Two soldiers, Matt, and the captain entered the lab while the rest of the troops set off in all directions.

Cal waited. He could hear radio calls coming in, reporting nothing found. After a while, the group exited the lab and stood outside. The captain checked again for any signs and there were no reports.

"Have you checked the roofs?" he asked.

"There are no steps or ladders on to the roofs," said a soldier

"All right. I have a helicopter coming shortly. Keep up the search."

Cal could hear the beat of helicopter blades approaching so he took off his clothes and changed his suit to camouflage with the roof.

Searchlights scanned each roof, sweeping side to side, backwards and forwards, until they got to the lab. He remained perfectly still as the lights passed over him, then he heard radio reports.

"Nothing to report."

"Okay, we will..."

"Wait! I have a heat signature at the front."

Cal cursed to himself and switched on a shield. Wind beat down on him as the helicopter hovered above almost within reach.

"No sorry, false alarm. Must be an anomaly from the detection unit."

"Okay, we will call it off. Return to base," the captain ordered.

Cal waited until the helicopter was out of sight before putting his clothes back on. He watched as the troops regrouped at the front of the lab and drove off, taking Matt with them.

That had been a close call and he felt angry and disappointed. Did they not realize he was not a threat? His mission was one that everyone should embrace, not hamper him at every turn.

Dropping down from the roof, he checked around every corner, his senses on alert.

Allen Cox pulled up by the fence. It was a dark night with no sign of movement anywhere. He sat with the engine running for a few minutes, then turned it off, wondering where Cal was. Did he have a watch or use an internal clock? Was he off somewhere else? He was about to drive off when a rap on his side window made him jump.

"Get in."

"No. Are you alone"? Cal asked. "I just had a visit from the military."

"I can assure you I came alone. I need to speak to you so get in."

Cal vacillated, staring all around, almost sniffing the air. Cautiously, he got in.

"What happened?" Cox asked.

"A bunch of goons came and forced Matt to open the door. They searched around and brought in a helicopter. I thought I may have make a run for it."

"Sorry about that. I had no knowledge of that and I am sure Jack didn't either. We only got back from Washington an hour ago," Allen said.

"How did it go?"

"I had a meeting with the president and he was intrigued by the hologram. I thought he was sympathetic but when I asked for assistance, he only said he would take it under advisement."

They sat quietly in the car. For Cal failure was not an option, and just making progress was not good enough. This chance he had been given was a one-time deal, perhaps even a godsend.

"I have some other news." Allen said.

"What's that?"

"Lara is in hospital. Apparently, she started coughing a lot so took your advice and saw a doctor. You were right and now she is in isolation with a lung infection. Apparently, it's also called camel flu. She did not like that."

"Is she far?"

"No, but we cannot see her in the isolation room."

"I need to see her," Cal insisted.

Cox started the car. "I'll take you, but you won't get in."

"We'll see."

The hospital was well lit and was the only indication of human activity for miles around. Even the car park was full and they drove around until they found a spot.

"Where is she?" Cal asked.

"Sixth floor, ISO ward, room 611. But you won't get in, I already tried."

"I will get in, but alone. I do not breathe so I cannot catch anything or transfer any infection. You should wait here."

He entered through the main lobby where there were many people. No one paid any attention to him.

Taking the elevator to the sixth floor, he exited to find the ISO ward on the right and went to the reception desk. The nurse looked up at his approach and before she could speak, he took her hand and she slumped over. He found room 611 and went in quietly. Lara was resting with an oxygen mask on and her eyes lit up at seeing him.

"What are you doing here?" she asked.

"It's alright," Cal said. "Allen is in the car park but I insisted on coming alone because he could get infected or pass it on. Listen, I need to ask you something but first, can I hold your hands?"

She gave him a suspicious look, held back for a while, then held her hands out. He took them and looked into her eyes.

"I see they are treating you well and there is a slight improvement. I can help, if you let me."

"How?"

"I can give your immune system a small boost and you will feel a lot better after a good sleep. But first, I need to ask you some questions."

"What about?" Lara asked.

"Dark energy."

They discussed it for a few minutes before Cal broke off.

"I need to leave now, I left a nurse asleep out there. Give me your hands again."

Lara held out her hands and he took them.

"You trust me, right?"

She nodded.

"You will wake up tomorrow feeling normal. Lay back and relax."

Cal sent neural signals through their hands and she fell asleep. Making sure she was comfortable, he left. He went back to the nurse and held her arm. Her eyes opened.

"You okay?" Cal asked.

"Yes, what happened?"

"You looked like you were nodding off."

"I'm fine." She looked indignant. "Can I help you?"

"Yes. A friend of mine, Lara Holden. How is she?"

"She is in isolation. You cannot see her but she is doing fine."

"Good that's all I need. I'll come back later when it's possible. Thank you."

Cal gave her a warm smile, turned, and walked out.

CHAPTER TWENTY-SEVEN

The octagon elder control complex was located outside the city boundaries. There was an entrance to the city and elders did not need to be in an air environment, but had an air feed for visitors. Central meeting rooms surrounded a compound used for ceremonies. Utilities for the city's underground ecosystem were on one corner, and medical facilities for humanoids and hubrids on the other.

The flyhov parkade, repair area, and air locks were on one side and visitor accommodations were on the other, next to the elder quarters. Furthermost from the city was the outdoor works units with heavy equipment and repair facilities. Humanoid or worker droids and drones were accommodated anywhere they were needed and did not need quarters. External and space control decks were at the outermost section and this was where Talan was monitoring the *Orlando*. Large screens showed the cosmos and in the centre display and most prominent was the discus shaped starship.

Commander Roach had commandeered the fastest flyhov in the fleet and was closing in on the *Orlando* before the starship gained interstellar speed. A tech with hearing audio controls turned to Talan.

"He just hailed the ship and asked permission to come onboard."

Talan said nothing and waited for events to unfold. The flyhov got closer until it seemed it would crash into the side. At the last minute, a docking bay gate opened and the commander entered.

"Let me know when the *Orlando* comes back to the station," he ordered before leaving the control deck.

Just as he entered the inner corridors, a voice spoke to him. *"Nyla to Elder Talan."*

"Yes Nyla, what can I do for you?"

"Sir, I think you should come to the central computer control room. There is something you need to see."

"On my way."

Darkness filled the room as Talan entered and he gazed around for answers. All of the computer screens were blank, and only desk lights gave illumination. Hunched over the main screen, Stella sat motionless, her hands resting on the touchscreens. Nyla approached the elder as he made his way to the middle.

"She has not moved since sitting down. The screens went blank shortly after."

"How long?" Talan asked.

"Two days, sir."

"Two days? Why didn't you inform me earlier?"

"I have been checking with control experts around the world. Theirs also went down at about the same time. Controllers say she has taken charge of the whole system. They were frightened to break in and ruin a computation sequence so have waited until now and finally asked me to get you involved."

Talan wandered around the room, thinking it over.

"Is there no way of externally checking her activity?"

"No sir. We tried but are getting blocked out."

"Then I will have to call her on internal communications."

"Talan to Stella."

Waiting for a reply, they stared at her but there was no sign of movement. After trying once more, Talan spoke to those listening.

"Give it another four hours then call me. She may be working on a significant breakthrough, so let's wait a little longer."

A couple of hours went by, then slowly screens began to come to life, one by one. Nyla had a call from the central computer control team and they confirmed systems were coming back online. Stella still hadn't moved and Nyla called Talan to return.

Entering the room, the elder went straight to Stella. He called her again and this time he got a message that she was unavailable.

He waited at a desk and used his hand to manipulate the touchscreen control units, then watched as his commands showed different parts of the elder complex. After checking all security cameras, he called up space control.

"Status on *Orlando*?" he asked.

"We tried to hail the commander but got no answer. Same with the fight deck. The ship is not turning around. In fact, it's speeding up."

"I knew it!" a voice shouted.

Talan turned to see Stella facing him with an angry expression.

"I knew that pair were up to no good. I told you there was a revolt going on and needed action."

The elder had his mouth open but no words were coming out.

"There is no army here," he said. "Only limited security and that is mostly to guide people onto trains or onto flyhov. We've had no use for an army for hundreds of years."

"I brought him back for you and you let that mealy-mouthed son of a bitch talk his way out of it."

"We had a trust system working here. Our commanders, officers, and security looked after people in their sphere of operation."

"Sphere of operation," Stella said contemptuously. "This world has gone to hell in a handbag!"

'Hell, in a what? What you talking about.' Talan barked back, the situation getting heated.

Talan seemed deflated, but she wasn't done.

"Your citizens are now in the hands of a pair of autocrats." She paused for effect. "One thing is for sure," Stella paused again. "You better start building *Orlando 2*."

He smiled when he realized she was calming down. "What did you find in your research?" he asked.

"Some answers and a possible solution, but I need to put together a presentation for all the elders. Can you arrange another council meeting?"

"Of course, but can you give me some idea?"

"The planet's energy has been extracted for the last thousand years and at this rate has only a thousand years left. I'll provide a better explanation soon."

"Alright, I can arrange that. How long do you need?"

"A couple of hours."

They went their separate ways, Talan to organize the meeting and Nyla and Stella to make a presentation. The two humanoids sat down and waited for their next assignment.

The room was set out as before with all the elders at desks inlayed with screens. A raised dais sat in the middle but this time there was a desk with a hologram resting on top.

Talan called the meeting to order.

"This is a full elder council meeting held to discuss the crisis that grips the planet. I believe Dr. Stella Cooke has some important information to pass on. After the presentation, we will have a round table discussion. When you are ready, Stella."

She stood to face her audience. Nyla sat at the desk to run the presentation.

"Thank you all for making this possible. I believe you will be enlightened and have a full understanding of the situation by the end of this presentation.

If you will first check the screens in front of you, there is a video of earth as it was one thousand years-ago and the same view today. They are very different, as you can see. It went from a lush, green, water-filled planet to a brown wasteland.

The reason is that the earth's energy is being absorbed by something unseen and before now unprovable.

Thanks to gravitational wave measurement technology of the LISA tools and computer generated theories and calculation, we have discovered that the planet's energy is being taken up by a cloud of dark energy."

Murmurings spread around the council members and Stella held up her hand to continue.

"Little is known about dark energy except that along with dark matter, it exists in the cosmic void. Now I can tell you it is formed like clouds that drift eventually form, or become part of, a black hole. One of these clouds attached itself to earth around a thousand years-ago. Whether it drifted here or was drawn, I cannot tell.

"Its energy is in the form of microwaves in the L-band of the spectrum, the same band used for navigation and many other uses. As such, it has gone unnoticed as it syphoned off heat and energy continuously for a long time.

I have no exact date for when it arrived. If you look at the hologram, I can show you it's extent around the globe. By measuring its effects on gravitational waves, we can see it does not fully envelop the planet, only about two hundred degrees. I cannot tell you how far into the void it extends, only how close and how far around."

The hologram displayed the planet with a cloud surrounding it, full on one side and partial on the other. Shown in black, it extended outward into infinity. It looked like a giant hand holding it in a fist.

"It has slowly crept in toward the planet, lowering the stratosphere and troposphere and making the atmosphere unbreathable. Artificial intelligence could not detect it because to our standard instruments, it did not exist. We had to reimagine it and calculate all the variables, including how much energy it has taken, and recalculate how much time before earth is a dead planet.

The figures are available if you wish to check them but we have only about a thousand years left before the planet is unusable by humans. It is possible that this happened before on Mars. I suggest a one-hour break, and then I will take questions."

The room erupted immediately into full discussions between delegates and elders.

CHAPTER TWENTY-EIGHT

Some elders were studying the figures, others discussed it amongst them-selves, and still others grouped around Talan asking questions. Stella and Nyla were at their desks in the middle of the dais when the elder leader called the meeting to order.

"We will now have a question and answer period to explain the findings and consequences of the hypothesis,"

"Stella," an elder said from the left side of the tables. "How sure are you about this? Are you convinced this theorem is right? For us to believe this coming from an ancestor is very difficult."

Stella stood down from the dais and walked in front of the elders.

"I know it is difficult, after all, what has happened to your intellectuals for the last two thousand years? The facts are that you have become too reliant on artificial intelligence. I do not blame AI for not being able to recognise an unprovable threat, or humanoids either, because it took imagination as well as the combined computing ability of the whole planet.

As I started to think about the possibilities with the central computer's support, AI began disputing and challenging each part of it by means of calculus and opposing conjectures until combined it started to become clear that discarding the palpable theories that did not work. We were left with the only feasible explanation. After that, we worked on proving it beyond doubt and that is what you have seen today."

"But can you explain why the dark energy is undetectable?" another elder asked.

"We do not have equipment to be able to see it in any form and that is because it has only just been discovered. Even in my time it was only a theory, not provable and I am sure we will be able to detect it directly. For now, we only know of it by its effect on other things like the atmosphere, magnetic fields, and electrical fields around earth. In the cosmos, it is indistinct from dark matter, so at this time we do not know how big the cloud is."

The discussion continued for another hour before the elder leader asked for concluding remarks. Stella paused to look directly at each elder before beginning.

"I am proud that we have come here today with some answers to questions that have eluded you for a long time. What is required now is that you all go back to your districts and individual experts in the fields and verify the conclusions of today's presentation. After all, every calculation and theorem is there for all to study and disprove if possible. It is imperative you have full faith in this theory. Now we need a solution to revive the planet."

"And do you have a solution?" Talan asked.

"I have proposal. I suggest a retrogress solution by way of a cosmic event."

"Are you suggesting what I think you are?" Talan asked.

"Yes, Talan. We looked at other solutions such as explosives but it was clear that the dark energy would just absorb it, you already tried that. Another way would be to try to transfer the energy from the cloud back to earth but I do not see a way to do that. The only remedy is to use shock waves to push the cloud away from the planet."

The elder next to Talan motioned to speak. "Can we try to find ways to bring the energy back to earth?"

"What about the lost water?" another asked.

"There is a lot to consider," said Talan. "Let us convene again after reviewing all the data and options. I will call a summit when everyone is ready. The meeting is now closed."

When Talan, Nyla, and Stella were the only ones left in the room, the elder motioned for them to stay.

"Are you serious about this solution? How do you mean to make it happen?"

"Let me show you on a hologram display. First, the planet needs water, yes?"

Talan nodded.

"And we need energy or heat."

He nodded again.

"There is only one source for both."

"Enceladus is a small natural satellite in Saturn's E-ring orbit. It is a small water planet with a hot core. If it is collided with earth, it should give us what we need. First, the shock waves should push away the dark energy cloud, the internal core heat will replenish earth's core and re magnetize the planet. The water is frozen on Enceladus but the impact should melt it."

"But how to you plan to make this happen?"

"If you look at the hologram, you will see we need to nudge Enceladus out of orbit so it takes a trajectory around Jupiter, then gets a sling shot from Mars to collide with earth."

They watched a demonstration created by the hologram as the satellite left orbit, swung around Jupiter, then got close to Mars before speeding up on a collision course.

Talan looked on, fascinated.

"We have to create an explosion of massive proportions close to the satellite to make it move off course," Stella said. "It has to be done in my era because it will take two thousand years to reach here. That is why it has to be a retrogress solution."

"Do you think you can make that happen?" he asked.

"We can build multiple fusion barrages installed on a spaceship flown close to it and set off at the correct moment."

"But is that possible in your time?"

"I'm not sure, so I need to go back and find out. The *Intrepid* is due here the day after tomorrow and I need to be on it."

"How did you decide on Enceladus?" Talan asked.

"It was a joint choice by the central computer and myself. We searched for the nearest possible satellite and the selection narrowed down to only one choice."

She paused. "I feel I should also tell you what happened during the research. When we were finished, the central computer asked me one question."

"What was that?"

"'Who am I?' Talan, I think it's conscious. Above and beyond the self awareness of normal artificial intelligence, it may be morphing into something more, a deity discernment formation of thought."

CHAPTER TWENTY-NINE

Wearing his white lab coat and sitting at his desk in T.T. Labs, Cal tried to decide on his next move. The scientific community had come up with little of any significance, they had shown interest in the data supplied and theorised on possible magnetic depletion interpretations also climatic changes due to environmental disasters but not much more.

Intrepid was due out again the next day and he nothing to show for his time here. Talan had said not to return, but he did not know why. He had to find some answers but did not know which way to turn.

"Allen Cox is on his way in," Matt said over his shoulder. "I just heard from the gatehouse and he has someone with him. I arranged with security to phone me if any people are heading our way."

"Good. Do you know who is with him?"

"No, could be from Homeland Security, so I guess you should either look busy or hide."

"I'll take a chance."

The doorbell rang and Matt went to let them in, head down. Cal pretended to be working until he saw it was Lara accompanying Cox. He rose to greet them but they came straight to him, smiling.

"You really look the part in that coat," Lara joked.

"And you look at lot better not being in a hospital gown. How are you?" Cal took her hand.

"She has never been better," Allen said with a smile. "I got a shock when the doctor phoned to say she could leave. They were astonished with the speed of her recovery."

"Yes, I can tell." He let go her hands. "What are you doing here?"

"We came to thank you and see if we can help in any way," Lara replied.

"I wish you could, but I'm not sure where to go from here. I checked on the microwave theory but cannot verify it."

"Mmm," Lara mused thoughtfully. "Why don't we have a round table discussion. That's what we do in the field when there is a problem. We can throw out some ideas and see what we come up with."

Cal looked to Matt, who said, "Sounds good to me. Lara, let me introduce you to the team and show you around."

As introductions were made, Cal pulled some chairs around two tables and waited. He noticed they were being shown the *Intrepid*. That didn't worry him, but wondered why if it was a top-secret project.

"You all know why Cal is here and his predicament," Matt began. "Having consulted with the top scientists around the world, he still has no answers. To be honest, I'm not sure some of the scientists took him seriously. It is not our area of expertise, but I know we would all like to help. Has anyone thought about the crisis facing the planet?"

"I have," Lara said. "I have thinking about the electromagnetic wave spectrum and how earth could have lost atmosphere, magnetism, and energy. There are more bands in the spectrum and that we cannot see them or measure them all. I read a paper a few weeks-ago that suggested the EM spectrum is larger than we have thought since the early twentieth century. The author argued that we may be able to detect these other bands in the geological record maybe there are more than we know. Is the planet losing its energy to space through different electromagnetic waves? Has anyone done research in this field?"

"I seem to remember a study that suggested the possibility of nanowave particles being heated by external sources such as electromagnetism, laser, or ultrasound in the RF spectrum," Daniel said. "Is it possible that an external force such as anti-matter or positrons are drawing energy this way?"

"Billy? You had something to say?" Matt asked.

"Yes, along the same lines. I read a research interest on computational heat transfer dynamics and visualisations had started on heat transfer by fluid motion, but also in atmosphere motion such as heat loss from tall structures and transfer to other structures. I would need to find that research and its progress."

"Is it possible that there is an adiabatic and advective process of thermal conductivity going on through microwave or nanowave spectrums that causes the planet to degrade?" Cal asked.

"As a geologist, I would say you could verify it from the known thermal conductivity values in rocks from today's values to those rocks of the future," Lara said.

"That's all well and good, but what is causing the phenomenon, and how do we fix it?" Matt asked.

"It's a good place to start. Anyone else?" Cal looked around the group.

"No good asking me," Allen said. "You lost me at wave length spectrums."

"Okay, let's call it off for the moment and do some research into what we discussed," Cal said.

The team moved apart and Lara approached Matt and Cal.

"If you let me go on the next *Intrepid* run, I could take some research of my own and compare it there, and possibly work with other researchers to get answers," Lara said. "Allen and I have discussed it and he does not want me to go but I have convinced him."

Matt looked at them both. "The risks are enormous. We have already lost one person. I could not let a member of the public take that chance."

"I had to ask," Lara said. "It's the chance of a lifetime for my research to be able to work on a future version of the planet. If you change your mind, I am available."

CHAPTER THIRTY

The destination pad for the *Intrepid* had a temporary station close by. Its equipment was sparse, with just a couple of flyhovs, medical equipment, tools, and general yard gear.

"It's like waiting for a bus," Stella said.

"What do you mean? Oh, like an ancient two decker bus on wheels, is that what you mean?" Talan asked.

"Yes, used to wait hours at bus stops, keep looking up the road to see if it's coming. This reminds me of those times but here you cannot see the transport coming."

Nyla smiled. "What will you do when you get back?"

"I will find out if we can get government cooperation to launch a space flight. There are a couple of things I need you to do."

She looked at Talan. "You must get approval from every faction of the planet. Otherwise, we cannot go through with this. I also need a space flyhov. If we get to Enceladus, I need a way to get back and there are no facilities to build one in my era."

"How are you going to get it there?" he asked.

"I will get an extension built to the back of the *Intrepid*. I want to load it on next week. Looks like we are doing this trip once a week. If I do not come back, just load it on. If there is no flyhov, then I will know there is no approval to continue the mission. Is that acceptable?"

"I do not know if I will get full approval by then, but once I do, you can have a flyhov. This decision is too important to be made lightly," Talan said.

"I understand," Stella said. "But what is the alternative? The extinction of humankind? I don't know, but as elders you must decide before it is too late."

Air shimmered outside the window like a mirage in the desert. Gradually, lucidity gave way to clarity as the blimp shape appeared. Dust swirled around it as it settled into reality. They waited while Nyla scanned the vehicle.

"There is a human on board. Sensors show a heartbeat. Only one."

"Who is it?" Stella asked. "It cannot be the hubrid."

"Nyla, please check it out. Make sure they have air and protection," Talan instructed.

As she opened the door to the *Intrepid*, a woman stood waiting to leave. She was wearing a suit and helmet and carrying a breathing pack. She greeted her.

"Hi, I'm Lara. Cal sent me."

"Nyla," she answered. "Follow me."

Walking to the station, Lara gazed around before entering and being greeted by the elder she recognised from the hologram. She guessed Stella was the other.

"Hi, my name is Lara Holden." She shook hands with all of them.

"Who sent you and why?" Stella asked.

"I have been helping Cal with research, and they did not send me. I had to sweet talk my way into it. Matt and Cal finally relented and I am here to help if I can."

"We figured it out but you can help by verifying the findings and the solution," Stella said. "Nyla and Talan will explain. I have to get on board in case it leaves prematurely." She turned to Talan. "I will only come back if I think it is necessary. You know what has to be done. Is that agreed?"

Talan nodded and she hugged Nyla before leaving the station to enter the *Intrepid*, they watched until the door closed.

"How did you get involved?" Nyla asked.

"A close friend of mine showed me a film he took of Cal displaying a hologram. I am a geologist and I could not understand how the planet could degrade in such a short time. I've done a lot of work on the effects of magnetism and heat transfer in rocks so I tried to come up with a reason. That's when my friend introduced me to Cal and we had talked until we came up with some answers. I am here to bring those to the table and help."

"We will wait until the ship has left, then show you some of the devastation on the way back to the city. There we will let you consult with our scientists and take it from there," Talan explained. "Talan to Stella, can you hear us?"

"*Yes*," she replied.

"Give us a brief summary of what you have, Lara."

Lara could not tell where the voice had come from or how they were in communication. Everything still seemed very strange. She took a moment to gather herself.

"We surmised that the planet was losing energy to an outside entity and it had to be happening in the electromagnetic spectrum. It was undetectable and our deduction was either dark matter or dark energy. The atmosphere, the magnetic degradation, and the desolation are all the result of the loss of energy. I was hoping to prove this by comparing rocks from the past and now."

"*You're very close*," said Stella. "*I think she can help. Did Cal send any message?*"

"Yes, I have it here." Lara pulled out the hologram book from her pocket.

"She has a holook," Talan said. "I will look at it later. Any other questions or requests before you go?"

"*Not that I can think of. Thanks for everything, especially the help from you, Nyla.*"

With that, the air around the ship began to shimmer and it faded away.

"Let's get you to some breathable air," Talan said as he led them back to a flyhov. He entered to the rear, allowing Lara at the front with Nyla piloting.

Lara was in awe at everything, including the flyhov lifting up and flying out, the utter barrenness of the landscape, and desolation everywhere she looked. They headed to a promontory with a cliff point on the peninsula and they pulled up on the edge overlooking what once was the sea. A flat muddy landscape fell away to the horizon, with occasional lumps of mud where there was once a hulk of wreckage.

"I cannot believe it," Lara said with a lump in her throat. "Is it like this everywhere?"

"Yes, and it is and getting worse," Talan said from the back seat. "Moisture is giving way to dry acrid wastelands where nothing can exist. Even we have trouble getting around. Nyla, let her have the controls. She might as well get accustomed to driving."

Nyla took over a mentor role and issued instructions as Lara took the joystick on her side. The flyhov launched over the edge and into the air. Heart in mouth, Lara struggled not to panic. Soon the craft came under control and flew around in a gentle circle back to the city.

CHAPTER THIRTY-ONE

There was an air of quiet anticipation permeating the lab as they awaited the return of *Intrepid*. Cal had never experienced the group connection before but could read the anxiety in their faces. Each checked their scanners or computers, then glanced at the space reserved for the ship, expectation written in their expressions.

An hour passed and activity ramped up. They moved as if in unison as the air around launch pad shimmered. Billy, dressed in protection gear, scanned the blimp for anomalies and radiation hot spots before giving it the all clear.

Daniel and Carrie went to open the door and enter the craft, but before they could, the door opened from the inside and a figure appeared.

Clad in a one-piece gray-green suit, Stella stood at the entrance, smiling.

"Good to see you all again."

The team was frozen in amazement. Cal got up to introduce himself but the others rushed by him. They gathered around Stella, hugging and holding hands. Each tried to embrace her and emotion ran high.

"Come sit down and tell us all about your experience," Matt said.

Cal at last managed to get to her.

"Hi, I am Cal244." They held each other with both hands and seemed to communicate on a different level.

"We met once but you would not remember. You were dead at the time."

The smile never faded but Stella's eyes gazed around at every person. She had a new perspective on each of them, and they in turn knew she was different.

"It's a long story," she said. "But I will make it short for now. The voyage started off alright, then shortly after moving, the cabin started vibrating badly. It got worse and there was nothing I could do. I guessed it was a malfunction of the gyro, but I passed out."

"It was the gyro," Billy said. "But we got it fixed thanks to Cal."

"Yes, when I met Lara, I guessed you fixed it."

"How is she?" said Allen in the back.

Stella looked at him, not recognising the face. Matt introduced him.

"Stella, this is Allen Cox of Cox Industries. He has also been helping Cal."

"Oh, well yes, she is fine. She will be given privileges afforded to an ancestor, right Cal?"

He nodded.

"When I woke up, I did not know at first that I had died. They explained what had happened and that they had changed me to a hubrid. I cannot explain what a shock that was and how angry it made me. They had me restrained so as not to harm myself or others. I had a mentor who had undergone the change and she helped me acclimate to this new form of mortality."

She looked at Cal. "I was able to connect with the qubit central computer and harness all the computing power available on the planet."

"Were you able to get some answers?"

"Yes, and we will go over that in detail later. First, let me tell you that earth is worse that even I thought. The devastation is beyond your imagination. The world is perched on a knife edge of complete collapse. There is a lot to go over and I need to sit down with Cal and discuss where we go from here. I know what caused the crisis and why they never found it. I also have a possible solution but we will leave it like that for now. I should let you get home to rest."

Matt urged the team to finish the shutdown of the *Intrepid* before leaving and asked them to return at 6:00pm.

"I need to consult with you," Stella said to Cal. "You can come back to my apartment with me. Matt, you have not done anything with my apartment. Have you?"

"No, I did have your body cremated and is in the process of transport back to your family in England with a sympathetic letter of condolence from us."

"I am on the run, Stella. I have to stay hidden. The military wants to find me and take me apart to study me, perhaps reverse engineer me. I cannot let them do that."

"I can explain." Allen Cox said. "I work with Homeland Security and Cal became a very big deal when he was exposed to the public. Now the president and military are involved and we have to keep him hidden."

"We need to talk, so I will sneak you back to my apartment. I need to get some clothes that will fit. I cannot walk around like this." She indicated the suit.

Cal grabbed his backpack from underneath his desk and, taking off the lab coat, followed her. Stella still had her vehicle parked there and Cal climbed between the seats to stay hidden. The only trouble they had at the gate was that the guard had not seen her for some time and wanted to chat. He noted that her car was still there but was told she was away on a mission.

CHAPTER THIRTY-TWO

Apartment block San Pueblo was located on the outskirts of town, one amongst twenty others, all similar but with one or two subtle extras to distinguish them. Joshua trees and desert plants surrounded Stella's block and she drove into the underground parking just as light was cutting into the darkness and warming up the ground. Pulling into her designated parking spot, they got out and made their way to the third floor. Apartment 322 was at the end of a corridor of bland cream coloured doors and off white walls. As she inserted her keys into the lock, the door opposite opened and a slightly older grey haired woman emerged.

"Sharon, how are you?" Stella said. "Thank you for keeping an eye on the apartment. Any problems?"

"No, just some junk mail I threw away for you and a couple of bills I slid under the door."

Her eyes were glued on Cal as she spoke.

"It's so good of you and makes me feel much better when I am away. I've just come by to pick up some papers. This is a colleague of mine named Cal."

He nodded by way of a greeting. Sharon had trouble taking her eyes away but then focused on Stella.

"Something wrong with your neck?" she asked.

Instinctively, she put her hand to her neck and touched the top of her suit. "No, no its a new workout top. Everything is fine. Any other news?"

"No," Sharon said.

"Good, well I'll see you later." Stella pushed the door open and they entered. Sharon went back into her own apartment and closed the door.

Picking up the mail, Stella glanced the bills and put them in a side table drawer.

"That woman recognised me." Cal said.

"How can she recognise you if she's never seen you before?"

"I was on TV and I am sure she knew who I was."

"What were you doing on TV?"

"Bank security camera s caught me." Cal confessed as if it were a crime.

"You robbed a bank?!" Stella said.

"No, I stopped a robbery. The criminals threatened people and I had no choice. You know I have to help innocent people."

She turned up her nose and sneered in annoyance. "You could not stay out of trouble, could you?"

"What else could I do?" Cal said sheepishly.

Stella pulled out a holook and gave it to him.

"There's a message for you from Talan. Check it out while I get changed into acceptable clothes." She entered a bedroom and closed the door.

The hologram from the future showed everything that had happened since he left, including the fiasco with the commander of the *Orlando*, Stella's interaction with the central computer and subsequent meetings with the elder council, and the recommended cosmic event to revive the planet.

Noises from outside prompted Cal to listen intently. He changed into the smaller clothes and stuffed the backpack with the others. Stella walked in to find a small boy wearing a hoodie and ball cap. She had changed into a dark grey business pant suit with a scarf around her neck.

"What the heck?" she said.

"The police are here. I told you the neighbour recognised me. I am your nephew here for a visit, okay?"

"How did you do that?"

"You mean you cannot go smaller or larger?

"No."

"Then this ability is just for workers who need to stretch up or drop down for access. They probably thought you would not need it," Cal said.

There was a knock at the door and a voice shouted, "Police, open up."

Stella opened the door. "Can I help you, officer?"

"We are looking for this fugitive, have you seen him?" He held up a photo and composite drawing.

"No, it's just my nephew and myself here. If you want to look around, feel free."

Hand at his hip holster, the policeman checked all the rooms in the apartment without finding anything and returned to the living room.

"Military have been advised and may come here depending on my report." He scrutinised Cal.

"Haven't I seen you somewhere before?" He examined the photo and looked at Cal again. "I know, I saw you at the mall the other day, didn't I?"

"Maybe. I go to the mall a lot," Cal replied.

"I remember. There was a report of a stolen handicap scooter and you were riding one. I think you better come with me."

The policeman approached Cal and reached out to hold him but instead he fell to the ground in a heap.

"Did you have to do that?" Stella said angrily. "And you stole a motorised scooter?"

"I did not. It was rented and I left it in the car park. Better tell his buddies he collapsed and needs help. He will be out for a couple of hours."

Stella left the room and came back with two more officers who went to assist their comrade.

"Sorry about this ma'am. There is an ambulance on the way."

One of the officers looked around. "He did not find anyone then?"

"No, but you can look again if you like," Stella replied. "I think he was about to leave when he collapsed."

Paramedics arrived and removed the officer on a stretcher. The other officers followed them out.

"Any other misdemeanors you want to tell me about? You know car theft, jewellery heist, or the like?" Stella asked.

"No. Well, I did escape from jail but went back. What about you and Commander Roach?"

"That was a revolt and Talan did nothing about it. There's trouble brewing for later, I would say."

"How later."

"About thirty years, when the ship comes back."

Cal bounded to the window and looked out.

"The military is here, we have to go. Grab your things."

"Why?" Stella stood her ground.

"They want to dissect me and if they find out you are a hubrid too, they'll do the same to you." Cal rushed to the door and held it open.

Grabbing her wallet, phone, and keys, they left and Stella motioned towards the roof. "There is only one way up to the apartment so they would get us going down." Stella bounded up the stairs two at a time.

The roof door was locked but she had a key and quickly unlocked it. They burst out into bright sunlight. The nearest exit was on the roof of the next block of apartments.

"Let's go," Cal said.

"It's a thirty-foot gap," she said.

"Easy, come on." Cal started running with Stella in tow. His clothes ripped as he extended his legs and grew taller.

Reaching the edge, they let go of each other and leapt. Clearing the gap comfortably, they landed on their feet and made for the roof door.

"No," Cal said. "Let's go a couple more apartment blocks over." He glanced towards the city. "That way."

Sprinting and jumping, they cleared three more gaps between apartment blocks before Cal pulled up.

"I hear a helicopter coming, we have to go down."

"I don't have a key to these doors," Stella said.

"You don't need keys anymore." Cal smiled and approached a roof door. "Put your hand on the lock and turn the mechanism with your mind."

Stella did as she was told and there was a click then a clunk as the door opened. They quickly went inside. Cal changed his ripped pants before making their way to the ground floor. They exited onto the street, checking for any sign of the military.

"Might as well go back to the lab," she said.

"How far?" Cal asked.

"About twenty miles."

"Any transport?"

"I am not stealing a car for you," Stella said.

"Can you carry me then?" he joked.

"On your bike, pal."
"I don't have a bike!"

CHAPTER THIRTY-THREE

Torn between the exhilaration of piloting a flyhov and a feeling of dismay at the desolate landscape, Lara guided the craft towards the elder complex in the distance. Low lying rolling hills devoid of vegetation surrounded an octagonal shaped concrete building that seemed to blend in naturally to the bleakness around.

"The entrance is on the right and an air-lock gate will open when you approach," Nyla said.

"You can drop me off there," Talan said from the back. "Then carry on to the science nucleus. Nyla will get you some accommodation there."

Slowly, they glided in, Lara apprehensive of where to go. Nyla pointed out a drop-off zone and Talan got out when they had stopped.

"Ask Nyla for anything you need. She will be your mentor and I will speak to you later," Talan said before walking away.

"The gate for the city is over there." Her mentor pointed out and they pulled up in front of it.

"Destination please?" A voice startled Lara.

"You do not need to drive in the city. Just state your destination and the flyhov will take us there."

Staring at Nyla for confirmation, she said, "Science nucleus." The craft took off without Lara doing any more.

"You can switch off your air now and take the helmet off. We are in breathable air now."

It was a relief to feel free again instead of the restriction of the helmet. They entered the city and Lara was speechless at what greeted her.

An underground city was never something she could ever have imagined. She saw tall buildings, a roof that looked like a natural sky, green fields, trees, and shrubbery on all sides. Her head swivelled side to side at tall glass structures with moving commercial advertisements playing across them. Fountains and statues were interspaced along the road, which seemed lacking in traffic.

They made their way to a low circular glass and mosaic fronted construction that looked like a sporting arena. A moving neon sign surrounded the top that said, "Science Nucleus: Guiding Your Future with Innovation."

"You have arrived at your destination. Have a good time." The flyhov door flipped open.

They entered into a large atrium. Signs gave direction to various science organizations and administrations. A humanoid approached.

"Good day, hubrid Nyla and friend. Can I direct or accompany you to a particular venue?"

"No, but you can get a visitor's pass in the name of Lara Holden. We will be at the geology campus."

The humanoid turned away and they went to a moving walkway, the sign above reading, "Geology and Archeology."

Lara was fascinated by people walking by. Their strange clothing seemed to change colour with body motion. They in turn stared at her dressed in a spacesuit and carrying a helmet and oxygen case. Dismounting the walkway, they were confronted by a translucent green door, Lara hesitated but Nyla walked straight through it.

"Green doors are holograms and allow access to the public," Nyla said.

Another humanoid stood in their way. "How can I help you, hubrid Nyla?"

"Who is presiding today?"

"Professor Aleck Parris, but he is taking a lecture at the moment. He will be available in about an hour."

"Please inform him we will be back then."

"Certainly."

They turned around and walked back through the green door. There were corridors off to both sides.

"Let's find you some accommodation and you can get out of that suit," Nyla said, turning to their left.

As they passed along radiant blue walls, Nyla explained the doorbell signs and availability. They came across an empty apartment with the sign, "Geoo32". Pressing the button, the door slid open and they entered. She motioned for Lara to put down the case and helmet. A droid approached and spoke to them in a robotic voice, walking mechanically.

"How can I help you today, hubrid Nyla and friend?"

"My companion is Lara Holden and she will be staying here for a short time." Nyla turned to Lara. "Would you like a drink or something to eat?"

"A drink please, coffee if possible, black."

"The droid is your personal butler. It will take care of the apartment, your belongings, and food or drink. Just ask for whatever you want. There is no menu, it will be cooked to your preference."

"Oh, I think I could like it here,"

"Let's show you around."

The apartment decor was minimal but pleasant with a bedroom, bathroom, and closet room. Walls of cream coloured synthetic vinyl with built in screens surrounded a living room with a work desk.

"Your coffee, Lara." The droid offered her a cup.

"Thank you. Do you have a name?" she asked, taking the cup.

"My name is Baer, or you may call me droid."

"Let me show you the desk," Nyla said as she sat down. Lara stood behind her sipping her coffee. "This is a touch desk and will display on the wall opposite. You will have access to all the records in the nucleus once the professor gives you a code, or I can help you navigate to anywhere in the world."

Nyla touched the top of the desk and it lit up. Simultaneously, a large display on the wall fired up. "The display on the desk is controlled by hand or mind. Placing your palm on the section on the right or left allows a neural connection and is easier to operate. Give it a try."

Lara sat down and placed her left hand on the desk.

Nothing appeared but a question. "Source?"

"Try asking with your mind for the news," Nyla said. The display changed instantly to a news anchor seated at a desk.

"Breaking news, another ancestor has arrived today. She is believed to be Lara Holden, an eminent geologist, and will be working at the Nucleus

Centre. Her goal is to verify the earlier work of Dr. Stella Cooke and help resolve the crisis."

Lara pulled her hand away and the display faded. "They know who I am already?"

"Yes, there are no secrets here, and as an ancestor you will be treated with reverence, respect, and privilege," Nyla said.

Lara sat at the desk and finished her coffee, bewildered at the attention. She wondered about the expectations on her and questioned her decision to come in the first place.

"Shall we see if the professor is available now?"

"Yes," Lara said quietly and got up. The droid took her empty cup.

Taking off the space suit, she wore jeans and front pocketed light brown shirt. She placed all her stuff in the closet and went to the door.

"Place a finger on the inside bell button and the apartment is assigned to you. You can leave an away message with the droid," said Nyla.

After assigning the accommodation, they went back to the geology department. Walking back through the green door, they met the humanoid.

"Good day once again, hubrid Nyla and Lara. A visitor admission seal has been sent up for you. Please keep it on you at all times, otherwise you may be denied access."

It handed her what looked like a coin with electronic signatures and she placed it in her shirt pocket.

"Professor Parris will see you now. Please follow me."

They turned into a corridor and the first office was marked with the professor's name. Entering, they were met by a tall black man with a bald head, a bright white smile, and warm dark eyes.

"So, glad to meet you, Lara. Elder Talan informed me you were coming and I want you to know if I can help in any way, it would be a pleasure."

They shook hands and he gestured for them to sit down.

"I am excited to be here, professor. I just hope I can help," Lara replied.

"Call me Aleck, please. I checked back in our records to find you and you know what? One of your hypotheses is in our student teaching lecture aids."

"What, even now? I cannot believe it," Lara said in astonishment.

"Believe it, Ms. Holden. You are now a celebrity and I want to ask you if you would give a lecture while you are here." He smiled pleadingly. "But only if you have time."

"I don't know, there are more important issues. Let me think about it and see if there is time later."

"Of course, now, your access code to records will be your apartment number, Geo032. I am sure Nyla will help you and you must be tired, so I will let you settle in and talk to you later," Aleck said.

"I have one question for you first," Lara said. "I have a loaded memory stick of data from the past I want to compare to today." She pulled out a couple of memory sticks from her pockets and held them up.

The other two began laughing and the professor took them from her.

"Ancient technology. Sorry to laugh but these are in a museum. I do have a guy who is into that history and I'm sure he can input the information into the system. Give us a short time, then check on your apartment desk."

They all got up and the women left. "Do you want to do some shopping before settling in?" Nyla asked. "There are some shops in the complex."

"Damn right. Shopping is an art with me. Let's go."

CHAPTER THIRTY-FOUR

Shopping was a nice distraction. It was like most shopping centres she was used to but there were electronic shopping booths where you could ask for anything and displays showed the goods. They would bring out the size and colour you required. Lara found an outdoor all weather suit that was great for work. When she asked how she could pay for it, Nyla motioned to the easy pay touch pad.

"Try it. You may have already been given some credits."

"Who by?" Lara asked.

"The elders. If not, I will pay for you," Nyla replied. "Go ahead, just touch the screen pad."

Touching with her index finger, the pad clicked and spoke.

"Thank you, Lara Holden, for shopping at Nucleus Central. Your credit is now..." There was a pause. "Unlimited."

"What!" Lara exclaimed. "I think I should get to work now and earn some of these credits."

Window shopping on the way back, Lara wanted to go into each shop but resisted the temptation. Entering the apartment, they were greeted by the droid. "Hello Lara and hubrid Nyla. Can I do anything for you?"

"What do you want to do? You must be tired by now," Nyla asked.

"I am, but wired on adrenaline I think. Will you just help me get started on the desk? I will have something to eat, then try to get some sleep."

"Of course, order your food and we will get started."

"Baer, I'll have a salad and smoothie fruit drink, please," Lara said.

The droid turned away and the women sat at the desk, Nyla to one side. Lara put her hand on the pad and screens and desk all lit up. "Source?"

"Think your code," Nyla instructed.

Geo032 brought up a menu of options from all the nucleus departments. There were far too many for Lara to choose.

"How do I find out if my own data is available?"

"In your mind, say 'My Data'. It should be there."

Instantly, the screen displayed the records she had transferred to the memory stick.

"Good. Now, how do I find comparable data from today's time?"

"It's simple," Nyla said. "It is like any data source and you cannot break it. Ask questions until you find what you are looking for. You may even be able to access files that are denied to others because of your unique circumstance."

Lara turned back and screens filled with data, both ancient and current. "This is great. It's so easy!"

"I told you! Now, if you want I will leave you to it. Your food is here and I will come back when you are rested. Just ask the droid to summon me."

"Won't you join me?" Lara asked.

"I do not eat, drink, or even breathe air, so I will just leave you to it," Nyla replied.

"Just one last question. How do I leave the desk to examine data on the large screen?"

"Whatever you want to do, ask in your mind."

"I guess I will get used to it. I think I'm too tired to concentrate," Lara said.

Nyla left and, sitting at a table, Lara consumed her meal with the droid looking on.

"Do you have to watch me?"

"Sorry," the droid answered and left the room.

After eating, she showered but found it disappointing as the water stream was weak, probably to conserve water. The bed, however, felt luxurious. It seemed to adjust to her form and temperature. Sleep came despite her distractions and it seemed only minutes before she woke up.

Darkness filled the room. Often, she knew the time instinctively, but now she had no clue.

"Time," she called without thinking.

"Four-fifty-seven in the morning," a voice answered.

Alarmed, she jumped up to find the droid standing in the doorway watching her.

"What are you doing?"

"I am monitoring for sleep deprivation, health issues, and comfort," Baer answered.

"Why?"

"It is one of my tasks to make sure you are cared for to the best of our abilities. Did you know you made a wheezing noise? It may be nasal constriction. I can get you examined?"

"No thanks!" Lara yelled as she jumped out of bed. Embarrassed at her nakedness, she grabbed a bed sheet.

"Lara, I am a machine, here to do your bidding. I will try to stay out of your way."

Calming, she said, "Too late to go back to bed. Baer, I will have a coffee after I shower."

"Certainly, Lara." The droid left.

Showering was no better the second time but at least she felt clean. She was pleasantly surprised to find her clothes cleaned, pressed, and ready to wear. Her coffee was at the beside and, taking a drink, she went to the desk. It came to life instantly at her touch and she logged on.

Refreshed and alert now, she concentrated on the task at hand as reams of data streamed by and her brow furrowed with worry. The results, each and every one, confirmed her worst fears. Twice more she re-examined the results and still could not believe it. She paused to consider the outcome of her findings. Stella's theories seemed to be verified but she would have to review her work. She called to the droid.

"Baer, can I have more coffee?"

"Would you like breakfast as well?"

"Can you make scrambled eggs and toast?"

The droid disappeared again. She felt like it was hovering over her all the time and it was perturbing. Stretching her arms, she got up and walked around, still considering her findings and the consequences. When the breakfast arrived, she sat down and first thanked Baer, then asked it to summon Nyla.

The food was surprisingly good, as was the coffee, and she felt better. Sitting at the desk, she pulled up Stella's work.

There was so much calculus it would take weeks working on her own to review and recalculate it all. Assuming the work was correct (she had no reason to doubt it), it suggested Cal and her were on the right track. She sat contemplating before Nyla arrived. Baer showed her in and they greeted one another like old friends.

"Nyla, I need to ask someone in electrical engineering a question. Do you know anyone there?"

"No, but I'm sure they will be helpful. Let's go."

Following signs and walkways, they went to what they thought was the correct department. Passing through a green door, another humanoid greeted them.

After explaining, they were passed to the head of the administration. Another humanoid but then got to see a Professor John Mason who ushered them into his office. He was a short stout white man, grey thinning hair but had a jovial welcoming smile.

"It is so good to meet you." He shook their hands and seated them at his desk. "I've seen you on the news but never thought I would get the chance to chat. What can I do for you?"

"I need some help," Lara said.

"It would be a pleasure."

She explained the suspected cloud of dark energy that surround the planet and the absorption of earth's natural properties.

"I thought of a way to verify it but it is out of my area of expertise."

"Explain your theory and maybe I can help."

"I want to know if we can detect electromagnetic energy in outer space."

"We can," Professor Mason said.

"And can you invert and absorb it to an accumulator?"

"Possibly, but what are you thinking?"

"If we equip one of your space craft, a flyhov, with an invertor and accumulator, then launch it above the atmosphere, we can measure when the microwaves start. It may give us the info to map this cloud of energy. If you pass through it, this will give us a depth and if you can gather energy in an accumulator, it can be discharged into your energy grid. Does this sound feasible?"

"I cannot say immediately, but I will investigate the possibility. Leave it with me."

CHAPTER THIRTY-FIVE

"Wait a minute. I'm going to phone Sharon to find out if the apartment is all right." Stella pulled up and took her phone from her pocket.

Cal stood on the sidewalk and scanned the surroundings, checking the skyline as well.

"Sharon, how are you? Stella here. Just checking, is my apartment alright?" She listened intently. "Are they still there?" She paused. "They're what? I'll be right there."

"The military are trashing my apartment. I'm going back to sort it out. You carry on without me."

"Think about it," Cal said. "What are you going to do? If you create a scene, there could be consequences. Trouble with the government will just draw attention and cause us grief."

"I cannot stand by while they destroy my life. You go on, I won't be long." Stella turned to walk back.

"Let's check our internal communication first, that way we can stay in touch."

"Let me go around the corner and see if it works here." She walked away. "Stella to Cal."

"I can hear you fine," he replied. "Make sure your outside speaker is muted and be careful."

Walking briskly, she walked towards her apartment. Cal followed at a discreet distance, checking for any unwanted parties. She bounded up the stairs two at a time and could see a uniformed soldier outside her door. As she approached, he held up his hand to stop her.

"This is my apartment. What the hell is going on?"

"We are searching for a fugitive, ma'am. You cannot go in."

The door opposite opened and Sharon appeared. Stella drew close to her and could see inside. Anger swelled inside at the mess confronting her. Pulling out her phone, she dialed 911.

"Yes, I have intruders in my apartment and request police assistance." She rattled off the address.

"Who is charge here?" she asked the solider.

"I am," said a voice from inside. "Captain Jeremy Poole. Please wait outside."

"I want to see the search warrant," Stella demanded.

"Don't need one. This is a matter of homeland security," he replied. "We're looking for a fugitive."

"And did you find anyone?" Anger laced every word.

"No, not yet but our investigation is classified and ongoing."

"Then why are you tearing up my apartment?"

"Looking for clues," he replied.

"*Wait a moment,*" Cal's voice said in her ear. "*I know the director of local Homeland Security. I will give him a call.*"

"What makes you think you will find anything?" Stella asked the captain.

"A tip told us the fugitive was seen entering this apartment with you, so we have to check every possibility," the captain replied. The phone in his pocket started ringing. "Excuse me."

He turned away to take the call but Stella could hear every word.

"Captain, this is Jack Branigan, of Homeland Security."

"Yes sir."

"Call off your investigation. We have further leads and information elsewhere. Apologise to the tenant and send a bill for any damage to us. Understood?"

"Yes sir." The captain ended the call and turned to Stella. "Sorry a mistake has been made and I apologise for any inconvenience. Please send a bill for any damage to us."

He pulled out a card and handed it to her. The military unit assembled and left, leaving Stella and her neighbor surveying the mess.

"This is all my fault," Sharon said. "I thought I recognised the man with you earlier."

"You did. He is working under cover and apparently knows the head of Homeland Security. Keep this to yourself though. It is a national emergency and we are working on this together," Stella whispered.

"Wow! Can I help in any way?" Sharon asked.

"Yes, can you arrange to get this cleaned up and a new door fitted with extra locks and security. Send the bill to this address." She handed her the card.

Only too pleased to make amends, Sharon took the card and they agreed to tell the police it was a false alarm. They said goodbye and Stella went to the basement to get her car, then drove out to find Cal.

"Where are you?" she asked.

"Drive around the block a couple of times. I'll check if you are followed."

She picked him up close to where they had parted.

"Paranoid, aren't you?" Stella said.

"We cannot be too careful," he replied. "I have already been in jail twice and I have no desire to return."

"What shall we do now?" she asked.

"If we have time, I would like to make a house call. Check on her and talk to the homeland security director. I will give you directions," Cal replied.

"What, are you a doctor now?" Stella asked.

"Just a friend. Carry on along here and turn when I say so."

At a sign for Legacy Woods, Cal told her to turn.

"You know someone from here? This is one of the best neighbourhoods in the city."

"It's a long story. Turn left here," Cal replied.

He guided her right into the Branigan drive. Getting out of the car, Stella surveyed the house as they went up to the front door and rang the bell. "Nice place. You always make friends in high places?" Stella asked.

They heard footsteps approaching and locks clicking before the door opened.

"Cal!" Irene rushed out and threw her arms around him. "It's so good to see you. Come in, come in."

Stella scrutinised the couple with a frown. They were acting like lovers, not friends. They walked through the house with arms around each other until reaching a sitting room.

"Look who's here, Mother," Irene called.

Laura got up and hugged Cal.

"Good to see you again. I was just speaking about you on the phone."

"Nothing bad I hope." Cal stood apart but held onto both her hands.

"My husband is looking for you. I think everyone is."

"Best call him back then and tell him where I am."

"Who is this with you?" Laura gestured towards Stella.

"This is the original time traveller, Dr. Cooke."

Introductions were made and they shook hands.

"Stella, hold both of Laura's hands and tell me what you think," Cal said.

"You have a small tumor," she said.

"It used to be larger, it will disappear soon." Cal said. "Laura, you feeling better now?"

"Much better, thanks to you. I feel like a normal person again." She smiled.

"Good. Now, please call Jack back and ask him to come to a meeting tonight at the lab at six o'clock," Cal said.

Laura went to another room to call her husband and returned quickly.

"He said he would be at the meeting. He seemed a little incredulous that the whole country is looking for you and you're hiding at our house.

"We have some time to spare before the meeting tonight, so I thought we could drop in," Cal said.

"We are happy you did," Irene said. "Please fill us in on everything."

CHAPTER THIRTY-SIX

T.T. Labs seemed crowded at six o'clock. The whole team was assembled now that Stella was back, and Allen Cox and Jack Branigan stood on the sidelines. A table was selected to seat everyone and the chief of Homeland Security was introduced to Stella. His curiosity piqued because he knew about her conversion to a hubrid.

After introductions, Stella began. "As you all know, I just got back and want to update everyone on what has happened and what is in the works for the future." She pulled out a holook and set it on the table. "I have edited it to condense content to the essential details and save time. I'll answer questions at the end."

The hologram opened with a view of the underground city and driving through the streets.

"I thought you would like a view of the city. See how nice they have made it and how lifelike it is to an open-air urban environment. The vehicles you see driving around are called flyhovs and are driverless underground, but can be piloted to fly outside."

"Amazing," someone whispered.

The scene changed to the outside while they were flying over a rocky barren landscape, then merged to travelling over a muddy sea bottom. It showed their approach to the research station.

"This is one of the monitoring outposts situated at the bottom of an ocean floor. In the background is what is left of the sea."

The panorama changed to a view of a disc-shaped spaceship and an approach to a docking air lock.

"This ship is one of thirty-nine, each stationed above the underground cities. They were built to evacuate the populations if or when a habitable planet is found. Each can hold one million or more inhabitants and is self-sustainable for generations."

Inside views showed them walking to the centre of the ship and getting into an elevator.

"The control room for the LISA is where we can get data on gravitational waves, which is what I want to show you."

Monitor screens showed various wave patterns.

"Lisa is a triangulated signal of geodesics that indicate gravitational wave forms. By combining the signals from all the ships, we can draw a picture of the waves around the planet." The view switched on the screens in the room as she spoke.

"As you can see, instead of them all being similar, they vary greatly from one side of the globe to the other. This indicates pressure or an outside influence brought to bear on the planet. Its effect is what changed the atmosphere."

The world as a whole came into perspective, showing a black cloud partially covering one side and some of the other half.

"Using the central computer, we came up with this model of a cloud of dark energy surrounding earth. The cloud has been drawing electromagnetic energy from the atmosphere and the planet, which is reducing the planet's ability to filter harmful cosmic rays and radiation from the sun. First it caused the plants to wither and die, and the animals followed soon after. The rivers and lakes dried up, and eventually even the oceans began to disappear and has driven humanity underground. If it was not for our perseverance, we would be looking at a dead planet, similar to what we see on Mars today."

Stella got up and looked around at their faces, letting it all sink in. "Any questions so far?"

It was quiet for a while before Cal spoke up.

"Were you able to verify this?"

"I spent two days hooked up to the qubit central computer. This is result of the combined computing power of the entire world. The results stand for themselves, and I believe there is a third party also trying to confirm the theory. Right, Mr. Cox?"

Allen nodded.

"Also, every astrophysicist on the planet is pouring over the calculation and theorems. Believe me, nothing will be done without verification. Which brings me to the next step: A retrogress resolution. Does everyone want to take a moment before we move on?"

Most got up to get a drink or take a bathroom break and settled back down, all the while staring at the hologram. Stella waited until quietness prevailed.

"What I am about to propose is radical, so please keep an open mind until after the illustration. What we need to do to resolve the crisis is threefold. We must move the dark energy cloud, restore energy to the planet, and renew the supply of water. Doing all three at the same time requires a cosmic event and that means a collision of earth and another planet."

The hologram changed to a model of the solar system with earth set in the middle.

"The nearest satellite with all the required attributes is Enceladus, which orbits Saturn. It is five hundred kilometers in diameter, has a hot core, and is covered in water or ice. Colliding with earth will send shock waves out, pushing the energy cloud farther into space. Enceladus' break up would heat the core and start magma flowing again, renewing magnetism to the planet. Ice turning to water will renew the oceans and restart the chemistry of the atmosphere." She hesitated. "Questions so far?"

"If what you say is correct, how do you plan to make it happen?" Matt asked.

"Million-dollar question, Matt," Stella said. "We need the event to happen before the planet finally dies and to do that we need to start the process now.

The calculations are that once set on a collision course to earth, it would take Enceladus two thousand years to reach here, so action needs to happen as soon as possible." She looked each of them in the eye. "How? By nudging the satellite out of Saturn's orbit with the greatest explosion ever created by humankind."

The group looked incredulous and shifted in their seats nervously. Stella held up her hand for calm.

"We pack a craft full of fusion explosives, fly it to an orbit around the satellite, and set it off at the correct moment. Let me show you the proposed action on the hologram."

They watched as the satellite went out of orbit, travelled around Venus, picked up a slingshot from Mars, and drove on to a collision with earth. Stella let the program on repeat for effect.

"You are really serious about this, aren't you?" Jack said.

"Deadly serious," she replied.

"Won't it destroy earth as we know it?" Matt asked.

"Another million-dollar question, it will radically change Matt. But what are the alternatives?"

"What are the logistics of all this?" Allen Cox asked.

Stella looked at him. "We first have to alter the *Intrepid* to carry supplies from the future, then we pack a vehicle to fly them to Enceladus. I was thinking of getting the space shuttle out of the museum and retrofitting it."

"That will not happen, I can tell you that," Allen said. "I already approached the president to get help for Cal and was turned down. Correct, Jack?"

"Yes," Jack agreed. "I was there for a meeting for Homeland Security and the order was to find Cal and reverse engineer him for use by the military. Too many hawks, to use an old expression, and not enough doves."

"That will not happen!" Cal said.

"I agree," Stella confirmed. "We have a program installed into our AI unit that will start a self-destruct mode if interfered with, and that would destroy everything in a ten-kilometre radius."

The mood in the room deflated like a balloon at a kid's party. No one spoke for some time until Matt drew the meeting to a close.

"I think you need to rethink this. Shall we reconvene in the morning?"

Each slowly wound up their affairs and made their way out the door until there was only Matt, Stella, Jack and Allen Cox left.

"I may have an alternative vehicle."

They all looked at him with anticipation.

"Cox Industries has an airplane in mothballs in Arizona that may work if you do not plan to bring it back. I had plans for it but I guess the planet needs to take president. I'd like to show it to you."

CHAPTER THIRTY-SEVEN

Stella and Cal stayed behind overnight. They had no need for sleep and decided to work on the modifications needed for the *Intrepid*. Each knew the dimensions of a flyhov 4, and the sizes of fusion engines and fusion explosives, none of which could be obtained in this era. Realizing that more than one trip would be needed, they drew up plans to accommodate the largest item, which was the flyhov.

Allen Cox had agreed to fly them to Arizona the next day along with Matt. The whole team would need to be involved in the modification not only of the *Intrepid* but also the acquisition of a vehicle to get them to Enceladus.

As the team arrived in the morning, the modified plans were laid out on a desk and installed on all the computers. Stella gave a talk on how to carry out the revisions while they gathered around the desk. After everyone was conversant on the tasks, Matt left with Stella and Cal to meet at Cox Industries to fly out from there. Upon arrival at the gate, they were directed to a hanger where a helicopter waited outside for them.

"Good morning." Allen greeted each one from the pilot's seat as he guided Stella to the front and the two men to the back. They put on headsets so they could converse more easily.

"Just in time. I logged a flight schedule with aviation control so we can take off right away."

Checking instruments one last time, he checked in with the control tower before lifting off. Gaining height and speed, they headed off in a westerly direction. He indicated the main points of interest along the way, mainly for Cal, as he may have heard of them but never seen them in person.

"I am taking you to an aircraft boneyard in Arizona," Allen said as they got closer. "The biggest site is Davis-Monthan, but it is the military's, so we cannot use that."

Hundreds of aircraft could be seen as they got closer. They were of all shapes and sizes and all parked in orderly rows.

"This one, believe it or not, is a small boneyard, used for commercial and some private use. Some planes are almost ready to be reused, some broken up for parts, and others to be scrapped. We have a hanger here."

It was obvious Cox had been here many times as he guided the helicopter straight to a hanger with a landing pad close by. Landing softly, the engine was turned off and when the rotors stopped, they stepped out into a dry heat with only a slight breeze. Instead of taking, them inside, he walked over to a golf cart parked near the hanger. Getting in, Cox drove them around the aircraft graveyard.

They passed row upon row of Lockheed, Boeing, and Cessna. They turned down another row and went back a few aircraft before coming to a stop in front of a jet covered in white reflective tape.

"This, ladies and gentlemen, is a Tupolev TU-154M, a Russian built Tri-Star. It's built like a tank." He said it proudly as if it were his prized possession. "These were built for rugged conditions, like to travel across frozen wilderness and land in rough airfields. They were modified and fitted out for various uses including passenger, cargo, and astronaut training."

They got out the golf cart and walked around it, taking in the size and layout.

"I had to travel to Bishkek in Kyrgyzstan to purchase it and flew it back myself. I had plans to turn it into a luxury private rental for one-off flights to anywhere in the world. Imagine what it would look like without wings."

The other three looked at him curiously.

He threw his hands in the air, waving towards it. "Like a rocket ship!"

Nobody jumped for joy but they could see what he imagined.

"Let me show you inside." As they approached, he propped a ladder to door.

The inside was gutted, with no seats, overheads, or galleys and they went right to the cockpit. It had the usual layout, with two pilot seats up front and two seats on either side for navigators and instruments. It was a forward set cockpit with good views over the front nose through a framed window.

The other three had a good look around while Allen waited up front, Cal tapped the sides and roof as if checking it structurally, then checked through the windows. Stella was at the rear trying to find access to the lower section and upwards at the engine bays. Matt just wandered around looking for flaws.

"Well what do you think?" Allen asked when they all returned.

"How big is the hold?" Stella asked.

"Let's take a look," he replied.

Back on the ground, they opened a side hatch to the cargo hold and Stella jumped inside. Standing, she walked the length and width, mentally measuring.

"It will hold a flyhov," she said, looking at Cal. "But it would need a drop down hatch at the back for easer access and also an entrance to the main cabin."

"Here is what I was thinking," Allen said. "We cover the front with the glue-on heat resistant tiles and refit the wings to make them detachable, say with exploding bolts. Then we fly it out of the atmosphere with your engines, drop off the wings when we are in space, and use it like a space ship."

Nobody spoke and they slowly made their way around the plane, all the time observing it, until they reached the golf cart. Jumping in, Cox took them back to the hanger and this time they drove inside. It was cavernous like all aircraft hangers and the cart went right to the back where offices were situated. Once inside, they sat at a desk and Allen made coffee for himself and Matt.

"What do you think?" Cal asked Stella.

"I think it is one option, and a feasible one. I don't know if there are others. We need to consider it but it all depends on the elders and if they will supply all our needs." "Here is my proposal," Allen said. "I love this planet and it may be the most beautiful in the universe. I would do anything to save it. If everything is as bad as you say, then Lara will confirm it when she returns. I will donate the plane, place it in this hanger for you to work on, pay all the expenses to have it converted, and even put up your team to work here. There are beds in the back and a motel just outside on the main road. I will transport you all back and forwards. There is only one condition."

"What is that?" Cal asked.

"That Lara and I accompany you to Enceladus."

Everyone stared at him, wondering if he was serious or not, but his determined expression said it all.

"It could be suicidal. You know that, don't you?" Stella stared him in the eyes, holding his gaze. "And what makes you think Lara will want to do it?"

"We are an item. She loves her work and is the most strong-willed woman I know. It would spoil our relationship to get married so we both get on with our work and enjoy each other when we can. As you may have noticed, there was no stopping her getting on to Intrepid and it is her choice, but I guarantee she will want to go. And how could I turn down an opportunity to fly in the cosmos?"

Stella turned to Matt. "What about you and the team? I know and trust them all. What do you think?"

"I am responsible for the project and so far, I have held back all the reports. Sooner or later, NASA will want to know. If we help you, then a third party will have to fund all the expenses and I will have to ask the team to vote on it. That would only be fair," Matt replied.

Cal stood. "I truly appreciate what all of you have done so far. Expecting the government to help was a great disappointment but you have all been terrific. Allen, your offer is more than generous, it's overwhelming, and at least we have a plan if nothing better turns up. We must wait for a decision from the elders and take it from there."

'I think we should return to the lab and press on with modifications to the Intrepid, get it ready for the next launch.' Stella suggested.

They jumped in the golf cart and drove off, back to the Heli-pad.

CHAPTER THIRTY-EIGHT

"Can I help you Lara Holden and hubrid Nyla?" The humanoid stood before them at the geology department.

"Yes, I would like to see the professor again, as soon as possible please," said Lara.

"Is it an emergency?" the humanoid asked.

"No, but I would like to see him."

"It's alright, follow me," said Nyla. She took her arm and walked around the greeting robot. "Sometimes you have to bypass the protocols."

Outside the professor's office, he spotted them through the glass and motioned them in.

"Professor Parris, good to see you again," Lara began. "Have you had a chance to examine my data."

"No, but I can pull them up right now." He placed his hand on the desk and the files appeared on screen. His head moved slightly as he read.

They waited while he digested the information with a frown appearing on his face. He glanced at Lara a couple of times.

"Are you sure about this?"

"Yes," Lara said. "But I want to go outside and take a couple of samples to be sure. Can we analyze them quickly?"

"Of course, I would go with you but I am tied up today. Would you like an assistant? I have a recently graduated student and she has a brilliant mind."

"If she can get the samples examined in a hurry, she would be welcome," Lara replied.

"I'll send for her."

Turning to her mentor, Stella said, "Nyla, can you arrange a flyhov for us? I will need to get my suit for outside."

"You can use one of our suits. They are more durable and have rebreathers built in. I was going to offer one to you anyway," Nyla said. She smiled. "We want your old one for the museum."

Lara was laughing when a young girl knocked the door and was waved in by the professor.

"Ladies, this is Shaidi Lotario, one of our honour students. Shi, this Dr. Lara Holden and hubrid Nyla."

Reddish wiry hair framed an oval face. Smiling eyes and a disarming smile greeted them warmly.

"Hi, I have heard so much about you, everyone calls me Shi." They all shook hands.

"Hope you are not shy like your name." Lara quipped. "Bet you've heard that one before."

They all had a cursory chuckle but Shi never answered back, just smiles all round.

"Let's get going then," Nyla said.

They made small talk in the flyhov, getting acquainted. Shi had only been on the outside once before on a school trip.

"That makes two of us then," Lara said.

"But you lived on the outside before, did you not?"

"All my life," she replied.

After that an air of contemplation pervaded as they made their way into the parkade. Nyla guided the craft to a check-in hall. At a desk, she told a young male attendant they wanted suits for the outdoors. He ushered them to a fitting room where a humanoid measured them.

"I want new suits with their names on," Nyla said. The attendant rushed off.

The assistant came back with a piece of paper and writing pen. "I need you to sign for them."

"No, you don't," Nyla said.

"You're right," the young man confessed. "I just want your autographs."

With a broad smile, he passed them the pen and paper and the two women obliged. He looked constantly at Shi, then left, almost walking into a door.

THOMAS CONNER

"You've made a conquest there," Lara said, laughing.

"No, I have not!" Shi replied, blushing.

The suits arrived and Nyla authorised their release by finger imprint. It was a snug but perfect fit for both women, with a slight hump on the back, and Nyla demonstrated some features.

"By pressing a button on the wrist, a clear hood pops over your head and the re-breather on your back starts automatically. To talk, just speak and it will be broadcast to the nearest company."

Guiding the flyhov 4 gingerly through the air lock doors, Lara drove with Shi beside her and Nyla in the back.

"I want to go inland, Nyla. Which way?"

"Turn right and it is all in front of you," she replied.

Rising to an elevation of about one hundred feet, Lara gazed around as they cruised at a moderate pace. Soon they came upon the ruins of a township and they slowed to explore what was left.

Stone walls without roofs were surrounded in blown sand up to windowless openings. Other structures were in a heap where they had collapsed and parts were sunk in desert debris. Road signs or business notices littered the ground. Lara dropped down and cruised the streets. It was like driving through a ghost town.

"What happened to the people who died?" she asked.

"Nearly all were cremated by request, their ashes scattered to the ground to be blown in the wind all over the planet," Nyla replied. "It's sad, really."

Lifting up once more, they journeyed onwards until a steep hill confronted them. Rising over it, they came across a vast plateau stretching in all directions.

"Can you take over while I look around, Shi?"

"I have never driven a flyhov before. In the city, they are all guided," she answered nervously.

"Do not worry," Nyla said from the back. "I will give you a short lesson. They are easy, right Lara?"

Shi made a few side to side, up and down erratic maneuvers, then sped up dramatically before slowing down. She got used to the controls quickly.

"This is fun," she said with delight.

"Good, just keep it slow and steady," Nyla said. "What are we looking for anyway, Lara?"

"Geophysical evidence of electromagnetic activity," she said.

"And what does that look like?"

"I wish I knew," Lara replied. "But something out of the ordinary."

Bright sunlight reflecting off the rocky surfaces made it difficult and Shi had to turn around so Lara could check something unusual, but mostly it was just rocky outcrops or something in the shade.

Nyla's eyes were better than the others and often she drew their attention to what was thought to be different. It was no surprise when she called them to look.

"What about those circles over there?" She pointed to the left.

Shi swung over and they noted a number of circles dotted around. They dropped near to the ground and flew over them.

"Let's land and take a look," Lara said.

The flyhov landed softly close to a few of the circles.

"You're flying like a pro now," Stella remarked as the front door slid open. The girl smiled.

The circles were bowl-shaped, shallow, and had a spiral-shaped pyramid of small rocky sediment in the middle. Checking around, they all looked the same and Lara stepped inside one for a closer look. She sat on her haunches to examine the spiral.

"What equipment do we have with us? Shi?"

"We have a core sample drill, various rock hammers, a scoop and sample bags, a portable particle analysis machine, and a couple of sieve shakers," she replied.

"Magnifiers as well? I don't have my own with me."

"Yes."

"Could we unload them here, please?"

As the others unloaded the back of the flyhov, Lara studied the walls of the circles, finding spiral tracks all the way around. She grabbed a magnifier when they returned and went to look at a small rock, only to find the clear hood in the way. Pressing the button on her wrist, it flipped up but she could not breathe so closed it quickly.

"Let's do a quick particle analysis while we're here and take a core sample," Lara suggested.

Using a scoop, Shi filled some bags from different areas. Lara scooped some from the middle spiral and went to drop it in the funnel of the particle analyser, but stopped.

"Do we have a micro-splitter with us?" she asked Shi.

"No, there are some back in the lab."

"Alright. We will do more tests when we get back." Then dropped the scoop sample into the funnel.

"You better work this, Shi, as I am not familiar with this tool." Lara motioned for her to come over.

The girl dropped on her knees by the small machine and pressed a couple of buttons to turn it on. It displayed a reading on a small screen almost immediately. Lara stared at the results.

After a couple of minutes, she rose and stood scowling into the bowl, glaring around every inch of its circumference.

"Come with me," Lara said.

They rose and followed her to another circle and stood around it, each waiting.

"What do you see?" Lara asked.

Staring into it, not sure what they were supposed to find, Nyla said, "I do not know."

"It looks to me like a MCV, a mesoscale convective vortex, or what's left behind after one. See the circling patterns of the vortex on the outside and spiral patterns on the central core?

It's a cyclonic updraft that has risen up into the troposphere or higher and I think it was electromagnetic in nature."

Nyla looked skeptical. "So, you think this is how energy is absorbed into a dark energy cloud? Do you not think they could be formed by normal dust devils or whirlwinds?"

"No. Whirlwinds just move loose surface dust and leave little trace. All of these rocks, soil, and particles are the same. Dead. By that I mean, there is no magnetism, no residual heat, and no inert energy. Let's get the samples back and do further tests. I need more data to confirm the theory."

CHAPTER THIRTY-NINE

Back in the labs at Nucleus Central, Lara let Shi take all the soil samples for analysis to confirm what she was sure she already knew. She and Nyla went to the professor's office to consult with him.

"You think these cyclonic updrafts are what's been draining the planet of energy? How sure are you?"

"I am convinced of it," Lara replied. "The only way to confirm it is by finding one in action and measuring the electromagnetic energy passing through. That may take time, first to find one and second to get readings, but there is no harm in monitoring the area for now."

He looked thoughtful and studied the data on the screen. He stroked his chin before finally putting his hands on his forehead and elbows on the desk.

"I can start a team on monitoring the area. Shi knows the location, right?"

"Right."

"Okay, I will set that in motion," he said.

"I have one more experiment to do, so can I leave that with you?" Lara asked.

"Yes," Professor Parris said. "Will you have time to give that lecture I requested?"

"I'll try," she said. Nyla and Lara thanked the professor and left.

They walked along the corridors back to electrical engineering. "I am getting to know my way around now," said Lara. "You don't need to help me anymore, unless you want to."

"I want to," Nyla replied. "Besides, Talan wants to monitor you and record any significant findings you make. Is that okay?"

"Sure. It saves me having to explain it all."

They reached electrical engineering, bypassed the greeting humanoid, and entered the inner lab.

Spotting Professor Mason working near a flyhov, they approached and waited until he was free. After a moment, he turned around and noticed them.

"Ah, there you are." He took off his safety glasses. "We still have some work to do but are close to getting a test vehicle ready. Is it just a quick experiment you want to do? Will that be enough?"

Lara checked out the vehicle and equipment set up inside. "I want to know if it is feasible to harvest energy from the cloud that we are sure is up there. A better method can be utilized at a later date."

They examined the electronic equipment to be used. A large cylindrical accumulator filled most of the space and two probes set outside connected to an inverter.

"I suggest doing this remotely or with a robot, as it could be dangerous with static flying around," Lara said.

"I agree, we will do that. The two probes you see on the side are to pass electricity straight through if we cannot convert and store it," John said.

"Will you call me or Nyla when you are about to do the test? I would like to see the result."

"I can call Nyla; she may be easier to contact than you."

After changing out of her suit, Nyla took her on a tour of the city. They went around major buildings and parks, and saw the wildlife centre, theatres, and restaurants. They ate, or Lara ate and Nyla watched, at a place serving fruits, salads, vegetarian dishes, and hot drinks with exotic names.

"Don't you have a big shopping centre?" Lara asked curiously as she finished her meal.

"That's what you really wanted to see, isn't it?"

"It's a hobby of mine when I am in town."

"Okay, I'll take you to the shopping district."

Driving through the city centre in a flyhov, a voice spoke from speakers inside the vehicle.

"Message for hubrid Nyla, message for—"

"Put it through," she said.

"Nyla, John Mason here. We are heading to the elder complex to test the electrical accumulator, if you want to meet us there."

"We are on our way," she replied.

"So much for shopping," Lara moaned.

"We will work it in later," Nyla said. She asked the flyhov to change course towards the elder complex.

They arrived and were greeted by the young male attendant they had met before.

"Where is your friend?" he asked Lara.

"Busy. Where are the test facilities?"

Taken aback, he pointed to a corridor at the side of the parkade.

"Only asking," he said under his breath.

Striding off, they left him with the flyhov to park. Offices on either side gave way to a computer complex and the professor was standing with a humanoid at a bank of screens by a window. They noticed a flyhov was parked outside the window as they approached. At the sound of their footsteps, both males turned.

"Ah, there you are." It seemed to be the professor's favorite phrase. "This is Tory. He will be taking the test vehicle out."

Nodding in greeting, the humanoid left.

"A man of little words," Lara noted.

"He knows what he has to do," Mason replied.

After a minute or two, Tory appeared by the flyhov and got in. The vehicle lifted up, turned around and took off.

They turned their attention to the banks of screens. One showed a view from inside the front of the test craft with Tory looking out. Another a view was from the back and the humanoid could just be glimpsed around the equipment. The rest of the screens were sensor reading graphs and digital read outs. A speed indicator and altimeter were side by side.

"Everything is turned on so as soon as the inverter starts picking up energy of any voltage, it will be recorded," the professor said.

Watching a recording of the altimeter, it passed through the atmosphere and almost immediately, the other screens began showing readings. Nyla made a note of the height and monitored the data. The professor started getting agitated and excited, bouncing from one computer to another.

"The accumulator is filling up," he said eagerly. "And fast."

They stared at the capacity screen and it was already near three quarters full.

"Turn it off," Lara said.

"Tory, turn off the inverter and accumulator," Mason said.

The humanoid was pressing switches and nothing changed. The capacity screen showed it was almost full.

"Turn it off!" Lara shouted.

Sparks started cracking around the craft and Tory desperately tried to stop the equipment. Then static electricity began shooting from his body to all parts of the craft.

"Can we turn it off from here?" Lara asked.

"No," the professor said.

The data recording screens flashed red with warnings of overload, Lara tried turning them off without success.

"We have to stop it, now!" Lara stated, almost shouting.

"Tory, get to the shunt switch between the collector valve and invertor and turn it off manually." The professor ordered.

Horrified, they watched as he got out of his seat with flashes of electricity flying in every direction. Falling to the floor he struggled to get up, his eyes glowing with electrical surges pulsing through his body. He pushed around the accumulator towards the back of the craft, fighting for every inch. Bending down, his hand closed on a large turn switch and he held it without moving.

"Turn the switch!" Lara called out.

It seemed to take forever and all his strength to turn it. He collapsed as the electric flow ceased.

CHAPTER FORTY

"Can we bring the craft back remotely?"

"I believe there is a way but I don't know how. Only an OCR maintenance technician does," the professor said.

"What is OCR?" Lara asked

"It's outside construction reclamation." Nyla said "I think that young attendant is part of that team."

"I'll go get him," Lara said.

She walked out the office and towards reception. When the assistant spotted Lara coming, he turned away.

"Hey, are you part of OCR?" she called after him.

Turning back, he faced her with unconcealed annoyance.

"What if I am?"

"What's your name?"

"Dax."

"Dax Haller,"

"Dax, we have a craft out there that is immobile and pilotless. Can you help us?"

"Not another one." He sounded exasperated

"What do you mean, another one? Do you get lots?"

"All the time. Almost one a day. They are shut down and we have to retrieve them, decontaminate, and reset them before putting them back into service. Pilots also are shut down, humanoids, robots and drones. Sometimes their memories are wiped and have to be replaced."

"Have you reported this?" Lara asked.

"All the time. Every incident is recorded with location, altitude, time, and anything else. And the reports are filed in order."

"Can you get our craft back then, please, Dax?" She gave him her best pleading smile.

Lara put her arm in his and walked him back to the control room, where he sat at a computer desk.

Placing a hand on the controls, he stared at the screen and tried to manipulate the image.

"This your craft?" He pointed to the screen.

"Yes," said the professor.

"It's dead," Dax said without looking up. "I will have to go fetch it with a recovery vehicle."

"It may be hot with static," Lara told him.

"They mostly are but we have a double insulated flyhov we call the 'Feldspar' because that's what it is made of mostly and a decontamination booth where they are grounded and made safe before we work on them."

"I would like to see that," Professor Mason said.

"Not a problem, you can come with me if you like," Dax replied.

"The accumulator will have to be discharged and the outcome calculated. That will take time, so can we meet up later to discuss the findings?" The professor stated.

"Of course," Nyla agreed. "We have to see Talan anyway."

"Say hello to Shi for me, will you?" Dax said.

Saying their goodbyes, Nyla and Lara headed toward the inner complex and elder council segments. A greeter met them as they got closer and guided them to Talan's bureaus and to a closed door.

"Elder Talan is expecting you."

Getting up from behind a desk, the silver-haired elder came around and shook Lara's hand before indicating for them to be seated.

"Lara, I have to say that I am impressed by the work you have done here. Nyla has kept me up to date on your discoveries and our scientists are eager to work on the results."

"Thank you, sir, but it's not completed yet. I think it may be possible to harvest some power back to the planet from the dark energy cloud. By depleting it of energy, moving it away would be easier." She looked between them. "I'm not sure what gain to loss ratio could be obtained but it has to be better than the loss that's happening now."

"I already noted that observation and that is what I want to get our scientists working on it right away. Getting heat back into the planet would go a long way to regaining magnetism through magma flow. You have made a great contribution and the elders would like to honour you."

"In what way?" Lara asked.

"If you would agree to it, we would like to do a scan of you and replicate you in the form of a humanoid for honour in an academy of science."

"I'm flattered." Lara felt like she was blushing. "But that's unnecessary."

"We would be pleased if you'd agree. We already have a scan of Stella but have not received permission yet to do the same for her."

"Let me think it over."

"Certainly. Now, I think you can do some shopping if you want. Anything you want is our pleasure to provide."

"Thank you, but there are a couple of things I want to ask. First, I have been asked to do a lecture in the geology department. Is that okay?"

"If you have time and want to do it, go ahead."

Lara hesitated for a moment. "I have been giving a lot of thought to the planet and I am sure that getting energy back into it would be great, but there is still an overriding concern."

Talan smiled but looked sad. "Water."

"Yes. There is H2O in rocks but I feel most of that has already gone so without it there can be no mother earth as it used to be. If a return to living on the outside is the primary goal, then water and atmosphere is paramount."

"It is what consumes our every thought and solutions are sought all the time. We know that and have been looking for a solution other than the cosmic event that has already been put forward. We want to give you an answer to take back with you when you return so meetings are taking place and I hope to talk to you before you leave."

Lara did not want to be scanned or have a duplicate of herself wandering around but gave in to Nyla's persuasion that she would never see it anyway. The mentor also arranged for her to give a lecture the next day with her help. Having settled all of that, they set off on a shopping therapy session.

***

The lecture auditorium was full to the brim when they got there. Seats stretched up way back and all she saw was a sea of faces. Lara felt like she was the entertainment in a gladiatorial arena. As they were getting ready, Shi approached.

"Lara, I completed the analysis of the samples we gathered and found exactly what you had surmised. They were bereft of any trace of medium or soil aggregate. Now the professor wants me to monitor the site. Is that correct?"

"It was, but things have changed. I want you to connect with Dax, the OCR technician. He has records and knows sites where electromagnetic activity is prevalent. I need you to monitor them and correlate findings with Professors Parris and Mason in electrical engineering."

Shi's eyes looked up in dismay. "Not that attendant?"

Lara smiled. "Look on the bright side: He is going to take you outside in the Feldspar. Working with two departments will boost your reputation."

Shi looked resigned and took a seat with the rest of the audience.

"Good day, everyone, my name Dr. Lara Holden and todays subject is Geoarchaeology and is a combined science using a multi-disciplinary approach. Using the latest techniques and subject matter of geography, geology and other Earth sciences to examine topics which progress archaeological knowledge and thought. The lecture is titled 'Getting Down and Dirty' and is lots of fun."

She nodded to Nyla and a huge screen behind them lit up, showing a couple of women mud wrestling. The audience burst out laughing and Lara felt better with the ice broken.

"Maybe not that much fun, but I hope you get something out of it. Let's begin."

CHAPTER FORTY-ONE

When Stella, Matt, and Cal got back, the team had made a good start to modifying the blimp. The rear section had been removed and part of the frame at the back. Frame parts lay on the floor marked with chalk to where they would have to be cut or have parts added and welded back to the new design.

Around four o'clock, Matt called a halt to have a team meeting, where everything was explained to those working on the craft. He asked them to think seriously about it overnight and have another meeting in the morning. Their absolute discretion and secrecy was required until it was all over. They could then go public about the mission.

At the end of the shift, Cal and Stella stayed behind to continue working overnight. When they were the only two left, they talked about the plan.

"If we go ahead with this venture, we will have to have a number of trips in the *Intrepid*, which means a list will have to be made," Cal said. "There's no way we can build engine replacements for the aircraft and no way we can make fusion explosives here. It would be too dangerous for one thing and too difficult to keep hidden. All the parts required will have to be shipped here, put straight into the craft, and kept out of sight." He paused. "Do you think this will work?"

"If it turns out to be the only option we have, then we may have to make it work," Stella answered. "I guess we better gather all the dimensions and make the final blueprints."

"At least we have the nights alone to work and to put a hologram together to send to Talan," Cal said.

"Do you think he will go through with it?

"I'm sure Talan and all the elders do not want to do it but I cannot see they have any choice. The point is that if the event does occur, then the planet will be uninhabitable for hundreds of years until the effects settle down. Then we have to start all over again, the environment will change, the land masses will probably move and it will be a completely changed world."

"I wonder why our government is so against helping you," Stella said.

"The military."

Together they continued working through the night and managed to get the framework finished and a hinged ramp installed at the back.

Around eight, the team rolled in one by one and got ready for work. Then Allen Cox turned up and went straight to Cal and Stella.

"I have been asked by the team and Matt to attend a meeting this morning and I think they want to have it without you two."

"Not a problem. We will carry on working," Cal said. Stella nodded.

The group went into Matt's office and closed the door.

"What do you think that's all about?" Cal asked.

"Not sure, but notice, I have been left out, looks like I am no longer part of the team." She considered this for a moment.

"Knowing Matt, he will not commit to any venture without the team agreeing to it. I cannot blame him. Why should he put his head in the noose for us? But if they do commit and we do have to make several trips with *Intrepid*, we should ask Talan if they could visit. I mean, anyone who wants to that is. Seeing the reality of the planet would go a long way to justifying their commitment."

Cal considered it for a moment. "I think Talan would agree but I'm not sure if spending a week away is totally necessary. If we could speed up the process and do a trip every two days, that might work."

"That would be a bit tight. It would mean extra work for the crew but it's possible."

They carried on working, measuring a platform to add inside as a holding base for cargo with brackets for tie downs. About an hour later, Matt opened the door and waved them in.

Inside, the team sat around a desk. Matt stood at one end as they stepped inside, no one looked happy.

"I said we would have a meeting this morning and I invited Allen because he also has a stake in this," Matt said. "The main concern is the legality of our situation. As you know, Cal has been classed as a fugitive and is being actively sought by police and military. To keep him here is a commitment that puts us all at risk. If he is found here, we will be branded as co-conspirators, which would jeopardize the mission. We talked it over and we all want to help without the possibility of going to jail. However, Allen has come up with a solution that may be viable and agreeable to all." He nodded to Allen to take over.

"Jack Branigan, as you know, is Director of Homeland Security for this area and has already committed help that would put his job in jeopardy. To avoid any more danger to him and to the team, I believe you, Cal, should leave here and work at the airport. Think about this for a moment."

Allen started speaking again. "Stella could stay here and oversee all the work on the *Intrepid*, while you could control the work on the airplane in the hanger. I can even get some of my own staff that I trust to help you. I have also reassured the team that Cox Industries' litigation team would help them if it came to that. What do you think?"

Cal looked into all their faces one by one.

"It may work. Can I think it over and discuss it with Stella? I'll make a decision later today."

Everyone nodded and with that they dispersed and got to work. Allen, Matt, Stella, and Cal stayed behind for a moment.

"I need to get some instructions from Talan," Cal said. "This could work but I need to stay here until the next *Intrepid* launch. When it comes back, we will know the elder council's decree."

"I think the team could live with that," Matt replied. "I will ask them individually throughout the day and we do need to get the blimp ready as the launch is only two days away."

After Matt, had left Cal turned to the other two. "Is this a Matt concern or are the team truly committed to the scheme."

"I think the team is fully committed." Allen replied. "But Matt is really worried about the project, he has already covered up a death that would scrap the deal and close the facility. So, he is walking a fine line through loyalty to Stella."

'We must help him as much as possible." She urged.
They all agreed.

CHAPTER FORTY-TWO

Work on the blimp progressed well. The frame, cargo hold, and outer cladding was finished on time. The launch was again set for 2:00a.m. and the team was sent home at noon to get some rest. They would return at 10:00p.m.

Stella and Cal went over the hologram, detailing dimensions and requirements for the aircraft. They examined the description of the fusion explosives to ensure they could be carried safely. The exponentially charged explosive material could not be armed until out of the planet's atmosphere so a trigger hook-up line was also needed. Finally, an appeal to shorten launch dates to either a two- or three-day span was requested. The holook was then left inside the *Intrepid* marked for the attention of Talan.

A buzz of anticipation prevailed as launch time approached. The team worked in unison to initiate a smooth send-off while Matt oversaw the whole procedure and Allen Cox looked on anxiously.

After the craft disappeared, the nervous anticipation dragged on for an hour before at last the air shimmered and the blimp appeared, became solid, and settled down. Shields were removed and safety checks and radiation readings measured before it was given the all clear. The hatch door opened.

Lara emerged dressed in a grey/green suit similar to the ones both hubrids wore. She carried what looked like a carpet bag made out of the same material. Stepping down, she smiled and waved to the group staring at her. Allen Cox rushed over.

"What have they done to you?" he exclaimed.

"Nothing, why?"

"You are wearing a suit like the others. Have they turned you into one of them?"

"No, don't be silly. They exchanged my spacesuit and oxygen case for a better design because they wanted it for a museum."

Gathering around she laid the bag on a desk and opened it, first giving a holook to Cal and then bringing out one of her own.

"I have lots to show you but first Talan said to tell you that after a huge elder council conference, they have agreed to the cosmic event. A flyhov 4 will be sent next time and a thorough check will have to be completed to ensure it is reliable for a trip to and from Saturn. So much went on that Nyla put together a hologram of the events. They even made a scan of me so that a replica humanoid could walk around a museum."

She looked at Stella.

"They have a scan of you and want your permission to do the same. I was hesitant at first, but Nyla assured me I would never see, it so I agreed."

"I have already seen my real self dead so a replica is not going to bother me, but I am still not happy. I will think about it," Stella said.

Lara laid down her holook and the hologram lit up. Everyone watched intently for about an hour.

"Are you sure about all this?" Stella asked. "That the energy from the planet is being drained through these swirling updrafts?"

"You saw for yourself what happened to the flyhov equipped to convert and store the electromagnetic energy. So yes, I am pretty sure that's what has nearly destroyed the earth," Lara replied. "There is so many dust storms and chaos in the weather that it may have been overlooked."

"It just seems so strange to me that all the scientists have not discovered it sooner or found a way to stop it."

"Maybe they have too much reliance on AI," Cal said.

"I think there is more to it than that."

Just then, Stella's cellphone rang. She looked at the caller ID, then answered.

"Yes Sharon." She listened intently. "Did you get the door repaired? Then let them in and tell them I will be there shortly. There had better not be a mess!" She hung up and turned to Cal.

"The military is at my apartment again. It seems they are determined to find you."

"Soldiers are also taking over the check-in gate and a full search is underway," Matt said.

"Time for me to get lost again," said Cal. "Allen, can you get that plane put in the hanger? I will hop the fence and find my way there. I have some money and credit card Irene gave me." He turned to Stella. "We will keep in touch, right? Go about your work as usual."

Allen and Stella agreed and Cal ran out the side door. Dawn was just breaking and a dim light gave some cover as he flitted from building to building getting nearer to the fence. Large army vehicles were driving up and down the roads, dropping off soldiers at junctions. He almost reached the fence when a couple of troopers turned a corner towards him and he barely got to a dark spot by a building.

His clothes got darker and his face blackened in the dim light. He pressed himself tight to the building as the footsteps got closer.

They were having a conversation. One turned towards Cal and looked straight at him, but they showed no sign of recognition and they walked straight by, barely two feet away.

Moving to the edge of the building, he glanced around it and noted the fence was still twenty feet away. He listened, looked all around, and then sprinted out and leapt over the fence in one bound.

"Hey you!" a voice called behind him.

Cal turned and pretended to be walking slowly along the road. The troopers came running up to the fence, calling him over.

"Hey you! Have you seen anyone on this side of the fence?"

Contorting his face, he tried to slur the words. "Oony yooou par of beuuuties." Falling to the ground, he tried to stagger up, holding on to the fence. "Goot anny change for a cofeeee."

"He's a waste of time. Been on the piss all night," said the soldier.

They turned away and Cal slowly staggered off until he was out of sight, then straightened up and sped up to a brisk walk. Little traffic was on the road and he made good progress without drawing attention. Soon he saw the shopping mall he had been to before. He was sure there was a bus depot there as well.

As he strode into the station, he spotted a Greyhound bus marked Phoenix on the front. He tried to get on but the driver stopped him.

"Ticket?"

"Can I pay here?" he asked.

"No, at the ticket office." He pointed. "And you better be quick. We leave at 5:30 sharp. You got three minutes."

At the desk, he found it cost over $300. He offered the credit card he had and hoped it would cover it. The desk clerk looked at him suspiciously as he swiped the card, then turned it over.

"You don't look like a Ms. Branigan to me."

"It's my sister. She is paying for me to visit Mum, who's ill. Please hurry or I'll miss the bus."

The desk clerk hesitated, then the printer spewed out the ticket. He handed both over to Cal, who sprinted over to jump on the bus.

"How long until Phoenix?" he asked.

"Six-thirty tomorrow night," the driver replied.

He found a seat near the back with no one around him, sat down, and went into sleep mode.

After two hours, the first rest break woke him up and he decided it was too long to pretend to be asleep. Descending the steps, he walked to a quiet spot and called Stella. "Can you talk?"

"Yes," she replied. "I am at my apartment and the military has left. Jack Branigan came around too and he asked me where you were. I told him you were out of the state but refused to tell him where. The less he knows, the better for him and his family, and probably for us too. Where are you?"

"On a bus to Phoenix. We are at the first rest stop. This is going to take forever."

"Best you stay low for a while, so don't fret about it, I looked at the hologram from Talan and everything is getting set up."

"Good. What are you going to do now?" Cal asked.

"Get set up for the next launch and see if we can do it every three days. I'm going to send Allen Cox back at the same time."

"Why?"

"He will need a suit and he is invaluable for the mission. If he sees how bad things really are, I'm sure he will be fully onboard, not that he isn't already but he needs to see for himself. Lara is totally in now as well."

"All right. I guess I will just enjoy the countryside. Keep in touch."

Back on the bus, he mulled things over. It was not going as planned but there was nothing he could do except, as Irene had said, go with the flow.

CHAPTER FORTY-THREE

Stepping down from the bus, he was glad the trip was over. He never wanted to do that again, even if it was expedient. He could go to the moon quicker.

At a local store, he found a map and memorized the route to the boneyard airfield. He would have to try to get a lift down the main highway.

About a mile away, he found an opportunity. A car was stranded at the side of the road and a woman was sitting on the sidewalk.

"Can I help, ma'am?" he asked.

The woman was middle aged, black, with wiry hair tied back. By the lines on her face, it was obvious she spent a lot of time outdoors.

"Not unless you're a weight lifter. I have a flat tire but no jack. Garage must have taken it out and forgot to put it back."

Cal checked around and found a log stump in one of the nearby desert gardens that were in front of every house.

The flat was at the left rear and he carried the stump over and set it by the car.

"If I lift it up, can you slide it under?"

She looked at him incredulously. "Are you serious?"

"Let's give it a try."

Turning his back to the vehicle, he slipped his hands under the wheel arch, bent his knees, and lifted until it was clear of the log. The woman stared at him for a moment before sliding the log under. He gently dropped the vehicle until it rested.

"How you do that?" the woman asked.

"It's just a trick I learned," he answered. He started to change the wheel, it was old technology but he soon worked it out, dropping the flat into the trunk then fitting the spare.

"You ready to pull it out?"

"Whenever you are," she replied.

Once again, he lifted the car but the woman struggled to get the log out. When she did, he dropped the car slowly onto the ground.

"You all right?" he asked. The woman was sitting on the log. She nodded but he could see otherwise. He held out his hands and she took them, thinking he was helping her stand. Instead, he held on.

"How long has the arthritis bothered you?"

She tried to shake him off but he held on.

"It's nothing."

"Sit down again and relax," Cal said. She did so and he kept hold of her for a while longer. A warmth spread throughout her before he let go.

"Better now?"

"Yes," she replied, thankful but confused.

"What can I do for you? I have no money."

"I don't want your money but I was hoping for a lift. Are you heading for Tucson?"

"Not quite that far but most of the way. It's the least I can do for you. What's your name?"

"Cal, what's yours?"

"Peggy," she replied. "Get in."

Cal replaced the log stump and got in the car. Peggy accelerated quickly and they started a conversation.

"What are you doing down this way? It's a long walk to Tucson."

"I'm a bit of an aircraft nut and was going to visit the boneyard close to Tucson, but I don't have a lot of money so was hoping to hitch a ride."

"I know where that is and it's not far from me. I'll drop you close by. I don't know what you did but I am feeling quite a lot better, are you a faith healer?" she asked.

"Something like that."

The gates were locked as he approached and warily he stared around, expecting to see cameras or guards covering the boneyard. Not taking any chances, he walked the perimeter, observing all the time. He still did not find any precautions in place.

It was early evening and not yet dusk, but it looked like everyone had gone home. Remembering the layout of the airfield as he got closer to the hanger, he became more cautious. The last thing he needed was to be caught entering without permission. He sniffed the air and listened, but did not detect humans or guard dogs. The fence was not as high as the one around the lab, and he easily jumped over it. He could see the hanger from the apex of the leap.

Crouching, he listened and sniffed again before creeping around to the building, searching for a side door. His hand gripped a door handle and he tripped the lock. He entered the darkened chamber silently.

His eyes instantly adjusted to the gloom and he noted the huge shape of the Tupolev standing in the middle of the hanger. He walked around it, examining the state of the plane. Some white tape was hanging down, a push/pull bar was attached at the front, and there were some scaffold ladders at the back and up to the entrance door.

He jumped up to the door and entered. Nothing had changed inside.

"Stella, can you hear me?" he asked into the intercommunications.

"Yes, where are you?"

"At the hanger in the boneyard. Have you spoke to Cox?"

"Talked to him today and nobody knew where you were, which is a good thing. What do you need?"

"I want to know the state of play and if I can work on the plane now that I'm here. Looks like some one has put scaffolding in place but that's as far as I've got."

"I'll call you back after I talk to him." Stella ended the internal call.

Cal walked down the scaffolding ladder to the floor and started taking inventory in the hanger. He found various jacks, lifting cranes, and hand tools around the sides. At the back, there were offices, washrooms, locker rooms, and two bunk rooms, one male and one female. Another side door at the rear revealed an entrance to the helipad, golf cart, and parking spaces for vehicles. He headed back inside, closing the door quietly. As he waited for Stella to call back, he strolled around, familiarising himself to every nook and cranny.

"Cal, you there?"

"Yes Stella, you okay?"

"Fine. I got hold of Allen Cox and he said he would fly up there tomorrow and bring Billy with him to help you. The rest of the team is staying here with me working on a schedule to turn around launch to three days or even two. Cox says you can work undisturbed there but to keep the noise to a minimum overnight. There are some working lights on mobile stands but keep the illumination down. I didn't tell him you could work in the dark."

"Good, thanks. I will start on the plane's hold, putting a drop down hatch at the rear. When the flyhov arrives, we need to hide it straight away. The best place is probably in the plane's hold."

"I agree. Did you have any problems getting there?"

"No, but I did have to use Irene's credit card. Can you tell her I owe her or could you pay her back?"

"Not a problem. Anything else?"

"Nothing. I'll get started working on the plane. Talk to you later."

He lifted the lid to the plane cargo bay, hopped in, and started measuring and marking to make a rear opening. He also noted he would have to make a hatch to the main cabin.

CHAPTER FORTY-FOUR

He heard whirling rotor blades long before the helicopter landed at the pad nearby. Shortly afterwards, the side door opened and Allen Cox and William Briggs entered, but he was surprised to find Stella with them. He greeted them with handshakes and a hug for Stella before guiding them to a desk littered with blueprints.

"I have made a list of parts and equipment required for this makeover. It's mostly steel, aluminum sheet metal, hinges, and various fasteners," Cal said.

"Give me the list," Allen said. "I will pass it on to Sierra, who will get it all under a Cox Industries purchase agreement and have it delivered here. If you need anything, just contact her."

Cal nodded and looked at Stella.

"I came along today to find out if you think we can complete this in a month," she said. "If you cannot, then we have to rethink our plans. I have spent some time doing calculations and checking astronomical data and if we are to succeed, we have to launch soon."

"How soon do you mean?" Billy asked.

"It will take 5.8 days to reach Enceladus at two astronomical units per day using the power of the fusion engines from the future, and that is cutting it close to when the satellite is at the farthest station of its orbit around Saturn. That's when we need to nudge it on a course for Earth. We need to leave here within a month."

Cal thought for a moment. "It can be done if we can get all we need in that time. Have you been able to get a turnaround timeline sorted with the *Intrepid*?"

"Yes," Billy said. "We can do it every two days, and if there is a problem it will go on the third day."

"Can you think of anything else you need?" Stella asked Cal.

"Last night I remembered there was a heat resistant paint or glue material that would save time rather than applying tiles. Do you know of it?"

Cal knew her AI was more extensive than his and he watched as she worked through her memory banks.

"Yes, it's applied to the starships, its heat and radiation resistant and is called heltherm. I'll ask Talan to send some. Anything else?"

"I'm not sure but I will call you if I think of anything."

"Right. Now, just to keep you up to date, Allen will be travelling out on the next launch and staying there for two days. He'll come back with the engines. Lara arranged it with Talan. She seems to have made quite an impression there.

We may send the rest of the team but we will take every precaution to keep the mission quiet, safe, and secure. If the flyhov is on the next return, I will personally bring it up here hidden in a truck or rental container. Whatever we can arrange."

Cal then showed Billy to some bunk quarters and living units, and they all surveyed the work load.

After an hour or so, Stella had made a couple of recommendations and they agreed that a hatch to the cargo hold from the cabin should be located at the rear where the galley used to be. Allen and Stella left shortly thereafter to prepare for the next *Intrepid* launch, and that left the men to get down to work.

The journey back was uneventful and Stella got back to the lab before the next launch.

Lara helped Allen to suit up for the trip, making sure all fasteners were sealed and air would not escape, then checked that the air supply case was working properly.

"You nervous about this?" she asked him.

"Nervous excitement," he replied. "Will I feel nauseated? I don't see any sick bags around."

"Don't worry, little boy, you'll be fine. Nothing to it, just relax. Okay?" She smiled.

"Say hello to Nyla for me, will you? She will probably meet you and show you around. Her job is mentoring new people, mostly hubrids."

He got up and lumbered over towards the ship. As he always did before flying, he walked around it, looking for any defects. When he reached the rear, he checked the rear loading hatch again. He had gone through the routine a few times to practice opening and closing it.

Before he entered the craft, Stella called out to him.

"Say hello to Nyla for me."

He nodded. Lara checked that he was securely strapped in, gave him a short kiss on the lips, and closed the lid to his helmet. In a few minutes, the *Intrepid* disappeared.

Sitting in a flyhov, Nyla waited for the swirling dust to settle around the craft before getting out to meet another ancestor. Approaching the craft, the side door opened and a figure appeared.

"Hi, I'm Allen Cox. Are you Nyla?"

"Yes," she replied. "How did you know?"

"Lara and Stella described you and said to say hello. They send you their regards."

"Thanks. I liked both of them a lot. Can you open the rear cargo hold? I need to load up this flyhov before we do anything else."

He did as he was asked and watched as the black woman got into the side door of a strange craft, painted yellow like a school bus without wheels. The front was rounded with a small window like a windscreen reaching from one side to the other. He watched her move to the front and sit down, then the vehicle lifted up and moved to the *Intrepid* where it reversed into the hold. She got out the side door and called to him.

"Do we need to secure it?" Nyla asked.

"I don't think so. It was a smooth ride here and nobody mentioned securing it," he replied.

The mentor looked around and found some straps, and then threw them over top of the craft and tied them off to some brackets.

"Best be safe. You were in an internal pod steadied by a gyroscope."

They walked towards another flyhov that had the glass front lifted up.

"Now I recognize that one," Allen said. "I have seen these on a hologram but not the one you just put into the blimp."

"No, that was specially built for interspace travel and has a more robust exterior to block stellar radiation and a different thruster for more speed, as well as air recyclers for humans." Nyla replied.

Sitting side by side in the front, Nyla closed the glass door and turned towards him.

"I left a holook in the *Intrepid* for Cal. Did you bring any information for us?"

"Yes, but it's inside my suit. Can we wait until I get out of it?"

"Of course, Now I want to make sure the craft leaves properly so we have to wait, but I will familiarize you with the flyhov."

She explained all the controls to Cox and they lifted off and drove around for a while as Allen got used to what the flyhov was capable off.

"Wow, it's really mobile and fast," he said, clearly excited.

They zoomed around faster and faster as he got more used to it, doing loops around the blimp but always keeping it in sight. Finally, the air simmered around its mass and it disappeared from sight.

"Head out that way. I'll show you the coastline before we go back."

CHAPTER FORTY-FIVE

Allen could make out a hexagonal concrete building in the distance. As they approached, Nyla pointed out an air-lock docking station. They eased in and the mentor guided him to a parking area, where they found an attendant waiting. The front of the flyhov slid upwards with a hiss and they alighted to a check-in desk.

"Dax, this is Allen Cox, a friend of Lara's," Nyla said. "He is to be scanned and fitted with a new space suit, as per the elders' instructions."

"I know," Dax replied. "Please follow me."

"Can you first give me the holook? I will pass it on to Talan, then come back for you," Nyla said.

He set down the air breather case and opened a pocket to extract the holook, then followed Dax to a locker room.

"You can take your suit off here and then we will take you next door for the scan."

"I will need to take that back with me, there may be others coming," Allen said as the handed over the suit.

"I know, Lara explained everything to me," Dax said.

"Is she really your sigi?"

"My what?" Allen said curiously.

"You know, sigi, what we call your significant other."

"Oh, yes. She is my girlfriend."

"You are so lucky. She is a hero here. People ask me about her because I met her. Ever since her lecture on geoarchaeology, which was broadcast worldwide, she has become a media phenome and people want updates on her work."

"Is, that, right?" Allen said, raising his eyebrows.

"I'll show you." Dax put his hand on a desk. A screen lit up and a news update came on showing Lara in a space suit pointing out MCV updraft scrolls.

"They are showing her lecture continuously at the Nucleus Central exhibition."

"Wow. I didn't know I was dating a celebrity," Allen said.

"Oh, yes. Let's get you scanned." Dax guided him next door to a machine that looked like a MRI.

Afterwards, Nyla met up with him. "Talan would like to meet you, if you would follow me."

Allen looked everywhere, scrutinizing every nook and turn, every open door, every room and office. At last they entered an inner sanctum and Talan rose to greet him.

"So, good to meet you." The silver haired Elder shook his hand and guided him to a chair.

"Nice to meet you too," Allen said. He noted the elder's hand was warm and slightly hard to the touch.

"I have studied the latest information from Stella and I want to thank you for your contribution to the mission. It was disappointing the government did not want to help, but as you have probably observed by now, the situation here is desperate. We have searched for solutions and if it were not for Stella and Lara, I know we would still be lost."

"I didn't know how bad it was until Nyla showed me around. I saw it on a hologram but could not take it in," Allen said.

"Your help is invaluable, and we want to familiarise you with the plan." Talan continued. "You are so fortunate to know Lara. She is a remarkable woman. Stella too, but Lara is gifted."

"How do you mean?" he asked.

"Stella is unique. She is endowed with AI way beyond anything we had before and is capable of great things now and in the future. But Lara, without any aids, has discovered how we were losing energy from the planet and set our scientists on finding a way to recoup some of it. That's no small feat in such a short time. We are incredibly indebted."

"I know she is an extremely strong willed woman who will not take no for an answer. Cal and I both tried to talk her out of coming here but she sensed an opportunity that was not to be missed. I'm glad she came now."

"So are we," Talan agreed. "Now, as we are using your equipment can we discuss the plan so far, how we are progressing and the next steps?"

They had a discussion for an hour before Talan drew it to a close and said.

"We planned to let you use the same apartment she was given. It's close to downtown, so feel free to wander where you want. Nyla will help you."

"Is it possible to visit a starship? I know you lost one, but is there another close by? I would be fascinated to see earth from above," Allen asked.

Talan looked at Nyla. "Does he have time?"

"Only if we fly direct to *New York One* and come straight back," she replied.

"Arrange it then, please." Talan shook Allen's hand again and they left.

"Your suit will not be ready yet so I will give you a quick trip downtown. There is someone I want you to meet," Nyla said as they walked back to the parkade.

"Let me know as soon as Mr. Cox's suit is ready, Dax. I am taking him down to Nucleus Central."

"Certainly. Say hi to Shi for me please."

"Dax, Dax, Dax. You certainly have the hots for her, don't you?"

"Hey, we are workmates now, so just say hi, okay?"

In the parkade, they jumped in the nearest flyhov and pulled into the city lane.

"Where to?" a voice asked.

Allen looked around.

"Nucleus Central," Nyla said before explaining the art of driving in the city.

He wished he had brought a camera but knew he could not take it all in. Allen had heard both Stella and Lara describe it but he was truly impressed by the underground city. Broad avenues lined with trees and a roof that looked like the blue sky above. Buildings and houses were designed to look different yet blend into a multi-coloured integral layout that was pleasing to the eye.

"Destination arrival, Nucleus Central."

Allen was overwhelmed by the brightness and benevolence the city surroundings exuded. A hiss as the door opened brought him back from his pleasant thoughts. They entered the auditorium and were greeted by a humanoid stepping into their path.

"Good day, hubrid Nyla and guest. Can I assist you?"

"Get me a pass for Allen Cox, a friend of Lara Holden."

"Right away. Shi would like to meet your guest. She will be here directly."

Nyla explained the different sections and the combinations of science departments and public uses. They were then approached by a young woman with a pleasant smile and shoulder length reddish hair.

"Allen, I am so pleased to meet you. Lara said you were coming and Dax called to say you were on your way. Welcome to our science centre. I would love to show you around but someone else wants to do it," Shi nodded to someone behind him.

He spun around and the shock nearly buckled his knees. His eyes widened in surprise and he was unable to speak until he grasped the situation.

"Lara, what are you doing here?"

"Nice to meet you, Mr. Cox. I hope you can help me gain knowledge of my originator, as my memory banks are bare of facts relating to her personality."

"I... I'm speechless," he stammered. "I can tell you what I know, if we have time."

"We are sorry to spring this on you," Nyla said. "But we wanted to surprise you. Humanoid Lara was just completed and we wanted your expert opinion on her. We have an assembly line of humanoids so could get her size straight away but her facial features took a little more time."

"She certainly fooled me." He examined Lara's face intently and walked around her, scrutinising up and down. "Perfect to the last detail, but I think I could tell the difference."

"How?"

He put his arms around her and kissed her.

"That's how," he said.

CHAPTER FORTY-SIX

The starship was a speck in the sky that gradually increased in size as they approached, but his gaze was torn between the ship and the planet. A brown haze covered the ground and flashes of an orange hue occasionally broke through. Notably, there was no blue, nor were there clouds floating above the planet in broken wisps.

He looked towards the poles and thought he saw white but it could be because he wanted to see ice caps. Nyla guided the flyhov towards an open air-lock and eased in before the gate behind them closed. They entered the ship through another airlock meant for humans. He pressed a button on his wrist and the see-through lid on his helmet flipped back. A humanoid dressed in a uniform of bright blue with red epaulets greeted them.

"Good day, hubrid Nyla and Allen Cox. You are expected. My name is Selah and I will be your guide today. I know you are on a tight schedule so I have been instructed to show you around before a short meeting with one of the ship's commanders. I normally give tours to humans who one day would be living here but I know you are more interested in the ship's operation. If you will follow me."

They followed Selah as she moved towards the centre of the ship, describing points of interest as they moved. Apartments, shopping centres, restaurants, medical facilities, and advice centres all lined the route to the central lift blocks. The guide pressed a button and they travelled upward quickly.

Allen was trying to process everything. Training done for Homeland Security helped as he visualised all he had seen so far. When the lift stopped, they exited to a command centre.

On one side was flight command and control, and on the other was ship maintenance, internal community, utilities, and where medical records were housed.

They were given a briefing on the different aspects and responsibilities of each department before being funneled through to the flight deck.

An officer, tall with blond hair and blue eyes, approached wearing a bright red uniform and multi-coloured ribbon adornments. He stretched out his hand in greeting.

"Hello, my name is Commander Mario Kier. Talan said to expect you, so I will give a quick tour and explanation of ship's flight control."

Allen stared around as he shook hands with the commander. A circle of computer desks surrounded an inner command centre with glass walls.

"Our starship is maneuverable in any direction because we have thruster engines situated all around the outside rim. Each engine is controlled by a flight officer at one of the thirty-six control desks and we can control direction depending on which engine or combination of thrusters we use. I believe you are an aviator, yes?"

"Yes," Allen conceded.

"But nothing like this."

"No."

"The combination of shape and engine placement make space travel easy, but although we can move up and down with thrusters on the top and bottom of the ship, we cannot land or take off. We use them to stabilize our orbital position. There's not enough power for a ship this size to escape earth's gravity from the ground, so we rely on shuttle flyhovs for travel to the planet. We also had to build the ships in space.

"Again, we had to use flyhovs, humanoids, and robots in the assembly, but as they did not require air, we could assemble a starship quite quickly. Each took about twenty years in total."

"Very impressive," Allen acknowledged. "How fast can you travel when fully loaded?"

Mario started walking them around the flight sections. "If we deploy one quarter of the engines, we can accelerate to ¾ light speed, but like any large vessel, it takes a long time to build up and an equally long time to slow down by applying thrusters on the opposite side of the ship."

Commander Kier took the time to explain the different aspects of the control and operation of the ship until they came around once again to the entrance, where Allen thanked him profusely and they left.

The timeline was tight so Cox asked they leave quickly as he wanted to view the city before returning.

Light was dim as they flew into what once was the great city of New York. Allen wanted to pilot the flyhov and Nyla relented.

"I used to fly into New York quite regularly," he said. "So, I know my way around."

He guided the craft along what used to be the Hudson River but was now just a dried-up riverbed, muddy brown in colour without any vegetation.

"Oh, my god," he whispered. "There is nothing here. No high rises, no central park, no Empire State... nothing to indicate a city was ever here. Only remnants of structures that have been dismantled."

Moving up the riverbed, he came across the plinth that once held a famous statue. He circled it as if looking for the famous icon.

"I loved this city. What happened?"

"It moved underground after the atmosphere became unbreathable," she said. "The population diminished to such an extent that at one time this place was almost deserted before they decided to start building alternative accommodation. The statue you can't find corroded away so a replica was built. It is the centre piece of the underground city."

"At least you tried to keep tradition alive."

"There are other institutions and traditional structures that have also been restored, including theaters off Broadway and Central Park," Nyla said.

Flying back over Manhattan, he noted the OCR teams dismantling and moving steel girders and pushing rubble aside. He cast his mind back to a trip around Las Vegas where he visited a mock New York hotel resort. He imagined the underground city would be like that; a poor imitation of the real thing.

"I guess we had better head back," he said dejectedly. "There's nothing more to see here."

Nyla took over the controls and turned south, Allen looked out the window in abject despair.

"You know." He started reminiscing. "I once saw this old movie where an astronaut crash landed on a planet and was enslaved. After a few adventures, he escaped and at the end of the film he was on a beach on a nice sunny day, his troubles were over and a woman had come into his life. Making a fresh start on a beautiful planet was all he could think about, any thoughts about getting home were gone.

As he turned the corner of a rocky promontory the beach in front of him had a huge hand sticking out of the sand and in this hand, was the torch of liberty. He fell to the ground sobbing with despair as he realised he was back on planet earth. That is exactly how I feel now." He said with moisture in his eyes.

CHAPTER FORTY-SEVEN

Stella and Lara anxiously waited for the *Intrepid* to be deemed safe to enter after it reappeared. Instead of going inside, they went to the rear and opened the hatch.

A gleaming yellow Flyhov 4 sat facing outwards. They jumped in and eased the craft into the spacious rear of the hanger. A crowd gathered to watch in awe as it maneuvered around, turning around and around, lifting up and down with no wheels and no steering.

After a couple of rotations, it stopped and Stella got out. She asked three others to get in and Lara explained the controls to them while taking turns around the hanger. Going inside the blimp, Stella retrieved a holook and slipped it inside her suit. When she came out, she went to find Sierra.

"Can you arrange a container to be dropped off here then picked up later when we have the flyhov loaded inside? Tell the company I will accompany the driver to its destination. Don't tell them where; just say it's in the Phoenix area."

"When do you want that to happen?" Sierra asked.

"They can drop the container here as soon as possible. I want to do most of the drive overnight. The drive is around twenty-six hours so if we leave early in the morning we can make it there early the next day."

"I'll see what I can do," Sierra said.

Stella watched the team try out the controls, then placed the flyhov back in the *Intrepid* and locked it up. Turning to Matt, she asked if he wanted to go on the next trip to the future.

"No," he replied. "I know it has been safely proven but I have family and if anything, went wrong… Ask Daniel instead."

He said yes eagerly so it was agreed and everyone went back to work preparing for the next launch. Stella went around and asked who else wanted to go. Carla and Katie said they would but suggested that Billy should be given a chance.

Retreating to an office, Stella opened the hologram and listened to Talan's message. Engines would come back with Allen Cox and the fusion explosives would need two trips, maybe three, along with trigger couplings, heltherm, and other accessories.

"Stella to Cal, are you there?"

"Yes Stella. Is everything alright?"

"The flyhov is here and I am arranging to bring it inside a trailer. I will let you know when."

"Good, that means we are good to go. I have the cargo hold hatch almost finished and it will be ready by the time you get here. What is coming next?"

"The three engine replacements should be next with Allen Cox returning in three days. After that it will be fusion blast armaments. There could be three more trips at two to three day intervals so it will be close."

"With Cox returning, we should be able to fly everything here and working non-stop, we can get it done. After we finish the hatch, we will start to remove the engines. Hopefully they will be a straight drop-in as they have in the blueprints."

"Okay, back to work. See you soon."

Later that day, a container was dropped off outside the lab but was out in the open so Stella stayed over and arranged for it to be picked up first light. Under cover of darkness, she unlocked the rear of the trailer, swung open the doors, and slipped the flyhov inside.

At six the next morning, a trailer tractor turned up and Stella left, accompanying the driver. At the main gate, she left a message for Matt that they had departed. The driver told her that due to driver fatigue restrictions, he could only drive for a certain time, but driver changes had been arranged through the route.

It was a long boring drive with just a few snatches of meaningless conversation to break up the monotony. The third driver was to meet them in

Arizona to finish the drive. In the middle of the night, they pulled into a rest stop. There was no café, only toilets and a large lot for trucks.

The lot was empty except for a car and as they pulled up, the car door opened and a large man got out and approached them. The first driver got out the truck and went around to meet him. They chatted for a moment, then came to the passenger's door and opened it.

"Okay lady, get out. FBI, we want to examine your load."

Stella jumped down.

"ID please," she said.

"Just open the back," the new driver retorted.

"Not without ID. If you are who you say you are, then there should be no problem showing me your ID."

The large guy put his hand inside his jacket but instead of ID, he pulled out a gun.

"Open the back, lady. We want to know what is so important that you have to accompany this container." He snarled.

"Okay, okay," she said submissively. "No need to threaten me."

The two turned to each other, smiling as if it were too easy, but as soon as they had turned away, the gun was in Stella's hand. Spinning around and under one, she had grabbed the gun from the other, and yanked it away.

"How did you do that?" the big guy said.

"If you guys are FBI, you need to go back into training. You're incompetent. Now show me your ID and you can have the gun back."

As they pulled out their hands, the original driver yanked out another gun. Stella twirled behind the big guy, put the gun to his neck, and grabbed the gun away from the driver. They were both astounded and speechless at her speed.

"Right, over to the car, both of you." Stella motioned with a gun.

Walking over to the car, she ejected the cartridges from the guns and tossed them into the desert.

"Hands on the roof, boys."

They complied and she patted them down.

"If you guys are FBI, then where are your handcuffs?"

"Inside the car," one said.

"Okay, get in and show me."

The big guy opened the driver's door and went to stretch in, but swung his arm around, trying to knock Stella. She had already ducked.

"Get in the car, dummy," she ordered.

He bent down and squeezed his big frame into the seat, then looked up at her with a look of fury.

"This your gun?" She held it up.

He nodded then watched as she hurled it off into the darkness.

"You look tired. You could do with a nice nap. You will awaken refreshed but forgetful." Stella grabbed his arm and he slumped over.

"Now, you want to tell me who is behind this robbery?" She smiled at the original driver.

"It's a group of us drivers who highjack trucks with valuable loads. We empty the containers and pretend we have been hijacked. The insurance pays and nobody gets hurt."

"Get in the other side." He obliged, hands in the air until he sat. Holding the door open, she looked into his eyes.

"When you wake up, the truck will be here and if you say anything at all to anybody, I will come looking for you. Understand?"

"Lady, who are you?"

"Your worst nightmare if you speak about this evening."

Stretching in, she took his wrist and he slumped down in a cataleptic state. She closed the door then, after looking around in the darkness, threw the gun away then started singing to herself.

"On a dark desert highway."

She started waking back to the truck, for the first time she felt good about her abilities. *"That you singing Stella."* Cal asked.

'E mm, yes, I was about to call you, must have switched on by accident. Got a little trouble here.' She replied.

"What's happened?"

"Oh, a couple of guys tried to highjack the truck but that's not the problem. Fact is I am going to have to fly the flyhov the rest of the way."

"How far away are you? Can you not just drive the rig the rest of the way?"

"I think I am about an hour or more away but in the flyhov only a few minutes. Its pretty dark so if you open the hanger door I will pilot it straight in."

"*If you are sure.*"
"Yes, get ready, I'll be with you shortly."

CHAPTER FORTY-EIGHT

Cal stared into the night sky, searching for the flyhov and listening intently. After a few minutes, he spotted her. It was almost invisible in the night sky but with his vision and hearing abilities, he was able to make it out clearly.

"Stella, I can see you and you need to bear a little to the right. The hanger door is open but the lights are off."

"I think I see it but switch the lights on for a second so I can zoom in on you."

The light came on, illuminating the open hanger door.

"Got you, turn them off again."

Even in the darkness, Stella had no problem guiding the craft through the door and around to the back of the hanger, landing gently behind the Tupolev. The hanger door closed and Cal came to the back as she was getting out.

"Had a bit of trouble then?" he asked.

"Yes, but nothing I couldn't handle. Found out the drivers have a hijacking ring going. They empty containers and pretend they've been robbed and the company claims the loss from the insurance company." She moved towards the aircraft.

"Nothing I could do, I mean, I couldn't turn them in, could I? Probably works out for the best for us. Now nobody knows our location. The insurance company will twig on to them sooner or later."

"Do you think you were seen on the way here?" Cal asked.

"I don't think so. I didn't follow the roads."

"If someone did see you, it will be passed off as a shooting star or a UFO. No one will believe a yellow school bus flew over them."

"True. Is Billy around?" she asked.

"He's asleep in the back. Poor guy has been going non-stop and couldn't keep his eyes open last night, so let him sleep a little longer," Cal said.

"Okay, let's see how you're doing."

"The cargo hatch is done. I think we should keep the flyhov out of sight, don't you?"

"I guess so. I just wanted to show Billy, but he can have a look later."

Cal dropped the side door to the cargo hold and they hopped in. He showed her the trap door into the main cabin and the switch to drop the rear hatch.

"We cannot go outside to make the transition to the flyhov so I made it so that when we drop down from the main cabin, the switch is right there. It can be worked electrically or mechanically," Cal said, demonstrating.

With the rear-hatch open, Cal jumped down, got in the flyhov, and gently eased the craft in backwards. They walked around, judging how much room they had.

"Let's give it a trial run," Stella said. "I will get in the main cabin and try the escape. Close the side door behind me."

Hopping out, she climbed the scaffolding into the main cabin, walked along the centre to the rear trapdoor, and lifted it until it rested against the rear wall. Looking down, she saw Cal standing close by.

"How are we supposed to get down there?"

"You'll be weightless. You'll have to push or pull yourself down," Cal said.

Pretending to be weightless, she dropped down and was close to the craft. Turning to her right, she pressed the release for the hatch and it dropped down. The door into the flyhov was on the other side so she squeezed around the craft, opened the door, and got in.

"It's a bit tight. Think we should come in forwards to give access for the flyhov door?"

He thought for a moment. "Let's try it when Billy is up and we can work out the best way. Meanwhile, let me show you the rest of our work."

"The engine covers are loose and just need to be lifted off. Most of the reflective tape is off with just a little left on the top, if you want to help."

With no one around, they jumped on to the top of the airplane and quickly pulled the rest of the tape off, dropping it to the ground.

"I will apply the heltherm last because the fumes are an irritant to humans."

They walked across the top to the rear engines and Stella lifted one end of a cover. Normally a crane would be used the remove them.

"It does not feel that heavy," she said. "Lift the other end."

Cal eased it up and together they had it free.

"Think we can jump down with it or shall we use the crane?" Stella asked.

"I don't have time to repair it if we damage it, so let's just do it the old-fashioned way."

The crane was easy to maneuver for them, so they soon had the engine covers on the ground and placed to one side. Just as they had done that, Billy appeared, a little bleary eyed and dishevelled.

"Morning." He yawned. "You guys have been busy."

"Sure have, sleepy head," Stella said. "Glad you're up; I have something to show you."

She opened the cargo hatch side door, revealing the yellow flyhov.

"Is that the larger version of the flyhov?" he asked.

"It's what they call a transport flyhov and is an interstellar version."

Cal hopped in, dropping the rear hatch, and piloting it out while Stella and Billy watched on.

"Looks awesome," Billy said.

"Come on, I'll give you a demo," said Stella.

They spent the next half hour flying around the hanger until Billy got used to it, to a point where he did not want to stop. Eventually they got him to park it forwards in the cargo hold and Stella once again tried the escape route. It seemed more convenient this way.

"What's next?" Billy asked.

"We can remove the engines to be ready for the replacements," Cal replied. "But Stella, should you not be getting back?"

"It might be difficult. I was considering waiting until Allen Cox gets here."

"Let me check for flight availability on the internet," Billy suggested.

He walked away to the office and Cal turned to Stella.

"It would be better if you were at the lab to oversee shipments. I cannot go and Billy and I are working well."

"Let's see if there are any flights."

Billy came back smiling. "Talked to Sierra. She is a genius at getting things done. She has booked you on a flight at 11:20 a.m. that will arrive at 4:00p.m. A taxi will pick you up from the main gate in half an hour."

"Looks like that's settled. I will get on my way and talk to you later." Stella said her goodbyes and left.

CHAPTER FORTY-NINE

Calling in at her apartment after the flight, Stella felt she had to freshen up, wash, change clothes, and apply some make-up. It was a routine she did every day. She might not have to do it anymore, but it still felt right. Even brushing her teeth was refreshing, although no food had passed her lips. Brushing her hair, she wondered if it grew anymore. She would have to ask Cal. Would she ever get used to this lifestyle? Was there any alternative? How long until this routine would become normal?

Arriving at the lab, everyone was already there getting ready for the next launch. It was like a well-oiled machine, and everyone knew their scheduled tasks. Even if they had to cover for someone else, it did not delay or compromise the procedure.

Lara was there already and was helping Daniel suit up, just as she had helped Allen before. Each closure seam was checked for leaks, each function of communication checked for performance.

"When you get there, you may have to help Allen load the *Intrepid*. That is the first priority in case there are any problems. Time is tight and when it leaves is not under anybody's control," Lara said.

"I understand," Dan replied.

"There will be distractions. Everything is strange and pulls your focus away from the task at hand. Nyla will be there to help and guide you. She is extremely well informed and acts as a mentor to us, but she is also reporting back to Talan and the elders at the same time."

"Got it."

"Nyla will not have a helmet on like you and Allen, so don't get fooled into a false sense of security. Don't open your helmet. She will tell you when it is safe to do so."

"Any more instructions, Mother?" he said, smiling.

She slapped the top of his helmet. "That's enough, mister. Just be careful and take it all in. It will only happen once in your lifetime."

"Is everything okay?" Stella approached them and pulled out a holook.

"Yes, it's fine," Dan replied.

"I have a message for Talan from Cal." She handed it over and he put it inside his suit.

"How is it going up there?" Lara asked.

"I think it's going fine. Billy is really helping and they just need the supplies. The flyhov fits in the hold. It's tight, but it fits all right. We tested the hatch and access to the main cabin, and that works. The engines were being removed today and hopefully Allen can supply the new ones and get them up there as soon as possible."

"Air freight is Allen's main business so I am sure it will. Did you have any trouble getting there?"

"You could say that." Stella relayed the story about her hijacking, and they were amused.

"After that, I think Allen needs to deliver all the supplies personally," Lara said.

The launch went as planned and as soon as the craft disappeared, they got ready for its return. Lara was nervous, she knew there was no reason for it, but she was anxious to see Allen again. The hour sped by and soon enough, the air shimmered and the *Intrepid* appeared. As usual, all the safety checks were completed and Allen Cox appeared, clad in a new gray-green suit.

"Hi everyone." He waved from the doorway and Lara sighed with relief.

Walking down the steps, he went straight to the back and opened the hatch. Stella, Lara, and the rest of the lab team were at his back.

"We could only get two engines in but they stuffed some heltherm around them." He turned to Stella. "We should still be on track but we may need to move the itinerary around." He gave Lara a hug.

"Are you going to be able to ship it up to the boneyard?" Stella asked.

"Of course," He stopped for a moment. "Either you accompany the stuff if I send a truck to fetch it or you can wait until I get changed and I will come for it."

"I would rather you did it personally," she replied. "I had a little trouble getting the flyhov up there."

"I will tell you on the way," Lara said. "You look tired."

"I am. Stella, give me some time to go home get a shower and rest, then I will be back. Is that okay?"

"Yes, you get some rest. I will carry on here and see you later."

"Here is another message from Talan." Allen replied and handed over a holook.

Allen went to the locker room and removed the suit he had been given, then he and Lara left together.

At their apartment, he started removing his clothes as soon as they had walked through the door, flipping his shoes off and walking towards the bathroom.

"I want a shower first," Lara said. "I've been up all night too."

"You want a shower for two?" he asked. "No, forget that. I know you like your modesty. You go first."

Wandering into the kitchen, he started coffee and checked the fridge for food until he heard the shower running.

"Give me a shout when you're finished," he called.

The bread seemed okay so he put it in the toaster, pulled out some eggs and a microwave bowl, and started on scrambled eggs. They were ready when Lara stuck her head around the corner.

"Bathroom's free."

"Come have some breakfast first," he said.

In a white dressing gown and a towel around her head, they sat down at the breakfast bar and ate together. Quiet filled the room as they stared at each other across the table.

"I have something to show you after," Lara said.

"Oh yes, I can't wait." He smiled.

"After your shower."

"Sure." He got up and trotted off to the bathroom while she put the dishes away.

When he was finished, he entered the bedroom with a towel around his waist, but Lara was not there.

"Lara, where are you?"

"Close your eyes," said a voice from the walk-in closet.

"They're closed."

She entered the room and stood in front of him.

"Okay, you can open them now."

His eyes opened, then opened wider.

Wearing a gown that would grace any red carpet, she shimmered in multi-coloured waves of low-light sparkling gems. The dress was full length with a high neck. Short sleeves dropped down to her biceps, revealing slender arms.

"Where did you get that?" he stammered.

"You know I like to go shopping everywhere I go," she said playfully.

The dress changed colour to reveal different aspects of her body, going lighter at the waist to make it seem smaller, differing shades under her chest to appear fuller in the bosom.

"I can change the colours to suit my mood or shape the contours just by thought."

"Wow, I have never seen anything like it. It's stunning and makes you look more gorgeous than ever. How did you manage to buy it?"

"It cost a lot of credits, according to Nyla but I got it free for services rendered."

"Take it off," he said sitting on the bed. "You're turning me on."

She smiled alluringly. "Doesn't take much, does it?"

Stretching out his arms, he tried to pull her over but she backed up.

"Don't mess with the dress." She smiled.

"Just take it off," he insisted. "Don't want to get it dirty, now do we? You know, when we start."

"Start what?"

"Let's just say I discovered your fetish," he said coyly.

"And what is that?"

"Mud wrestling."

She laughed. "Who told you that?"

"Nobody. It was all over the auditorium lecture. You should have told me; I could have hauled a load in."

"I'm not into mud, that was only to warm up the audience."

"How about some wrestling anyway?" He patted the bed to suggest she sit beside him.

With a demure smile, she sat and leaned over to kiss him.

"Don't touch the dress. I will kill you if it get's damaged." Gently, she eased it up over her head and laid it down carefully.

Lying down, they kissed gently and put their arms around each other. He kissed her neck and shoulders.

When they got back together after being apart for work, it was like a first time all over again. This time it was different. The future had a shadow cast over it. Life seemed short and without answers, only they mattered in this moment. They both felt altered by events that had reshaped their lives beyond recognition and this was their first time alone to express that.

They kissed gently then passionately, until breathless, they broke apart and kissed gently again. He eased over her, careful not to put his full weight on her.

"I love you," he whispered in her ear.

"You never say that," she said. "Why is that?"

"You know I love you. Do you really want me to keep repeating it like a love-sick teenager? I would give you anything, you know that."

"Anything?"

"Yes, but what I really want is to make you happy."

"Then make me happy." She eased her hand down between them and gently guided him in.

He always took his time at this stage, not wanting to hurt her or cause pain, but she pulled him on to her. Both knew this time was special and more meaningful than ever before, and each tried to please the other, kissing became short and interspersed with bouts of frenzied movement.

She thought if ever there was a time to conceive, this was it, and she clung to him like a vise. He responded by becoming more and more urgent until they both burst into a climax that they had never experienced before.

Collapsing back on the bed, they kissed and said they loved each other. He put his arms up and she nestled in his shoulder. Soon his chest was heaving with a regular beat of sleep. She smiled to herself.

"Typical man, never waits to find out if the woman is finished." She whispered closing her eyes.

CHAPTER FIFTY

Cox industries had a small fleet of cargo planes used to ship freight all over the country. They were sometimes hired out to shipping companies whose own fleet may be out of commission for maintenance or repair.

The collection was mostly Boeing newer models but a few older types, and he had a Lockheed L-188 Electra on loan from a friendly rival and he commandeered this for a month to fly the cargo up to the boneyard. For personal reasons, he also took leave for a month, saying he was working on his own project, which all of his staff knew about.

The Electra was a turboprop plane with good cargo hold dimensions but was an older model and only a few were still working, so he felt comfortable taking it out of the fleet.

With the fusion engines on board and Stella for company, he landed in the boneyard and taxied up to the Cox hanger.

He used the journey to get Stella acquainted on co-pilot duties. She had the knowledge within her but not the experience, and eventually she even piloted the plane for a short time.

Darkness was descending as they used a forklift to move the engines to the back of the hanger, placing them close to the old engines. After setting all the freight in place, Billy and Cal started removing the packing.

"I cannot fly back tonight," Allen said to the group. "There are restrictions on some night flying. I could make excuses but that would draw attention to us. I'll submit a flight plan for first thing in the morning."

"There won't be any more supplies for another two days anyway, so it makes no difference," Stella said. "I can help Cal tonight while you take it easy. Why don't you and Billy go out for supper while we work here?"

Billy smiled at Allen. He did not need much of an excuse to get a break. They could tell by the grime and weariness on his face he needed a break.

"Sure, not a problem. I know a nice place just outside the gate," Allen said. "Let's go." He hustled Billy onto the golf cart and drove out to the gate.

Alone, Stella and Cal continued unpacking the engines.

"Allen is fully on board for this mission. I think Lara was more interested than him when she saw the hologram video.

But now he has seen for himself the devastation of the planet, he was full of it on the way here, telling me he had been to New York and there was nothing left of it. I know he is after some technical info to put into his own business but he would do it now out of loyalty to planet earth," Stella said.

After a few moments of reflection Cal replied. "He has fully funded this endeavour with not only this plane, but with money and time. He deserves to get something out of it, but what, I'm not sure. We can ask Talan."

He turned back to his work. "If we can attach the crane to one of these engines," he swung the hooks and lifted brackets over the top, "we can see if they will fit."

They hoisted it up and dropped it into place, bolting it straight in exactly how the old one was mounted. He finished just as Allen and Billy returned.

"You guys don't hang around, do you?" Billy said.

They gathered in a group beside the engines.

"We don't have time to hang around, Billy, but we are making good progress. Stella and I are going to carry on through the night, if you pair want to bunk down in the back."

"I could carry on," Billy replied.

"No, I need you fresh in the morning," Cal said. He turned to Allen. "There isn't enough time to do anything with the wings. We are just going to coat them with the heltherm and pray they don't fall off."

"What's the chance of a test flight?" Cox asked.

"Good question." Cal looked to Stella.

"It would be prudent," she said. "But it will have to happen before we start loading the consignment."

"Let's get the engines in and see what time we have. We certainly don't want anything going wrong when the mission begins," Cal said.

A new sense of urgency came over them, but they tried not to rush because mistakes would ruin everything. With a deadline set and supplies to be coordinated, everyone buckled down to get the job done.

The next day, Stella and Allen few back to Orlando while Cal and Billy continued fitting the engine and preparing the body to apply the heltherm. Billy would help fit the mechanicals, then fly back to the lab after the third engine was in place. Stella would stay behind to apply the coating to the body, since the active ingredients were toxic to humans.

With two of the engines in place, Cal started hooking up the controls while Billy finished the body preparations.

The lab was in full swing for the next voyage. Sierra would go first and stay while Dan came back with the third engine and the last of the heltherm.

Carla would then go while Lara looked after her duties, so the pair had long discussions on flight control, which was Carla's duty, then with Stella on flight navigation to Enceladus.

Lara had helped with navigation on Allen's journeys but never anything as complicated as interstellar travel. She would also be helped by Stella as the calculations required demanded complete accuracy.

Intrepid came back in a routine now familiar to the whole crew. Daniel arrived with the last engine and more supplies but he was a changed man. Even in greeting everyone on arrival, he was different. He didn't seem depressed, but was certainly unhappy.

He sat down with the group to discuss his trip.

"It is unbelievable," he said. "I cannot describe the desolation of the planet. Nothing has any resemblance to today. A brown desert covers the whole world and has dried up rivers, seas, and oceans. There are no living plants, no animals or birds, or lizards or insects. You have seen it, haven't you?" He looked at Stella and Lara.

"Yes," they agreed.

"Surely, we can learn from this and put measures in place to avoid this from happening."

"With Lara's help, I fully intend to put the facts on record and place them in care before we take off for Enceladus, just in case something happens to us," Stella said. "Then we'll make this public and inform the scientific community. The world must come together and put solutions in place for the future. We will explain what we have discovered about dark matter and dark energy which causes the desolation."

"I didn't quite get all that," Daniel said, confused. "But I get the gist of it and hopefully we can find solutions."

"Good, then let's get this done."

CHAPTER FIFTY-ONE

Lara and Allen removed the third engine, loaded all the supplies in a truck, and took off to fly them up to the boneyard. After going through the procedure to prepare *Intrepid* for the next trip, the crew went home for a rest.

Stella went to a local computer store and bought the latest model laptop with the most up to date firewall installed, plus a secondary firewall package as protection from intrusion. Adding a maths keyboard software and detached hard drive, she paid for the purchase and went to her apartment. Sharon assured her that no one had returned and the apartment was the most secure in the building due to the extra locks.

Stella unpacked her purchases, plugged in the laptop, and waited for some battery power to be charged before she began. Her intention was to put all she knew on file and produce a theorem to explain the effects of dark energy, dark matter, and the theory behind the effects that caused the devastation.

She added the maths keyboard software, then switched off Wi-Fi and made sure she was not connected to the internet. Her intention was to write the complete theorem down, transfer it to a separate hard drive, and keep the computer switched off at all times when not in use.

She began with an explanation of everything she had witnessed in the future, how it occurred, and what could be done to retard the process. It could not be underscored enough that the human race was in danger of extinction due to the moribund state caused by the dangerous phenomenon. Then she started to write the mathematics to prove the proposition, the endless equations she extolled were so complicated she realised that at intervals explanations had to be inserted for even the best mathematicians to follow.

Even then, the software did not allow for some of the equations and she resolved to write it down and scan it.

It was a frustrating and longwinded process that took more time, and before she knew it, morning light began filtering in through the window. She realised it was time to go back to work and downloaded her work and closed down the laptop.

At the lab, preparations for the next trip were progressing well. Lara and Allen had delivered the supplies to the boneyard and were now at home resting. Whenever she had a break, Stella pulled out her theorem and continued writing, hoping to complete it before going home.

Carla was next to go and she seemed nervous. At lunch break, Stella reassured her there was nothing to worry about. It also meant that only Billy was left and she would have to travel up to help Cal finish the preparations.

She finished her tasks early and told Matt she had work to do at home and left, borrowing a scanner to finish her download.

At home, the equations were scanned into the laptop to merge with the rest. With the complete program finished, she downloaded it twice to the external hard drive and memory sticks. There was only one other scientist in the world she trusted her work to, so she inserted the sticks and paperwork into a bubble envelope and addressed it.

Taking a break, she walked to the local post office and sent it via secure mail, registered and delivery guaranteed. On the way home, she resolved to put some information down regarding fusion power that would help Cox Industries. She wasn't sure if she would give it to Allen or not, but at least it would be available if the decision was favorable.

The whole night was spent writing the fusion part of the composition, detailing each stage of manufacture of amalgams and combinations thereof to produce the two parts of fusion compounds. Each stage she knew had to be correct in every detail, as any deviation would have catastrophic results.

Then the fusion power procedure had to be explained. For robotic application's it had to be used in very small minute, Nano units, and for industrial use it had to be in microgram units. Then for more powerful use, such as spacecraft power, it was to be in macroscopic units.

For explosive use, a separate trigger device had to be used that would blow up and instantly merge the fusion mixtures into an uncontrolled detonation of force dependant on the quantity and volume of available compounds.

Having completed the tasks, it became clear that she was tired, not physically but mentally, and that startled her. It was the first time any fatigue had surfaced. Then she remembered that different modes were available to her, so she lay down and switched to sleep mode for two hours.

When she woke up it was to a feeling of relief more than being refreshed. She had felt troubled that the information inside was solely her responsibility. The changes in her life had happened to her so quickly, the lifestyle, the knowledge, brain capacity and now the accountability. The responsibilities now lay a burden on her, from leaving the team to become a leader, to liaison with a future era, becoming somehow answerable for the future of mankind was all too much that she had to share it.

This way the information would be in a third party's hand, filed away on memory sticks and computer drives, which she would place in another's keeping. If the mission failed or something happened to her, there was back up for someone else to take up the mantle and protect the planet.

Returning to the lab, she found preparations for the next trip almost complete. They would finish, then leave for a rest before coming back in the evening. She approached the team leader.

"Matt, I will go up to the boneyard with this cargo and help Cal finish the plane. Billy will come back and go on the next *Intrepid* voyage. There will be one more or even two after that if you would like to go."

"No, it's fine," he replied. "My family means everything to me so there is no way I would jeopardize that, also as team leader I do not want to be some other persons worry and I would rather be in control of things here, but thanks for thinking about me."

The *Intrepid* left and returned without incident. Sierra returned with it and explained her travels to the group. She confirmed what the others said but also said how impressed she was with the underground city, even to the point that she could live there. Stella opened the rear hatch and found it full of rectangular containers, each with a separate trigger explosive taped on top. She decided not to call Lara and Allen straight away, as they were probably asleep. Instead, she went into an office and tried to contact Cal.

"Cal, you there?"

"Yes, what's up?"

"The *Intrepid* cargo hold is full of fusion explosives. How are you progressing?"

"We have the third engine fitted and I am connecting up the controls now. When Billy gets up, we will install the engine covers and then it is virtually ready to fly."

"I would like to do a test flight before we start to load any fusion material."

"I agree. If you give me another couple of hours, it should be ready for Allen to take it out."

"That's what I was hoping for. I will come up with the supplies and Lara so we can all test the craft together. Then Billy can return with them and I will stay behind to help."

"Sounds good. I will see you later then."

CHAPTER FIFTY-TWO

Allen parked the Electra L-188 alongside the Cox Industries hanger and they all disembarked and entered the building. Billy and Cal were waiting for them at the back beside some desks. The old engines were stacked in the far corner.

The Tupolev looked immaculate with all the tape removed, engine covers installed, and original markings still prominent. They took a stroll around it, taking note of the condition of the plane. The rear exit hatch looked seamless, as if it were a natural part of the structure.

Climbing a ladder for access, they entered the main cabin and walked the length to the rear to inspect the escape hatch.

"Everything is in order for a test flight, Allen," Cal said. "But there is one other supply we need."

"What's that?"

"We need tie down straps for all the fusion cylinders. They will be stacked from the floor to the ceiling along both sides where the seats were. We cannot have them floating around in zero gravity."

"There are some straps in a back stockroom that will fit to the seat anchors in the floor. There may not be enough but I will bring some more from headquarters on my next trip."

"Good. Do you want to try her out?" Cal asked.

"Yes," Allen said, excited. "I will have to submit a flight plan to the aviation authorities first, so I will go do that while you unload the fusion cylinders from the Electra and stack them at the rear of the hanger, out of sight."

Stella and Cal worked inside the Electra, guiding Billy to move the forklift under the pallets and secure the cylinders while Lara showed him where to drop them. It did not take long and the two men draped the load with a tarpaulin to hide them from view.

Allen returned in the golf cart.

"We have a window in an hour and a half so we have to go through the pre-flight checks now. Cal, are you familiar with the controls?"

"Yes, I tried them when I connected the engine controls."

Allen handed them two-way radios. "If you all take up positions in the cockpit, I will check the operation from outside."

Allen was so used to pre-flight checks that it did not take long. Entering the cockpit, they discussed their roles.

"I will pilot us out, since they know me at the control tower. Cal, you can co-pilot. Stella, will you help Lara with navigation and take over as pilot later to get familiar with the controls? Billy, are you okay just going along for the ride?"

They all nodded.

Settling into their positions, the engines fired and slowly Allen eased the Tupolev out of the hanger.

"Are you sure we should leave the hanger open like that?" Stella asked. "Anybody could wander in."

"I will go back and guard everything," Billy said.

"You sure?" Allen asked.

"Yeah, we cannot afford any prying eyes now. I'll drop into the cargo hold and get out through the rear hatch if someone will make sure it's closed after me."

"I'll go." Stella got up and followed him down the cabin, returning shortly afterwards.

They taxied out to the runway to await their turn and receive instructions to leave.

"Flight TU154, you are cleared for take-off. Have a safe flight."

Everyone heard the instructions over their headphones.

"This is TU154. Thank you, Wally," Allen replied.

The fusion engine noise was barely audible even when Allen pulled back on the throttle and they were pushed back in their seats as speed increased.

"V1," Cal called. "We are airborne."

Allen dropped the throttles down a notch.

"What are you doing?" Cal asked.

"We are going too fast." He operated the landing gear. "It could rip off the landing gear if we are not careful."

"TU154, this the tower. Allen, you took off in a third of the runway. How did you do that?"

"Upgraded the engines, Wally. Surprised even me. Got everything under control."

"Okay, have a good flight."

Turning west, they headed towards the ocean, increasing speed and altitude as they went. As soon as they reached the shoreline, Allen eased the throttles back and they were pulled back in their seats.

"Wow!" Allen said. "This thing really has power. We are approaching its previous max of 975kph and we are at 40,000 ft."

"It will do a lot more than this," Cal said.

Just then, the plane started to vibrate, getting worse with speed until their vision started to blur. Allen leaned over to throttle back but Cal put his hand over.

"Its harmonic vibration," Cal said. "Engine to frame oscillations are at the same frequency at this speed. Go faster and we will pass through it."

Allen looked at him skeptically but did not say anything. He pulled the throttle further back. The vibrations got worse, then suddenly smoothed out to a normal flight pattern.

"We are already past max speed for the aircraft and height. Any faster or higher and we will be spotted and assumed to be a fighter aircraft." Allen levelled out but kept the speed constant.

"Take over." He motioned to Cal.

Maneuvering up and down, decreasing and increasing speed, he got familiar with the controls, then went higher and faster.

"Don't get too high. We are already above normal aircraft traffic and performance. Radar monitoring will be tracking us, ease back and let's turn around. Stella, you want to swap with Cal?" Allen asked.

He took over as they swapped seats and then Stella tried her hand at the controls, quickly acquainting herself to handling the plane. She made a U-turn and directed them back towards land.

Allen took over again as the shoreline came into view. He flew at normal passenger aircraft height and speed until, within range of the boneyard, he began the descent.

"Allen, can we try a reverse thrust of the engines?" Cal asked. "We will need them to maneuver in space."

Throttling back, they gripped the controls and eased the throttles to the reverse position. It felt like someone had applied emergency brakes on a car and they were all thrown forward.

Allen quickly pulled the throttles back to neutral and gained control of the aircraft.

"I think they work, don't you?" He smiled.

"Had to check."

The landing was normal and Allen taxied back to the hanger, where a tug was waiting to back the Tupolev into the hanger.

"A successful test flight," Cal said after they had switched off and Billy had closed the hanger doors after them.

"It was a good flight as long as no faults are found. We will have to inspect everything," Allen said. They walked around the aircraft, examining every inch, but no one found any concerns.

CHAPTER FIFTY-THREE

Billy used the forklift to move the fusion cylinders into the main cabin doorway where Cal and Stella took them off the pallets. Starting from the rear, they manually moved them into position and strapped them down securely.

Normal human strength would not have been enough but the two hubrids didn't falter, stacking the cylinders until they reached the roof. Overhead bins had been removed earlier with the seats so they concentrated on packing it all in. When they were finished, the cabin was about a quarter full so they knew three more loads were required.

Lara and Allen had slept through this and Billy said he would catch a power nap on the way back. They left early in the morning in the Electra, arranging to bring the next load as soon as it arrived.

This left only the heltherm coating to be applied and now that there were no humans around, they could apply it without worry. Using a static charge method to get complete coverage, they started and soon found out it would take a long time because of the size of the area to cover.

It was tedious, boring work and the smell was acrid with chemical fumes filling the hangar. They opened the hanger doors slightly for ventilation but it did not help much so they buckled down and kept going. To take out the tedium they talked, with the conversation first all about Stella's upbringing and childhood, then Cal did reluctantly disclose some of his early days.

His parents were teachers and university professors so he had spent all his life learning. It was a way of life for a lot of people in his era as robotics did most of the manual work, even to the point of manufacturing themselves.

The opportunities were endless for Cal and he took advantage of taking on new careers every time he graduated. Sports and arts were huge and he excelled at every new adventure.

Marrying an academic, they worked closely and agreed never to have children, giving them more freedom to develop as human beings. But when the time came, his wife decided not to be a hubrid, even when offered an elder position. Her qualifications guaranteed seniority but she shunned the chance. Like so many others who believed strongly in an afterlife, her faith pushed her towards a natural death.

A dying world seemed to drive many on the same path of a childless life dedicated to self-awareness and spirituality. Cal felt that a responsibility to mother earth was just as important and he thought himself accountable to help save it for future generations. This drove him to take the chances of travelling back in time to change the future by an act of retrogress.

Stella explained she had been born in a small English town to working class parents, but to her that meant nothing and never stopped her.

Studying hard to get to university and then getting a scholarship, she was motivated to make science, maths, and physics a priority before getting a post with NASA to work on the viability of time travel.

Heltherm coating dried to a clear translucent green that was hard-shell to the touch and when heated with a blow torch still felt cool.

Stella was impressed but also extremely glad when they finished. It had taken over twenty-four hours to complete, and she hoped it would do the trick.

Soon enough the next load turned up with Lara and Allen. Carla had come back and Billy transferred to the craft and left. There was a message from Talan but it was only routine, suggesting the next loads and asking if more were needed. Carla had been quite vocal about her trip and was glad she had witnessed for herself the fate of the planet.

Allen got to work with the forklift. Inside the Electra, Stella and Cal supervised the unloading and Lara guided the drop off close to the plane.

After emptying the cargo plane, they switched to the Tupolev cabin and began stacking the inside with fusion cylinders and securing them tightly.

About half way through, Stella's cellphone buzzed and she pulled it from her pocket to read a text message.

"I need to go back to Orlando. Cal, a friend of mine needs some help."

"That's okay," he replied. "You can go back with them. Just try and come back with the next load. It will be awkward moving this around on my own."

Allen decided to fly back late that day. He figured there would be no trouble with an empty aircraft; they did it all the time with normal freight to meet deadlines. Stella helped co-pilot the craft while Lara rested in the back, they had been up all night with the *Intrepid* trip, then brought the load up and now was flying back all within a day. She knew Allen would need a good rest before starting again and she would let him sleep.

They parted when they landed, Lara and Allen going home and Stella returning to the lab. She drove straight there and checked on the preparations for the next trip. Everything seemed in order so she asked Matt for a private conversation.

"I need to ask for a favour for someone," Stella began. "A friend of mine who requests secrecy wants to go on the next trip."

"Sorry Stella, but we have broken all the rules for this mission as it is. No can do."

She looked at him with consternation and began again. "If I tell you who it is, can we keep this between us?"

"You can tell me and I can keep a secret, but I still cannot allow this person to go."

She came close, leaned in, and whispered in his ear. When she backed off, his eyes were wide in astonishment.

"You are absolutely sure they want to do this?" he asked.

"He has seen all the data. I sent him a copy and now he's asking a favour. He wants to be called by the pseudonym 'Sherlock' and kept secret from anybody else."

Matt was stunned as he thought over the implications.

"Sherlock may not even come back," she said. "The science is so far out there that he is drawn like a magnet."

He wavered, pacing back and forth.

"How would you arrange this and be able to keep it secret?"

"I thought about it and on the next trip there is no one to go, so I would bring Sherlock up here in my car, then ask everyone in the room to leave while I set him up inside the *Intrepid*. I would also send Talan a message about him."

He paced back and forth for almost five minutes. Stella let him think.

"When everyone goes home for a rest before the flight, I don't know what happens in here." He fixed her with a knowing gaze. "If a prominent scientist disappears, I know nothing about it and will swear to that until my dying day. The answer to your original question is no. Got that?"

"Yes sir."

CHAPTER FIFTY-FOUR

Stella was alone in the lab when people drifted in, ready for the evening launch. Matt arrived and looked straight at her but she gave him a blank look. It took no time at all for the stations to be up and running and ready to go. Carla, last to come back, was full of details of the underground city, elder complex, and the desolate planet outside.

Launch time arrived and the *Intrepid* disappeared. An hour later, it came back with maybe a few more scorch marks around the sides. Stella opened up the rear hatch and found it full of cylinders, plus a trigger harness and firing timer to run the full length of the cabin.

Billy appeared in the doorway and smiled at everyone. He stepped down and handed Stella a holook.

"Talan said maybe one more load. He would get it ready in case but to let him know how much before loading it in."

She nodded. "Did you have any problems?"

"No, I loaded the back while Nyla checked the inside for messages from you."

"Good."

The turn-around procedure started as soon as the debrief from Billy was complete and after flight safety checks finished. Dawn had barely lifted when a box van with Cox Industries written on the side turned up and they began loading the supplies.

Stella would fly up with them to help Cal load the fusion cylinders and start laying the wiring harness for the trigger. If all went well, the mission would be able to start a couple of days ahead of schedule. It all seemed to be under control.

"Famous last words," she muttered as a military vehicle pulled up. They were closing the rear doors to the van when an officer jumped out and approached them.

"Can I see what's in the van or do I have to get a search warrant?" he asked, giving Stella a knowing look.

She recognised him from before at the apartment. "No, not at all." She opened the doors wide.

"What are they?"

"Oxygen and helium cylinders for our experimental work."

"Do you have the paperwork for them?" he demanded.

"Of course, it's inside. Follow me." Stella went back inside to her desk. Turning towards him, she held out her hand. "Sorry if we got off on the wrong foot last time. My name is Stella."

He took her hand and froze. Their eyes locked and something passed between them.

"Perhaps we can go out for a drink sometime." He smiled at her.

"Yes, I'd like that."

"Well, everything is in order here so I'll leave you to it." He pulled out a card and she took it, smiling.

As the Hummer drove away, Lara and Allen crowded around her.

"What did you do?"

"What did you say?"

"Oh, a little of everything. A little flattery, some hypnosis, and plenty of electrical stimulation," she answered. "Come on, let's get this stuff out of here."

The flight up to the boneyard airfield was uneventful and soon they were transferring the fusion cylinders into the cabin. Stacked neatly and tightly secured, they did an inventory and a trial layout of the trigger harness. Everything was fitted and the trigger was the correct length.

"There is something else we forgot to bring with us," Stella said to the group. "Food and water for you two."

"You're right," Lara said. "What do you have in mind?"

"We stocked up with food and water from NASA thinking we may be going away for longer. It's basic space program stuff but will get you through it."

"Then that will have to do," Allen answered.

"What about you, Cal?"

"What about me? I don't need any food or water."

"No, but there is an open seat if you want to go back for possibly the last time."

"There are loose ends I want to finish here so we can get off as soon as we have everything ready."

"Okay, does anyone else have suggestions for things we may need?" Stella looked at all their faces.

"We must not forget to bring the suits," Lara said.

"Do we know how many more cylinders we can get in here?" Cal asked.

"Yes, and I'll put it in a message to Talan. Anything else?" She looked at Cal, who shook his head. "Alright, then we can go back."

The flight back was uneventful and upon landing they separated, Lara and Allen going home for a rest and Stella going to the lab.

She prepared a message to send back and put it in the *Intrepid*, she also thought about going back herself but after consideration, ruled it out.

She knew enough about the situation to realise the mission was now the priority and whatever was transpiring on the stricken planet was secondary.

Before Allen and Lara arrived with the van, Stella had pulled out the suits, food, and water for the mission. They loaded everything in the box van before gathering together as a group.

"Hopefully this is the last time we have to do this," Stella said. "No more secret journeys or keeping things to ourselves. I want to thank you all for your cooperation and hard work, especially Matt for allowing this mission to go ahead. Even though you have not seen the devastation of the planet, the rest of us know that what we are doing is the greatest thing we will ever do for humanity. Now we can get ready to publish our findings and prepare for the veneration of all the hard work we have put in."

She went around hugging everyone and they in turn hugged each other. They wished each other good luck before the Cox Industries van drove away. The team returned to finishing post trip procedures before going home.

CHAPTER FIFTY-FIVE

Walking through the cabin of the Tupolev, they checked that every fusion cylinder was securely tied down and that the trigger explosives were seated in the correct position.

Food and water was stowed in lockers behind the cockpit and another quantity in the flyhov in the cargo hold. Fold up bunk beds were also stowed away in the hov.

Before carrying out pre-flight checks, they had a meeting in the office. On a mission this complicated and dangerous, no mistakes could be made.

"I want to fly out of here during the night," Allen said. "People around here know me and we have kept out of the limelight until now, and I want to keep it that way. There is no one in the tower past normal working hours and definitely not after midnight so we could take off unnoticed."

Cal looked around at each person. "Stella, how about the timeline and navigation?"

"I am going to sit down and do all the calculations again to confirm a timetable but if we start early, I can readjust speed on the fly to make sure we arrive at the correct elliptical tip of Enceladus' orbit."

"Can I help with that?" Lara asked.

"No, but you can go over the calculations and navigation to verify the data."

"Calculations yes, but navigation in the cosmos? Not sure about that," Lara said.

"Are we all sure that the plane is ready, fully equipped, and nothing left to chance?" Cal asked. They nodded. "Then let's take a break. Allen and Lara, rest up. Stella, re-do the figures, and I will go over the plane once more. At midnight, we will carry out pre-flight checks. If all are agreed, we will take off tonight."

They all nodded and split up. Lara and Allen lay down at the rear bunks but could not sleep. Cal went over the plane in meticulous detail and Stella immersed herself in calculus.

Midnight crept around and they grouped together.

"Are we all agreed to go?" Cal asked.

They nodded, the humans more nervous than the other two.

"Then let's suit up and go over the pre-flight checks."

Each checked the other's suit as they fitted into them. Lara and Allen had to be more careful that the suits were sealed so air could not escape.

Cal got into the cockpit first and operated all the controls while Allen checked functionality. Lara got into a communication seat behind him.

When the checks were complete, they dropped the rear cargo hold door and Allen entered. Stella operated the hanger door and the plane eased out slowly, then she closed the hanger door behind and jumped in beside the flyhov.

Making sure the cargo hold door was closed and fully latched, she squeezed through the cabin and sat behind Cal. With all lights extinguished, slowly and as quietly as possible, they taxied to the main runway under the cover of darkness.

Lined up with the runway stretching out before them, Allen called out a communication check and they all replied.

"Last chance to pull out."

"Let's go," Cal said.

Allen pulled back on the throttles and noise levels increased until he released the brakes. They shot forward, pushing them back in their seats. White lines and spaces disappeared under them until the front lifted and all they could see was a dark sky. The landing gear retracted with a loud thump and Allen slowly increased speed and altitude. The fusion engines thrust the Tupolev faster and higher.

Once again, they hit a stage of vibration as they approached and sped through the plane's maximum designed velocity.

"Are we still on the correct heading?" Allen asked.

"At this heading we can break through the atmosphere and still be on the correct alignment to our destination," Stella replied.

Cal reviewed the instruments. "What's that on the radar?"

Two blips seemed to be closing on them.

"We have been spotted," Allen said. "They are probably fighter jets scrambled when ground teams detected an unidentified craft."

"They are hailing us," Lara said.

"Switch to all open communications," Allen ordered.

"This is United States Airforce. Identify yourselves and state your business."

"Say nothing," Cal said outside his helmet mike.

The jets quickly caught up with them and drew alongside. "Identify yourselves and state your business."

Cal pulled back on the throttles and they sped forward, reaching the lower limits of the stratosphere. The jets lagged behind as the atmosphere got thinner and their speed dropped off.

"You have been locked onto by missiles of the United States Airforce. We command you to slow down and follow us to land."

Nothing was said and the humans held their breath, each now looking at the back of Cal's head.

"You have ten seconds to comply before we shoot you out of the sky."

"Time to find out if this aircraft can take it," Cal said. He pulled the throttles back to maximum.

There was a loud boom and bump and they hit the back of their seats. G force pulled so high the humans struggled to stay conscious. Vision blurred and their bodies compressed under the load. No one was able to touch the controls and it felt it was never going to stop until it suddenly smoothed out and they were out of the atmosphere.

Radar showed no sign of their pursuers and they stared around in disbelief. The void around them was filled with distant stars and twinkling lights. They tried to look back but could not. Stella got up and went to look through a cabin window but floated up to the ceiling. She put her hands up to control her ascent, then pulled herself along until she was able to look through a side window.

"Well, the wings are still intact," she said. "I guess we made it past the first hurdle."

She clambered back to her seat, strapped in to avoid floating, and checked the instrument read outs.

"We are on the correct heading for sure but, Cal, how do we determine our speed? The instruments don't work here."

"Engine data," he replied. "I installed a meter when I installed the engines." He pointed to an instrument in the middle. "It measures speed in percentage of astronomical units. It is steadily climbing and should reach 1.25 A.U. or better. Once we reach maximum speed, you will have to calculate the time to reach Enceladus, which is approximately 8 A.U. You said five days, so that is correct, but we will have to adjust as we get closer."

CHAPTER FIFTY-SIX

Nobody spoke for an hour, maybe two. They were struck by the vastness of space and even if their speed had reached 1 A.U. or more per day, it felt like they were standing still. They were each lost in their own thoughts of how small and insignificant they were.

What were four souls in the immensity of time and space, in the unlimited twinkling of stars and darkness of the cosmos? Humility or pride, intelligence or ignorance, strength or weakness meant nothing. Were all these stars just a synapsis of joining chromosomes to a higher being, or a spiritual guide to another even more complex intelligence, or just some flotsam in a vast dark ocean full of waves of gravity?

Cal was the first to break the silence, his thoughts interrupted by the needs of the mission.

"As we discussed in meetings before we should work out a routine on how to spend the time on this journey. After all, there is no need for all four of us to be awake all the time."

"What do you propose now then?" Stella asked.

"I packed some bunk beds and straps to hold down Lara and Allen while they sleep."

"What if I don't want to sleep, or can't?" Lara asked.

"Stella and I can induce sleep for a given time and we can go into a standby mode for a fixed time. Only one of us needs to be awake."

"But I'm not ready for sleep yet," Allen said.

"Not now, but after a few hours when boredom sets in," Cal replied.

"I don't think I can ever be bored with this," Lara said.

Silence descended again and Cal checked instruments. Allen and the rest stared out the windows.

Dry throats and empty stomachs eventually drove the humans into moving from their stations and Lara retrieved some food and a couple of water bottles.

After sipping some water, they emptied some into the plastic bags of food, shook the contents to mix the concoction into an edible substance, and ingested it through straws.

"Not gourmet but I guess it will sustain us," Allen said.

Lara frowned. "Glad you could stomach it. I'm not sure I can keep it down."

"How long have we been awake?" he asked.

"Lost count," Lara replied.

"I will set up the beds for you," Cal said as he unbuckled his seat strap. Instead of rising normally, he drifted upwards and guided himself by hand along the roof.

He got out the beds he had stowed away, and placing them inside the hov cabin, secured them down with tie straps. He then returned to the cockpit.

"Are you ready? We are going to use the ones in the flyhov. It has an air supply so you can take your helmets off and be more natural. What do you think?"

"Sounds good to me," Allen replied.

Shortly after, he called the two humans to the back and they floated down and dropped into the cargo hold.

He motioned them to lie down but they floated through until above the beds.

"The straps are just to stop you floating around inside here," Cal assured them. "You can easily undo them if need be."

Once in position and making sure they could not drift away, he instructed them on what he would do.

"First, there is air inside the flyhov so you can remove the helmets and relax."

"I was thinking you should sleep for four hours at a time, what do you think?"

"We can try that if you like," Allen said.

"I would like to awaken normally. Will that happen or do you wake us?" Lara said.

"Yes, you will wake up normally," Cal said. "When I put you under it is a form of hypnosis designed to set your immune system and recovery sleep function into action. You should awaken refreshed and rested."

He took Lara's hand and she drifted away, then followed with Allen. Closing the flyhov and floating back into the cockpit, he strapped in to the pilot's seat.

"Shall I go first?"

"If you want," she answered.

"I will do four hours as well. I think we could work out a routine to fill the time."

Stella nodded and watched as he closed his eyes. His body relaxed in the seat and his head rested on his chest.

Four hours on her own seemed like a long time, but then she thought about the humanoids who Nyla explained had been fired off into the far off reaches of the universe looking for a habitable planet and spent years in standby mode. They would awake as if coming out of sleep, only to find nothing in the darkness had changed, only their location in the cosmos.

She checked the instruments again and relaxed. There was something niggling in her mind but she could not place it.

Searching through her AI did not help, yet there was still a doubt so she decided to place the question in the back of her human brain, knowing her subconscious would find it.

She heard a bump then a creak, which made her jump. Stretching up and looking around, nothing appeared out of the ordinary. Another bump made her turn. The sound seemed to come from the other side, then another and another.

"Cal, wake up."

Instantly he was alert and senses heightened.

"What is it?"

"I heard a bump, a creak, and some more bumps."

As if on cue, the noise came again. Cal listened and heard more in rapid succession.

"Debris. It is space rubble or fragments of rock in our path," he explained. "We should be okay. It would have to be very large to damage us."

"I don't like the sound of that," Stella said.

"There's nothing we can do. I have encountered stuff like this before. It just bounces off, maybe leaving a small dent in the bodywork."

"You sure? What happens if a big piece hits us?"

"The only vulnerable place is the nose cone. Even if it penetrated, it would not stop us and we are not about to lose air, are we? If the wings get damaged, no big deal, they do not contribute to anything anymore."

"I wish I had your confidence."

"We will be fine. I am going back into standby mode." Cal relaxed and went limp again.

Stella could not relax and winched at every click, bump, or bang. Occasionally, a louder bang made her jump, but the noises seemed to be coming from the sides and not the front—not that it made any difference to her. She did not think nerves bothered her anymore but the thought of being hit by something large made her uncertain.

CHAPTER FIFTY-SEVEN

A routine formed as the humans awoke feeling full of energy. They wanted to do something but with only time on their hands, six hours was enough before going back under for another four. Stella felt more comfortable going into standby mode because she did not have to worry, leaving that to Cal.

Swapping sleep cycles and modes, the time passed as hours turned to days and days to anticipation.

After the cabin oxygen depleted and they switched to full suit rebreathers, time became more tedious for the humans. Eating and drinking was a chore, having to open the helmets to swallow every ounce of nutrient through a straw. They were not reluctant to go under anymore.

Slowly Saturn became visible to the naked eye, unmistakable as the rings surrounding it stood out with aureole circles so bright they seemed spiritual.

Enceladus was conspicuous as one of the brightest objects in the sky as all light was reflected off its icy surface. They almost didn't need their navigation instruments.

"I know we are on the right heading, but are we on the correct course to get within its orbit?" Cal asked.

"We have to start slowing down and make minor adjustments in two hours and thirty-six minutes," Stella answered. She studied her calculations on the navigation computer.

Boredom now changed rapidly to anticipation as the time approached for some work instead of sleep. They all sat at their stations and Lara studied a second computer read-out of the navigation stats, noting an intersection of paths that required change.

"When I say, you can reduce the engine thrust to neutral," Stella said.

As the paths intersected on the navigation screen, she ordered the change and Allen throttled back to the centre position while Cal watched their speed decrease. Stella and Lara studied the course and soon Enceladus was evident on screen. A line showing their indicated intersection was off to the right.

"We have to correct to the left."

"Do you want us to slow or speed up?" Cal asked.

"What do you mean?"

"If we reverse thrust, the left engine that will slow us as well as change direction. Or we can power up the right engine to speed up and still change our heading," Cal said.

"Reverse thrust on the left until we are on course, then I can work out a time to reach the moon," she said.

Allen pushed the left side throttle forward slowly and only in a small increment at a time. The women watched as the line of their indicated course moved first to the moon then to the left, and Stella indicated to throttle back.

She went back to recalculating and working on speed reduction to reach their destination without overshooting it. She had the pilots make small reverse thrusts at different intervals.

The closer they got, the more light emitted by the moon enveloped them, causing the helmets to drop a shield to protect their eyes. It seemed brighter than the sun as they drew close and made adjustments to hold station at a close enough position without being drawn in by its gravity. Though low at 0.0113 g, they did not want to be pulled in. However, it did allow them to run close at forty thousand feet above the surface.

"Stella, how long until we need to detonate?" Cal asked, turning to face her.

"Our window of opportunity is three hours from now, or if we miss that, we will have to do another orbit of Saturn, which is a little over a day."

"I think we all would like to do it sooner rather than later," Allen said.

"Allen, can you make sure we hold station while the rest of us prepare for departure? Stella and I will arm the triggers. Lara, you make sure the flyhov is operational and transfer any food and other supplies," Cal said.

They agreed and the three departed the cockpit, leaving Allen to control the plane and hold it steady. Lara went first to the rear, opened the hatch, and pulled herself through headfirst.

Starting at the rear, Cal took one side and Stella the other. They plugged in the trigger wiring to each individual detonation device. As they finished one, they swapped sides and checked the other's harness was fully seated into its connection before moving up one pair of cylinders.

Slowly, they worked up the length of the cabin until they reached the front. The final piece of the harness was plugged into the detonation timer.

They waited until Lara came back. She had passed them a couple of times transferring food and water.

"How are we doing, Allen?" Cal asked as they entered the cockpit.

"We are creeping ahead slowly and I have to keep using some reverse thrust," he replied.

"How much?" Stella asked.

Allen looked at his watch. "You have been almost an hour and we have moved ahead five hundred metres."

"So, if we thrust back one thousand metres and set off the timer in an hour, that will give us an hour to get out of here," Stella said. She confirmed it on the computer.

Cal checked the numbers and agreed, so Allen applied reverse thrust until they were at a thousand metres behind the designated primary point for maximum effect.

At the half hour mark, Cal indicated for the others to get into the flyhov and make sure it was fired up. They had a half hour to call it off and reset. He waited and did not receive any confirmation.

"Stella, is it a go?"

"Yes, the flyhov is running and checks out okay."

He did a countdown for the others' benefit, and then hit the firing button, setting off the one-hour countdown. He floated down the length of the cabin, quickly checking the triggers as he went.

At the hatch, he jumped down and went straight to the rear hatch door switch. Pressing the button, it did not move. He pressed it again but still the rear loading hatch remained closed. He tried the manual release. Nothing.

"I think the hatch is frozen shut," he said to the others who were seated inside the flyhov.

They stared at him blankly. He went to the door and tried to push it open, with hands on the roof and feet pushing down. It remained closed. Stella got out and went to the other side of the door and they tried pushing together. No movement.

"I think we are in trouble," Allen said to Lara.

"Go out and help them," she replied. "I will steer the hov."

He got out and went to the door switch, pressing the button repeatedly while operating the manual switch.

"The latch is released. I can see it's open," Cal called.

"So is this side," Stella confirmed.

Allen went to the middle part of the hatch and started pushing as hard as he could. It would not budge.

Lara was getting frustrated and got out to help. She went to the middle by Allen and yelled, "If we all count to 3 and push down together, maybe we can shock it open."

They began relaxing and pushing in unison, thumping as hard as they could with their feet. On the fourth push, there was a crack followed by a bang and the hatch fell open. They tumbled out into the cosmos.

CHAPTER FIFTY-EIGHT

Enceladus was so bright that they instinctively closed their eyes and turned away from the fierce glare. Cal had stretched to grab any part of the plane but was short and went flailing in empty space. Lara was close enough to Allen to clutch a leg and hold on. Stella was way off to one side and out of reach.

Lara pulled herself up Allen's body until they faced each other with a grim look on their faces. Looking around but away from the blinding light, she could see Cal was almost in reach.

"Can you push me towards Cal but hold onto my leg?" she asked.

"I'll try." He grabbed her foot and tried to push.

Lara stretched towards Cal, who saw her coming and pushed out a leg for her to grab. With her arm swinging, she contacted him and clung on for dear life. Allen floated up hand over hand until he got hold of Cal's other leg and both eased up until they were face to face.

They looked towards Stella, who was way out of reach and seemed to be immobile. She gave no indication of awareness. Cal turned to the Tupolev, only to find it inching away from them.

"Stella, you okay?" Cal called, but got no answer.

"If we climb over one another towards the plane, maybe we can reach it," he suggested.

Without hesitation, Lara clambered up Cal until he had hold of her feet, then Allen did the same, right up to the tip of Lara's hands. Cal did the same until his feet were in Allen's hands before Lara started again.

After completing the maneuver twice more, it was evident that like a mouse in a wheel, they were getting nowhere.

Cal pulled them altogether and called again to Stella.

"Stella, can you hear me? Are you all right?"

She didn't answer and they all looked at one another in despair.

"Lara, can I ask you a question?" Allen said in a desperate voice.

"What is it?"

"I have always wanted to ask you this but now may never get a chance. Will you marry me?"

"What!" She almost screamed. "You wait until now to ask me?"

"I have wanted to ask you over and over but was scared I might lose you."

"No! The answer is no! It's a stupid question at the stupidest of times."

"Oh."

Cal supressed a snigger, not wanting to embarrass them. He watched the plane edging farther away.

"I am sorry I got you both into this."

Their heads swivelled towards a movement of the flyhov. Shocked, they watched in amazement as the craft backed out of the cargo hold and moved towards them.

As it drew close, Cal reached out and grabbed at it. The smooth surface gave no grip but enough adhesion to be able to pull along towards the door. They opened it quickly and scrambled in. Lara jumped into a control seat and started guiding it towards Stella, who started moving as soon as the flyhov was under control.

The men pulled her inside and closed the door behind them. Stella moved over and sat beside Lara.

"Too late to outrun the blast. We have to shelter behind the moon. Hold on." She slammed the joystick fully forward.

The G force was so great the humans passed out and slumped in their seats. Cal straightened them.

The Tupolev was out of sight when they slowed down enough to get a bearing. Still not sure, she kept going until she was certain they were sheltered. Slowing to a hover, Stella leaned over to check on Lara, who was just coming around.

"I'm sorry, I had to do that to get away. Are you all right?"

"Woozy but okay. Are we safe here?"

"We have to watch our distance to Enceladus when the blast happens. It should be pushed towards us."

"How long?" Allen asked from the back.

"Twenty seconds." She counted down until there was a flash above the blinding light that already enveloped them.

Stella looked at the instruments and stole a glance at Enceladus. It was getting larger. She turned the flyhov away and accelerated. If she had a rear-view mirror, her eyes would have been glued to it. Instead, she had to use the instruments.

Pulling away to two hundred metres, she slowed and turned around to face the moon. It was still getting bigger but not rushing at them. Turning next to the left, she piloted the flyhov until they were clear of it.

"Can one of you take over?" Stella asked.

Lara was already in the front and offered.

"Good. Hold position so I can check telemetry, headings, speed, and orbital travel."

"Go ahead."

She pulled out a screen from the front of the craft and held it in her hands without touching it or any keyboards.

"Did you connect to the navigation-screen remotely before?" Cal asked.

"Yes. I did not think it possible but I had to try. Lucky for us, it worked and I was able to control the flyhov only because it was so close I think."

They waited patiently as she made calculations. "Cal, Enceladus has left orbit and is moving on the right course. I think we can call it a success."

"Yes!" The team shouted and hugged each other.

"Does that mean we can go home now?" Allen asked.

"Your wish is my command." Stella smiled at him.

"I have had enough excitement for one day, thank you," he said.

They all laughed with a laughter that was fueled by adrenaline in the humans and relief in the Hubrids, and was not likely to subside anytime soon. Stella plotted a course and steered in that direction slowly accelerating.

CHAPTER FIFTY-NINE

Four days into a boring return journey home, the crew was weary and looking forward to getting back to terra-firma. Apart from the sparking, twinkling lights from the myriad of stars, they were still surrounded by a void of nothingness. The two humans were asleep or resting under the influence of neurologic stimulation, floating around in the rear. Stella was in standby mode and Cal was piloting the craft.

Without warning, there was a bump that brought Stella instantly awake.

"What was that?"

"I think I accidently nudged the reverse thrusters," he replied.

"How could you do that?"

"I leaned forward as I caught the first glimpse of earth. Look." He pointed out of the front glass.

She saw a bright blue dot in the distance.

Turning around, she could see the two humans were sleeping soundly, floating up and down like buoys on an ocean swell.

"We will let them sleep. No point waking them until we get closer to home." She faced forward again and concentrated on the mother planet. "Be careful, okay?"

"Yes," he replied like a scolded schoolboy.

Once described as the blue marble, earth from space drew the eye to its constantly changing surface atmosphere of swirling white or grey clouds over deep blue. Shades from azure to aqua changing markedly according to both time, daylight and place, from brilliant turquoises and light greens, through ultramarine, navy blues, to dishwater greys and muddy browns. All fascinating to Stella's eyes as she admired its changing hue's and rotating sphere, a new appreciation and pride for her planet swelled within her mind.

If asked now where she emanated from, the answer would not be England or UK or even USA but her home planet "Earth."

Each country and region, she knew, had its own culture, language and biodiversity, so complex as to render it unique and individual yet viewed as a whole it was beautiful and exquisite. Humanity, no, she, had a right and a duty to protect it, as mother earth had borne her, fed and nurtured her then she was indebted with her life.

Deep thoughts made the time pass until stirring in the back of the craft brought her out of it.

"Are we there yet, mommy?" Lara said, smiling.

"Almost! Look, little girl, you can see it from here."

Lara's head popped between the two pilots.

"Wow, it's incredible." She turned to shake Allen. "Hey, wake up sleepy head. We're nearly there."

A bleary-eyed human blinked to clear his vision. He wanted to rub them but could not through the visor, which he had closed for privacy but now quickly flipped up.

"Great, can't wait," he said.

"Don't sound so enthusiastic. That is the most fantastic place in the universe." Lara pointed out the front window.

"I know, I know. I just want to get home, that's all."

"How long?" she asked Stella.

"A few hours. I'm not sure how you want to do this, Cal."

"I want to go in under the cover of darkness so we will have to get in orbit first, then go around to the dark side."

"Dark side," said Lara. "What, you think this is Star Wars?"

"That's well before my time, but no, little Ewok, the side not lit by the sun. Also, we want to avoid being seen by the space station or any other satellites. Can you work out a course, Stella?"

"Aye, aye. Anything else, commander." She saluted.

The mood was getting lighter as excitement built. Stella pulled out the navigation screen and started calculations.

"We can start slowing down in three hours. Until then, you will just have to admire the view."

"What do you want to do when we get there?" Lara asked, turning to Allen.

"Get a shower and feel clean again. You sure miss it after a couple of days."

"What about you, Stella?"

"The same but changing into some normal clothes so I feel sort of human like."

"And you, Cal? What do you want to do when we get back?"

"You will be home, but not me. As much as I love your era, I need to get back to mine."

Earth got bigger as they slowed and approached the outer atmosphere. The land masses were clearly visible as they moved over them faster than the earth's rotation. Stella called instructions to Cal as she studied the navigation screen, applying reverse thrust almost continuously.

Then a front plate dropped down over the screen, blocking any view. Stella glanced at Cal.

"It's a heat shield. The pressure of the thermosphere would burn us up without it. In my era, we don't need them to go to the space stations because the atmosphere is almost gone."

They slowed until they were travelling at normal aircraft speed and the heat shield popped up again, revealing their location over Asia.

Soon they were speeding over the Pacific and approaching darkness over land. Like diving into a pool of dusky liquid, night enveloped them.

"We are coming up from the south over Mexico, so we are not over American air space for very long," Stella announced.

City lights shone underneath that grew more expansive as they entered USA and headed up the Florida coast.

"Are we going straight to the lab?" Stella asked.

Cal nodded.

"Thought so. Then take a heading to the left until we see Orlando and drop down."

Familiar landmarks became visible and Stella directed him by pointing.

"You want me to take it down?" she asked.

"Yes, but slow it right down to make as little noise as possible," Cal said. He released the controls to her.

There was little moonlight as she came in from the rear of the complex and settled down in front of the hanger door. Cal got out, went inside, and opened the door so she could ease inside.

Once inside, everyone got out and the humans stretched their limbs, getting their muscles to work again and acclimatize to earth's gravity. Cal walked over to the *Intrepid* and opened the rear cargo hold. Getting back into the flyhov, he piloted it straight in and closed the hatch after getting out.

Lara and Allen went off to the locker rooms to get out of their suits and Stella spoke with Cal.

"What now?" she asked.

"Can you arrange a trip as soon as possible?"

"See what I can do," she replied. "Anything else?"

"No. I guess it is almost over for you now. Any plans?"

She shook her head, as if it were an anticlimax after all they had been through. "You think it's going to work?"

"Collide with earth, you mean?"

"No, change earth back to some sort of normality?"

"I cannot control what will happen, it will change completely but I hope it will be habitable." He smiled sadly.

CHAPTER SIXTY

The lab team had set up for the evening trip but around midnight people kept arriving. Lara and Allen were followed by the whole Branigan family—Jack, Laura, and Irene—who came to say goodbye to Cal.

It felt like a party atmosphere, as if everyone had sensed this was the finale. All their hard work had come to fruition and after tonight the success of the venture would come to light.

The men wore suits and ties and the women were smartly dressed. Stella wore a blue business suit over her hubrid skin.

Irene had on a summer print dress just above the knee, her hair in a ponytail. She put her arm around Cal's waist, her face close to his.

"I have a present for you." She held a coloured paper bag.

"You didn't have to do that," he replied, holding the bag open to look inside.

He smiled as he pulled out a stuffed toy squirrel and hugged it close.

"I will treasure this always. Thank you so much."

He leaned down to kiss and hug her, then held her at arm's length.

"I see you have been taking the supplements. Feeling less tired now?"

"Of course, full of vim and vigor. Want to try out that kiss again? See how it measures up?"

If he could have blushed, he would. "Not now in front of everybody. You're embarrassing me."

They both laughed together like teenagers, drawing the attention of Stella and Laura. Irene's mom gave him a tight hug and when they came apart, he held her hands for a moment too long.

"Complete recovery then?"

She nodded. "Thanks to you. I feel like a new woman."

"You look like one too. I once told you I could see where Irene got her good looks from and I meant it."

"Flattery will get you everywhere, but now you're making me uncomfortable." Laura smiled.

He leaned towards her and whispered in her ear. "You can even start another family. You're very attractive and still young where I come from."

"Now you've gone too far," she whispered.

Splitting apart, Cal smiled at her, took his leave, and went around shaking people's hands and thanking them, making small talk along the way. After speaking with everyone, he called for quiet to say a few words.

"I want to thank you all for going above and beyond. I know we have pushed your own agenda and research along the way, but to complete my mission was incredible. Doing so without the aid of the government makes it even more extraordinary." He glanced at Allen and Jack. "You have put your own careers at risk and for that there are no words to describe my gratitude. I know I will never see you again or the world as it is now, and that makes me extremely sad, but I hope our efforts will bring the world back to its glory. Once again, I thank you all."

There was some light applause but they all felt the same sorrow.

Lara moved to stand in front of Cal.

"While I have your attention, I would like to make an announcement."

All eyes focused on her.

"First, let me say on behalf of everyone here that it has been life changing to meet you, Cal, and we wish you good luck on the next stage of your endeavors."

They gave him another round of applause.

"Now, Allen, if you would come up front."

He looked confused but came forward to stand by her.

"Get down on one knee," she commanded.

Looking even more confused, he did as he was asked. Lara pulled out a small box and handed it to him.

"Now you can ask the right question at the right time."

He opened the box and gasped.

"Lara Holden, we have been through a lot together and my worst fear is that I would lose you, but now in front of everyone here, I want to tell you I love you with all my heart and ask you to spend the rest of our days together. Will you marry me?"

"Yes, I will." She smiled and held out her hand for him to slip on the ring. They kissed and she held up her hand to show everyone.

"In case you are all, wondering I purchased this for services rendered to the elders, and you are all invited to the wedding, even you, Cal, if possible."

Cheering erupted and the women all gathered around her to admire the ring. Cal went up to Allen.

"Nice surprise, Allen. Better than the last rejection, don't you think? I am so pleased for you both. This makes leaving a lot easier."

"Thanks." He was a little taken aback from what just happened.

The euphoria in the room died down a little as launch time approached and soon Cal stood at the entrance to the craft. Everyone called out goodbyes or good luck and he disappeared inside.

The countdown went as scheduled and soon the air around the *Intrepid* shimmered and the craft disappeared.

Now all that was left was to wait for it come back. In the meantime, Jack Branigan approached Stella.

"That was quite the trick you pulled off," he said. "I was at a meeting with Homeland Security and military brass when they showed a video of your escape from the scrambled jet fighters.

You have them running scared, not knowing if you were some secret Russian spy plane with a new technology, or maybe aliens. The way you just disappeared like that... How did you do that?"

Stella frowned. "What do you mean 'disappeared'? What kind of disappearance? We accelerated away from them."

Jack pulled out his cellphone. "I have it here on video. It has been leaked and will probably be shown on news programs as a UFO sighting."

Stella watched the Tupolev in front, and then suddenly the plane just disappeared. The niggling thoughts that Stella had sent to her subconscious to work through now came screaming out at her.

"No!" she shouted, her mood turning from mellow to fury as her face distorted in anger.

"Billy!" she called across the room. Everyone turned around in astonishment.

"Billy, you have been monitoring the astronomical society, haven't you?"

"Yes," he replied. "Nothing has been said but they're probably confirming the data."

"Check where Enceladus is now, please."

He went to the computer and looked from screen to screen.

"It's in its normal position around Saturn."

"I knew it!" Stella said. "I just knew there was something wrong." She turned to Matt. "Don't be surprised if the *Intrepid* doesn't come back, or if it's in pieces when it does."

"Why?"

"Because we have been duped!"

"What do you mean?" he asked.

"We have been conned and used for their benefit."

"Why would the *Intrepid* not come back?" Matt asked.

"They have no further use for us," she replied with a scowl. "I am so mad. They knew more than they let on and thought we would not help them if we knew the truth. They probably knew how to jump the bubble and how to time travel.

The Tupolev made a jump when we left the fighter jets and the flyhov made the same jump on the way back, where in time and space we went to I don't know. Or even why they deceived us at all.

They already knew they couldn't go back and engineer a retrogress solution, so that's where we came in. I think the only thing they did not know about was the nature of dark energy and Lara and myself enlightened them.

The *Intrepid* will not come back because they do not want me to go back there and antagonize them."

Everyone glanced around the room, incredulous at Stella's outburst.

"In a way, I'm glad because it means our era is safe," she continued. "And the only good thing for us is what we have found out. If I had not died, we wouldn't have access to their technology. But I tell you what, I will get to the truth and go back and confront them!"

EPILOGUE

Orlando 2 was a smaller craft than the regular starships because it was built in a hurry, but also it did not have to carry as many people. After a message was relayed back from the *Orlando* 1 that the planet they had reached, Gliese, was habitable and two and a half times larger than earth with oceans and a pleasant climate, everything changed.

Meetings were held and elders around the globe put it to a vote with the whole population in agreement to leave and journey like pilgrims to a new world.

Only *Orlando* 2 remained, manned mostly by hubrids, humanoids, and robots. A few humans also remained driven by a loyalty to the planet. Their mission now was to monitor earth after the cosmic event.

Cal had secured a reserved cabin on the outside of the ship with a window view. On his desk sat a stuffed squirrel and a holook. Often, he would play the hologram of himself and Irene kissing and at the same time turn the toy around on top of the desktop.

He had become a recluse since returning and because of his record, was left alone and treated with the utmost courtesy. Sometimes he just wandered the ship aimlessly and appeared to be lost in thought. Orders from Talan were to leave him alone.

Sometimes he passed the humanoid replicas of the T.T. team, now commandeered to help run the ship instead of museum exhibits to amuse the public. He saw them as like wax models that would never come to life—just another sting in the tail of complex guilt issues.

He tried to cope with what had happened and went over every event, justifying his actions as being good for humanity.

The closeness of the relationships built a loyalty that hurt when he left. He knew exactly what he was doing, and yet he continued.

It was history now and he knew he should move on, cope with new problems and plan for the future, but somehow, he could not. His only reasoning that it would all come together when Enceladus collided with Earth.

Corrections and adjustments had to be made so the trajectory of the planet and moon would come together at their point of greatest advantage.

The responsibility to work that out had fallen to the latest hubrid, and Cal had only met him a couple of times. Sebastien Hallstead was a tall, fair-haired slim man with a dark, disconcerting stare.

He and Stella had been friendly in the scientific community and now he had the latest AI unit. Cal knew he was as intellectual and powerful as Stella, but he did not share her demeanor.

Trust was not an issue, but there was not the same comradery that he shared with her. Only one person knew his real identity, that was Talan, and he had been asked to keep it secret. The man wanted to keep to his nom de plume, but Talan insisted there were to be no secrets.

Explosives had been set up in a couple of flyhov to go off as Enceladus passed by to alter its course and send it to its desired target at the Marianas trench, the deepest part of the ocean.

It was calculated that it would reap the greatest benefits to have it collide there or east of that location to cause the least damage to the land masses around. Animals and humanoids to look after them were left on the planet with the hope of being able to save species without having to use the frozen embryos that were placed in underground vaults.

"Cal, are you there?"

"Yes, Talan."

"ETA is in a couple of hours. Would you like to come up to the bridge and monitor the event?"

"Be right there."

Cal left his quarters and caught an elevator up to flight command. Entering, he noted Sebastien hunched over a desk with both hands on the keyboard touch pads. Shi and Dax spotted him coming in and gave a friendly wave. They were the only ones who regularly visited him.

They had gotten to know Stella and Lara and liked to come in and chat to him. They were so pleased when he had told them Allen and Lara were engaged. Shi told him their plans were to get married, have children, and then become hubrids like him.

They spoke highly of Sebastien, as they visited him as well, and although he never revealed anything of his past, he did praise Stella. Both had become scientific addicts through their knowing the women and now were part of flight command and assigned monitoring duties.

Talan, dressed in silver as usual, was standing in the middle control tower next to a man in a red as Cal approached.

"Good day, Talan, Commander Innes." He nodded to the man in red.

"We are going to move farther out to avoid any debris flying our way," Talan said. "Sebastien said that Enceladus had sped up as it was shocked into course variation, so we are taking no chances."

Cal nodded, then studied a monitor screen. Sebastien left his desk and moved towards them, waiting for leave to speak.

"Yes, what is it Seb?" The commander asked.

"We are on target and collision will be in one hour fifty minutes." He turned to Cal. "You know this is a gamble, probably the biggest risk ever taken in the history of humankind."

Cal glared at him. "And if we do nothing? Do we let the planet become a second Mars?"

Sebastien held his gaze. "Cal, I have gambled everything on your cast of the dice. Let's hope it works."

"I don't think you had much choice, and my stakes are as high as yours." Cal broke away and studied the screens.

The main screens showed a dark brown-coloured earth slowly rotating, the outline of the land mass shown in relief. There was no sign of Enceladus yet. The nervousness in the room was palpable and intense. Some of them had waited hundreds of years for this moment.

Cal was one of those and now doubt crept in. What if it was a disaster? What if earth was broken up and drifted away in pieces? What if the climate, although restored, was too harsh for humanity? All these scenarios and more ran through his mind until he remembered Stella's words: "You don't have a choice."

A gasp all around the room drew his attention to the screens and he watched as a streaking white light took less than a couple of seconds to appear, then slam into earth.

The planet shuddered and seemed to move.

"That's going to shift the earth's axis," Sebastien said, turning to Cal.

"We knew that coming in." He replied.

Great gushers of debris and fragments of earth's mantle spewed outwards like a gigantic volcano.

Clouds of dust, dirt, ash, and embers began to form in the next wave of lava that was thrown out, along with the tephra. Explosions multiplied.

As they watched, the atmosphere seemed to shimmer as a wave of propagating disturbance rapidly approached them. When the shock wave hit, everything that was not secured down went one way and the ship moved in the other. Furniture and people were thrown to the outer wall with such force as to render some unconscious, then the ship flipped and pandemonium ensued, followed by darkness.

Moments later, the lights came back on as the ship's systems rebooted. Cal stared around as humanoids went to the aid of people who were either shaken or unconscious. Nyla helped Shi, who lay in a crumpled heap, and Dax was struggling to stand.

Cal went to sit in the pilot's chair.

Firing up one side of the ship's engines, he maneuvered the craft into a loop that would bring it back into its original position at the top. He stopped the flight and settled it into a steady orbit. Switching to auto-pilot, he exited the console control centre.

As people and crew were getting back to some form of normality, Talan called for a meeting in the commander's office with Cal, Sebastien, a couple of elders, and the ship's commander.

"Sebastien, can you pull up a view of Earth from here?"

He sat down at the main control centre desk and manipulated the compute desktop until a vision of the planet appeared on the screens. They saw only a huge ball of dark grey cloud enveloping the globe.

"Is it still in one piece?" Talan asked anxiously.

Sebastien executed some more directives and data streamed along the bottom of the screens.

"I would say yes at the moment, but it will take some time to get a full assessment."

"Any orders?" Commander Innes asked.

"No, just maintain stations for now," Talan answered.

"The main event is over," Cal said. "Now we have to wait until the dust settles and sensors can determine the state of the planet."

"That could take many years," Seb said.

"We have the time," Cal replied.

Printed in Canada   THOMAS CONNER